DRAGON FRUIT

A Selection of Recent Titles by Karen Keskinen

The Jaymie Zarlin Mysteries

BLOOD ORANGE
BLACK CURRENT
DRAGON FRUIT *

* *available from Severn House*

DRAGON FRUIT

Karen Keskinen

This first world edition published 2016
in Great Britain and the USA by
SEVERN HOUSE PUBLISHERS LTD of
19 Cedar Road, Sutton, Surrey, England, SM2 5DA.
Trade paperback edition first published
in Great Britain and the USA 2016 by
SEVERN HOUSE PUBLISHERS LTD

British Library Cataloguing in Publication Data
A CIP catalogue record for this title is available from the British Library.

ISBN-13: 978-0-7278-8624-8 (cased)
ISBN-13: 978-1-84751-728-9 (trade paper)
ISBN-13: 978-1-78010-789-9 (e-book)

Typeset by Palimpsest Book Production Ltd.,
Falkirk, Stirlingshire, Scotland.

ACKNOWLEDGEMENTS

A raised glass of Santa Barbara County Noir and a resounding *Cheers!* to my talented and skilled editor at Severn House, Faith Black Ross. Faith, how fortunate I am to find myself seated at your table! Thanks also to my agent, Becca Stumpf, for sticking by me through thin and thick. Becca, you are *still* whip-smart, warm-hearted, and wise! Also, I want to express my appreciation to Leonard Tourney, for his keen-eyed assessment of the manuscript at an early stage; and to Sasha Gray, for generously sharing her thoughtful insights regarding a life-path I needed to better understand.

This time around, my gratitude and a tip of my hat to various members of the Reich clan: Ted and Wendy, true leaders in their wide circle of family, community, and friends; Adrian & Danielle, who somehow manage to solve the mysteries of science while sunning on Florida's white sands; Matthieu & Gerly, forging all our futures through solar engineering in Silicon Valley; Brigitte, translating computerese to rest of the world with one hand while navigating the icy waters of San Francisco Bay with the other; Dr Ellen, helping some of those who need help the most; Chris, rowing his way *all the way* to the top; and Kyle, hell-bent on quests few of us can match. Thanks also to my old pal Mary Susan Richardson, for her steadfast friendship and forgiving nature. I am grateful to each and every one of you for your support, inspiration, and love.

I wish also to express my gratitude to Rev. Suzanne Dunn and Rev. Jeannette Bertalan Love, pastors of the Catholic Church of the Beatitudes, Santa Barbara. Thank you for being the good sports that you are, and allowing me to portray a Woman Priest in this book! It has been an honor to witness you both as you journey towards equality for all, through faith and inclusive love.

PROLOGUE

February
The Beach at More Mesa, Santa Barbara

He curled into his sleeping bag to hide from the voices. So, they were back. They'd followed him from downtown and now they were harassing him again, here on the steep hillside overlooking the Pacific.

Darren opened his eyes. The voices had never spoken in Spanish before.

He pulled the sleeping bag flap from his head and lifted up on an elbow. Then he rose to his feet and looked over the dense thicket of coyote brush to the path.

They were out there all right. Not in his head. A three-quarter moon glared down on the men as they struggled up the cliff face, each bent forward under an over-sized load. They slogged up the path step by labored step, sighing as they climbed.

When the three men had passed, Darren turned to look down at the beach directly below. An open boat, around twenty feet long, was drawn up on the sand. A pair of big outboard motors were tipped up at the stern. A panga boat – Darren was pretty sure that's what it was. And the guys that rode in them – they called them *pangeros*.

There was something special about the boat. The stern remained in the water, and a thick ring of blue phosphorescence, shining with a strange light, circled the rear of the boat like an unholy halo. What did that mean?

Four times in all the men ascended the narrow path. Three times four: twelve bales in all. And on the fourth ascent, a voice shouted in English from up on the cliff top: 'Move it you fucking assholes!'

Darren froze.

He knew that voice. That blaring voice, and the mouth and the face that went with it. The cop was mean. He was one of the reasons Darren had left town and walked all the way from the marina to this cliff below More Mesa.

Now he tried to not breathe.

But not breathing did something to his throat. He coughed, he couldn't help it. And then the night grew still. He prayed over and over: *Please God, don't let them find me . . .*

For once his prayer worked. He heard the cop say something in English, then repeat it in Spanish. One of the men answered, but already their voices seemed farther away.

Darren waited five minutes. He was pretty sure he had the place to himself because an owl called, soft yet loud: *hoo, hoo-hoo . . .*

He stepped out of the bag and inched closer to the path. He wanted to take a look at the panga boat, to see if the pangeros had left anything useful behind.

Just as he stepped into the open, he heard a crashing above. One of the men must have returned. Darren slipped back into the brush just in time. A minute later a pangero tore down the zigzag as fast as he could go without falling. He came within a few yards of Darren, but the guy was concentrating on his feet and the path and saw nothing.

Darren watched as the man ran across the sand and crouched over the small boat. When he straightened, he held a bundle under one arm. Then the pangero turned and set off east along the south-facing beach, jogging into the dark.

What was going on? Darren thought he'd heard something weird: the cry of a cat. So the man had what, picked up a *cat*?

Most things in the world weren't what they appeared to be. You might as well just accept it: Darren knew that by now. He'd learned it the hard way.

He still wanted to see into the boat, the little boat crowned by the ring of blue fire. But he hesitated: somebody else might show.

Sure enough, a minute later, another crash sounded above him. He turned and looked up the trail. Now a tall woman in heels was making her way down. She too was moving as fast as she could, and as she passed by Darren's hiding place, her long black hair swung forward, obscuring her face. She slipped and nearly fell, then caught and righted herself and clambered on.

When she reached the sand, the woman kicked off her heels and raced across the beach to the boat. She sank to her knees and bent over the hull.

All was quiet for a time. Then, the woman screamed.

The scream was terrible, anguished. Darren felt like his heart had stopped. He remembered a scream like that: he'd heard it the night his mother had found his sister hanging from a rafter in the garage.

He put his hands over his ears to block out the unbearable sound, just as he'd done that night long ago.

The tall woman remained bent over the open boat. She seemed to have a flashlight now. Maybe it was a phone. Darren watched as she climbed into the boat, knelt down and shined the light into every corner.

Then the woman lurched to her feet. She had something small cupped in her left hand. She focused the flashlight beam on the object.

After what seemed like a long time, she stepped back onto the sand. She trudged back across the beach, one dragging step after another, and climbed the path.

Darren didn't want to look into her eyes as she passed close by him. But he did, he couldn't help it. He peered through the scrub and looked into her face, and he saw the suffering written there. He recognized that raw torment, he remembered it in his mother's face. Some shadow of it had never gone away.

Except . . . except in this case it wasn't *her* face, or *her* torment. It was *his*. That was one thing Darren was pretty sure of: this woman wasn't a woman, but a man.

ONE

The morning was pure and bright, as only a morning in the first weeks of spring can be. I biked to my downtown office, skimming through the streets like a bird. It was a poem of a morning, lilting, full of promise.

I pulled my Schwinn up in front of the bungalow court at 101 West Mission. As I straddled the bike and doubled the band on my ponytail, I studied the sign that read, among other things, SANTA BARBARA INVESTIGATION AGENCY. Something large, an owl or a gull, had splattered the board. I was in such a magnanimous mood that I felt honored: mine was the only business on the board that nature had thus anointed.

But as I wheeled my bike into the courtyard, somehow the morning's promise soured. I don't believe in premonitions, so I can't tell you what it was that altered the mood. Maybe it was just too quiet. No tiny frogs chirped in the old concrete fountain my office manager, Gabi Gutierrez, had resurrected. Nothing scuttled in the leaf litter or chattered from the flower bracts of the giant bird of paradise.

I cabled my bike to the wrought iron banister and climbed the three steps. Pulling open the screen door, I let it bang against my back as I shoved the key into the stiff lock of the main door. Inside, all was dark and still.

I left the solid door open to let in the fresh morning air, drew up the blinds and lifted the window sashes. It was still early and Deadbeat, my neighbor's parrot, had yet to take charge of his outdoor perch. The African Grey was indoors, no doubt scheming under a tablecloth.

I walked through to the kitchenette and raised the blind looking out to the concrete block wall at the back. I noticed that the hot pink bougainvillea, which had been attacked last fall by an invasion of bougainvillea loopers, was making a bid for survival. As were we all.

I was about to fill the coffee carafe at the sink when I heard the screen door squeal open, then close.

'Um . . . Hello? Anybody here?'

I set down the carafe and turned to peer into the office. The figure of a curvaceous woman filled the doorway. I say filled the doorway because she stood well over six feet tall. I'm no shorty myself, and she towered over me. Her face was in shadow, and the morning sun shone all around her like a white-gold aura.

I'd had my own aura done once. It had proved to be purple and black.

'Hi. Come on in.' I walked back into the office and stretched out a hand. 'Jaymie Zarlin.'

The lady's four-inch heels struck the old oak floor like hammers driving in nails as she stepped forward to greet me.

She extended her own hand, as a countess might. But when I took it into mine, I felt a small shock of recognition. In spite of its limpness, the hand was large and strong. I looked into her face, and at that moment, I knew that she knew that I knew. She tilted up her chin as if to say, *so what*.

'I'm Jesús María Robledo.' She tried to smile. 'They call me Chucha.' Her low voice was silk-soft.

I found it hard not to stare. Who wouldn't? Chucha was gorgeous, dark and exotic, with fine aquiline features and long black hair. Her nose was arched, and she looked like an Aztec queen. In spite of the cool February air, she wore a white peasant blouse cut low enough to display a good four inches of cleavage. Her black pencil skirt could have been spray painted on.

When I realized I was staring, I looked away. But Chucha was no doubt used to being stared at and didn't seem to care. Besides, it was plain she had something serious on her mind.

'Please sit down.' I indicated the couch, walked over and shut the front door, then took for myself what my office manager called 'the hot seat.'

I watched as Chucha arranged herself on the couch, hiked her blouse up and her skirt down. Then she fixed me with her gold-brown eyes. 'I don't know how to say this. It's so hard. And . . .' She swallowed and stopped.

'Lots of clients feel that way in the beginning. Don't worry, you won't be telling me anything I haven't heard before.'

Her eyes welled with tears, but this time she managed a smile. 'I'm not so sure about that.'

I wasn't so sure myself. 'Start anywhere, Chucha. You don't need a beginning.'

She nodded and rubbed a knuckle along her chin. It was a masculine gesture, unconscious. 'Maybe – maybe I'll start with this.'

She unsnapped the clasp on her handbag, reached in and withdrew a ziplock bag. She stared at it for a moment. Then, meeting my gaze, she leaned forward and handed it to me.

I unzipped the bag and withdrew a white cotton handkerchief that had been folded over several times. I pressed the handkerchief with my fingertips: something was wrapped in the cloth. For some reason, now the room seemed very still.

I unfolded the handkerchief: a small silver cross nestled in the fabric. The edges of the cross were filigreed, and in the middle, running down the center of the cross, four letters were etched: *MACB*.

'You'll have to explain, Chucha. I can see it's a cross made for a child. But what does it mean?'

'I don't have a clue.' When she shook her head, her long black hair fell forward and obscured her face. 'I found it this morning. I found it in . . .'

Then Chucha began to cry. She tried to hold it in, but her shoulders shook with long racking sobs.

I got up and went over to sit beside her on the couch. I took her hand, and she drew a ragged breath. The woman was trying to get ahold of herself.

'Sorry,' she muttered.

'Don't be.' I got up, went over to the desk and picked up the Kleenex box. I handed her the box and she pressed a tissue to her eyes.

'I can see it's hard to talk about, Chucha. You've had quite a shock. Take your time.'

'I've had a shock, yes. But not because—' Chucha sat up straight and flicked her hair behind her shoulders with both hands. 'Not because I found that cross. I've never seen it before. It's because I didn't find—' She bit her bottom lip.

I perched on the corner of the desk and waited. I could see Chucha had something she needed to say, something that was almost too disturbing to put into words. But even so, it had to be said.

'Ms Zarlin, I'm telling you this because I know you find missing people. I heard about you, people say you won't go to the police. Is – is that right?'

'Call me Jaymie. And no, I won't tell the cops.' A knot had formed in the pit of my stomach. I told myself to be cool, not to commit. Chucha was reeling me in fast, and so far I had no idea what all this was about.

'All right.' She knitted her long, elegant fingers together. 'What I didn't find was what was supposed to be there, in the boat: my baby, my little girl. *Now* do you see?'

The knot in my stomach pulled tight. This person had a kid? Chucha was right: this wasn't something I'd encountered before.

'I'm beginning to see. You had an arrangement, right? To pick up your daughter in a boat. Where?'

'On the beach below More Mesa, last night.'

'More Mesa.' I nodded, but kept my expression neutral. 'I understand the police confiscated a panga boat down there this morning.' I'd read that on Edhat. Roger the Scanner Guy had reported it first thing.

Chucha leaned forward, holding my gaze with her own. 'Yes. That was the boat. They phoned me at 3:30 a.m. and said my Rosie was waiting there for me, no problem. Just like I'd paid for.'

'I see.' So this lady did have a daughter. I hoped I was covering my surprise, but she shot me a hard look.

'It happens, OK? I'm human. I get lonely sometimes.'

'Be patient with me, Chucha. I'm trying to understand.'

'Sorry. I know you are. I – I'm going crazy.' Chucha got to her feet and paced down the room. Her long legs covered the distance in three or four strides.

'I have to trust you, I know that. So here is what happened. I went to visit my family in Mexico. And there was a girl, Leticia . . . She got pregnant. The baby was mine.' Chucha halted in front of me.

'I named her Rosamar. Rosie for short. Leticia, she didn't care what I called her. After Rosie was born I would always send money, every two weeks. Then one of my cousins, she called me. She told me Leticia was spending the money on herself and her new asshole boyfriend. Rosie, she was crying all the time. She was too skinny, and she was always dirty, you know? Leticia never gave her a bath.'

'So you decided to bring her here.'

'Of course.' She set a hand on her hip. 'Wouldn't you?'

'Yes. Yes, I would. But maybe I'd go and get her myself.'

'Maybe you would, since you're not a tranny like me.' Chucha sniffed. 'Oh, and no papers either, even though I came here when I was five. I'm not exactly the kind they give visas to. And believe me, border patrol don't look the other way if I try to cross in a car.'

'I'm learning. So, what did you arrange? You had her kidnapped, right?'

'Yes, I had to! Leticia loved getting the money every two weeks, understand? She was mean to Rosie, but no way was she going to let her go.'

'How did you work it?'

'My cousin has a friend who knows somebody, a guy who smuggles marijuana into California. The guy said he'd grab Rosie and bring her north in his boat. He said it was safe, he'd done the trip to Santa Barbara two times already. He would call me and tell me when I should go to the beach.'

'The beach at More Mesa.'

'Yes, that's the one he wanted to land on. The one under the cliffs, past Hope Ranch. The one with the really steep path down.'

'So, you paid for your daughter to be brought north in a panga boat.' I tried hard not to sound judgmental. 'And the pangero is a marijuana smuggler.'

'Yes, I know. It sounds crazy! But the guy in charge, the one I talked to on the phone? My cousin's friend said he has kids, he's not a bad man. And he sounded OK. He told me he would take good care of Rosie. I paid him half. He was gonna meet me when the boat landed, and then I'd pay the other half.'

There was one thing I was already sure of: a much bigger game was in play. The guy Chucha had dealt with wouldn't have been the one in charge of the smuggling operation, not by a long shot. Most likely he was just someone who saw a chance to make a buck on the side.

'So when you got there, the beach was deserted. You must have had a terrible shock.'

'Yes! The boat was there, but it was empty. I used my phone for a flashlight, I looked all over the boat, to see if I could find anything, anything that belonged to my baby.'

I looked down at the cross in my hand. 'You found this instead.'

'It was down in a crack. I noticed it because my light shined off it. Maybe one of the guys on the boat lost it, you know? He could have been carrying it to think of his own daughter.' She dropped down on the couch and put her head in her hands. 'I don't know. I guess I hoped that cross might be a clue.'

'Chucha, you've phoned your cousin, right? And the pangero. Have you made contact with him?'

'I called the guy right away. What a surprise, his number don't work anymore! I called my cousin, and she called her friend, and they both tried to find him. My cousin, she's still trying. The name he gave us? It's not his real name, we know that now.' She looked up at me. 'I've been so stupid. It's all my own fault.'

I looked out the side window. I felt cornered, pinned down by what Chucha was asking me to do. I needed to somehow convey my sympathy without implying I'd take on the case. Because I already had a good idea of what had gone wrong.

The most likely explanation – that the child died in the course of the passage and her body was thrown overboard like yesterday's trash – was the last thing in the world a mother would want to hear.

'I very much hope you find your daughter.' I folded the handkerchief around the cross and held it out to her. 'I'm sorry, Chucha. But there's not much I can do.'

'No.' Chucha held up a hand. 'You keep that. Somebody might come looking for it one day.' She frowned. 'What you just said, that you can't do much? I'm sorry, it just isn't true.'

I placed the folded handkerchief on the corner of the desk, got to my feet, and walked over to the window. The woman from the office next door was fastening Deadbeat's tethered leg to his perch.

'Jaymie, here's my problem,' Chucha said to my back. 'If you won't help me, who will?'

Late that afternoon I was fluffing up a stack of papers on the kitchen table when I heard the front office door open, then close.

'Miss Jaymie, I'm glad you're still here! My third house today, it took so, so long. Mrs Gustafson, she left all the dirty—' Gabi Gutierrez, my office manager, partner, and sometimes wise auntie, stepped into the kitchenette and halted.

'Uh-oh. I am reading your face. What is wrong?'

I pushed back my chair and got to my feet. 'So, a big day for Sparkleberry, huh? How about una cerveza.'

'Yes, that would be nice. I am going to stretch out on the couch, then maybe you will answer my question. Are any of those home-made tortilla chips left?'

'Sorry.' I closed the fridge door with an elbow and walked back into the main room, holding a pale ale in each hand. 'Those chips were my lunch.'

Gabi took off her sneakers and swung her legs up on the couch. 'I am so tired. But it's a good tired, you know?'

I offered her a bottle. 'This should perk you up.'

'Hmm. I like Mexican beer better. Bohemia, that's my favorite.'

'No problem, I'll drink it.' I withdrew my hand.

'Very funny, Miss Jaymie.' She accepted the beer, twisted off the cap, and took a long sip. 'I deserve this, you know?'

'Yeah, I know what you mean. Me too.' I dropped down in Gabi's desk chair. The desk had once been my own, but that had changed the day Gabriela Rufina Martinez Gutierrez salsa-ed in through the door.

Damn, the beer tasted good. I shut my eyes for a moment and listened to the everyday sounds: the rumble of going-home traffic out on Mission, and under it, the chatter of birds gossiping in the courtyard. The late afternoon sun flowed, like a river of gold, through the open front door.

'Miss Jaymie, I am looking at you and you know what I think? I think maybe you should go get a haircut. Your hair is such a nice color, dark brown and a little bit red, but that ponytail, it don't look so good. You are thirty-eight years old, it's time to get rid of the ponytail. Miss Jaymie? I am sorry but that's what I think.'

I opened my eyes and set down my bottle on Gabi's blotter. 'I had a visitor this morning. Her name is Chucha Robledo.'

'Chucha Robledo . . .' Gabi set her own bottle on the floor and began to unwind her yards-long purple and pink crocheted scarf. 'I think maybe I know who she is. Is she the girl that's a man?'

I wasn't surprised Gabi knew about Chucha. My office manager was related to half the population of Santa Barbara. The other half she seemed to know all about, too.

'Yep. She's the one.'

'I see her in my neighborhood, you know? On Haley. She kind

of, how do you say it? Stands out.' Gabi folded her scarf and placed
it on the arm of the couch. 'Lots of people know who Chucha is.
I think she does makeup, for weddings and quinceañeras.'

'I liked her. She seems like a nice person.'

'Yes, I think maybe she is. Some people are mean to her, though,
even some women. I think maybe people who are not . . .'

'Positively positive?' I said this just to tease. *Positively Positive*
was Gabi's favorite self-help book. She'd recently purchased the
workbook, too, and the office was positively oozing with good
intentions these days. I never thought I'd say it, but there were times
I positively yearned for Gabi's sharp tongue to return.

'Please don't laugh.' She leaned forward and began to unlace her
florescent pink sneakers. 'Some people are afraid of anything
different, know what I mean?'

'I know what you mean.' I got to my feet and walked to the open
doorway. A hummingbird flashed rubies and emeralds as it plied a
patch of white-flowered sage.

'Like maybe your eyes, Miss Jaymie. The way one is blue and the
other one is a little bit green. You are pretty, but some people, they
might get bothered by that.' Gabi sat back and folded her hands on her
stomach. 'Now tell me what Chucha said. And start at the beginning.
We are investigators, so please don't leave even the little things out.'

When I'd finished telling Gabi all about Chucha's visit, I opened
the filing cabinet and took out the handkerchief. I flipped open the
folds, exposing the tiny silver cross, and held it out to her.

'Chucha found this in the boat. She said she'd never seen it
before.'

Gabi peered at it through her newly-acquired half-moon glasses.
'*MACB*. Miss Jaymie, you shoulda put that in the safe. Otherwise
why do we have a safe, know what I mean?'

'I would have, if I knew how to open the damn thing.' The
combination changed every few days, for what Gabi referred to as
security reasons.

Gabi waved away my objection. 'This cross is from Taxco, I am
sure about that.' She flipped it over with an intricately manicured
fingernail. 'So Chucha said she never saw this before?'

'Right.' I handed her a sheet of typing paper and pulled my phone
from my pocket. 'Put it down there for a minute. I'll take a few
snaps with my cell.'

Gabi was quiet, observing me. When I'd finished photographing the cross, she spoke. 'Here is what I hope. I hope another baby is not missing.'

'It's occurred to me too. But we don't have any reason to think that's so.' I refolded the handkerchief around the cross and handed it to Gabi. 'You're right about one thing. We should put this away in the safe. We can give it to Mike the next time he drops by.'

Deputy Sheriff Mike Dawson dropped by often now. We were back together again, and though I still choked on the word, you could call us a 'couple'.

'Don't we gotta hold on to it? Till we solve the case.'

'Gabi—'

'A little girl, Rosamar, is missing. That is what you said.' She lowered her chin and gave me a hard look. 'And also, maybe a little child with the initials of MACB.'

'Gabi, listen to me. I haven't taken the case, and I won't.'

'What? You solve murders and you find missing people too, everybody in Santa Barbara knows that.' Gabi's voice rose into the stubborn red zone. 'Chucha needs you to find her baby, Miss Jaymie. One thing I can tell you for sure, she will come back again right away.'

I tipped up the bottle and swallowed the last trickle of beer. I could be damn stubborn too, when I had to. 'You do know what happened, right?'

'I think I know what you are thinking.' Gabi swung her legs back to the floor and sat up straight. 'Maybe Rosamar died, and the pangero, he put her body into the water.'

'Yes, I'm afraid so. Chucha still owed him half the money. If her daughter was alive, he'd have been waiting there on the beach with his hand out. I don't want any part of this, Gabi. I feel bad about it, but there's nothing I can do.'

'I know you feel bad. But Chucha, like I say, she will come back here no matter what.' Gabi placed her own empty bottle on the worn oak floor. 'We have to help her, even if we are gonna find out bad news.'

Then, for the second time that day, I was asked the same question.

'Who else is gonna do it, Miss Jaymie? Tell me the answer to that.'

TWO

Next morning the sky was again a sweet and delicate blue. Thank the gods, we'd had a winter with rain. The drought was foiled, at least for the time being, and all was right with the world.

I played catch with Dex for twenty minutes or so, till the three-legged heeler flopped down to inform me playtime was over. Then I jumped on my bike and coasted down El Balcon.

I thought I was headed for the office, but the old blue Schwinn seemed to have other ideas. It carried me along Cliff and up Las Positas, then left onto Modoc. My rational mind ordered me to get back on track, but I knew where the bicycle was taking me: out to More Mesa.

A sharpish breeze off the ocean fanned my warm face as I left the housing and pedaled across the rough muddy track. The fields, thick with wild radish and mustard, had just begun to burst into bloom, and the yellow, pink, and white pastel landscape was as pretty as an impressionist's painting. I rode past a clump of brush adorned with pussy willow catkins, and couldn't resist. I had to stop my bike long enough to stroke the catkins, soft as kittens' ears.

I dismounted at the cliff's edge and looked out over the channel. Santa Cruz Island's dark and austere form was shrouded in a skirt of white mist. From here, the island seemed close to shore.

I cabled my bike to an ancient lemonadeberry bush that was tall as a tree. Then I began to make my way down the steep path to the beach.

Part way down, at a switchback, I stopped to scan the beach below. The police must have removed the panga boat, as the beach was empty. The tide was way out, exposing rocks and pools. I didn't expect to find much, and for a moment I wondered why I was there, wasting my time.

But I knew why. Gabi was right: Chucha would return to talk to me today, no doubt about it. And although my decision to not get involved was the right one, it couldn't hurt for me to learn something about what had taken place. To do that, as always, I had to examine the scene with my own eyes.

I took a few more steps down the track, then halted. I'd heard something to my right in the brush. Not the usual scuffling sound of a towhee scratching through leaf litter. No, this was a larger sound, the kind of crackling noise an animal might make.

I turned and looked, staring into the thick brush. Something took shape in the leafy maze: a pair of eyes. Human eyes.

'Hi,' I said. And I waited, to see if the guy would answer me. I was pretty sure it was a man. I could make out the sleeve of a gray sweatshirt and a stubbled chin. But there was no reply.

Well, the fellow had every right to be there. Maybe more right than me, as the hillside was most likely his home. I continued on down the path, stepped onto the dry sand and crossed the beach to the water.

When I reached the high tide line from the previous evening, I halted and scanned the wet hard-packed sand. It would have been nice to have discovered a set of tire tracks from a police truck and boat trailer, but the sand was swept clean by the surf in all directions. I calculated: there could have been two high tides since the cops had come and confiscated the panga boat. At this point, it wouldn't be easy to determine exactly where it had come ashore.

A gaggle of whimbrels skittered away as I crossed the wet sand and headed for the exposed rocks. This was a minus tide by a foot or two, and the pools revealed shag carpets of waving anemones, darting rockfish, and bumbling hermit crabs. Only a few starfish, though. Starfish were suffering a dieback in the channel, for reasons biologists couldn't yet fathom, but which no doubt had to do with the usual 'humanizing' effect.

I walked westward, skirting the water's edge. I wasn't sure what I was searching for. Some object, maybe, that the police overlooked.

After walking two or three hundred yards, I stopped and looked back at the path down the cliff. I was too far to the west now. The pangeros would have lined up their landing with the path.

I turned and made my way back to my starting point, then headed east. In that direction, as it turned out, I didn't have far to go.

The scrapes on the exposed rocks were fresh. I dropped to one knee. You could see where an aluminum hull had torn off a long swath of sea lettuce, exposing the sandstone beneath. I bent down to study a glint: sure enough, there was even a streak of dull silver paint embedded in the rough rock. The tide hadn't been strong enough to wash it away.

So now I knew where the panga had landed. Early-rising beach walkers would have reported the abandoned boat straight away. Then the cops would have retrieved it as quickly as possible, by driving along the packed sand at low tide. Although no tire tracks remained, I guessed they'd driven on and off the beach from an access point to the east, maybe at Arroyo Burro.

But that didn't matter. All that mattered was to discover if the SBPD had missed any clues.

Hopping from rock to rock, I peered into the tide pools. The miniature salt water worlds gleamed crystal clear, vibrant with red and green seaweed. I saw shards of broken tile and sea glass, but they looked like they'd been in the water for a long time.

What was I searching for? I had no idea. But the police could be sloppy. I'd visited enough crime scenes to know they always left something behind, if only a blue latex glove.

I returned to study the scrapes on the rock, then headed for the high water mark to see what might have washed up on the beach at that point. There was the usual flotsam: a plastic fork with broken tines, an Arrowhead water bottle. And something more.

I'm not sure why they even caught my eye: they looked like nothing more than fragments of seaweed. The three small reddish-green fruits were ovoid in shape, like skinny ribbed eggs. When I picked one up in my hand, I noticed a few soft spines were still attached. *Dragon fruit.*

I'd tasted dragon fruit once: the flavor was delicate, delectable. But what the heck were they doing here in the sand? Dragon fruit weren't the sort of snack you'd take on a picnic. And besides, February wasn't a month for beach picnics, not even in Santa Barbara.

For no good reason I could think of, I slipped the fruit into my sweatshirt pocket. I didn't imagine they had anything to do with the case. But their presence on the beach was a mystery – and mysteries, great or small, made me wild.

Angel Mendoza and I nearly collided in the courtyard. 'Good morning, Miss Jaymie. How are you?' Gabi's boyfriend was a plain-looking guy, but he had the sweetest smile this side of heaven.

'Hi, Angel. I'm good. Did you bring Gabi a rose today?'

Gabi and Angel were sweethearts. But they were moving out of the courting stage to a deeper level, and I'd noticed Angel's flurry of floral tributes had slowed.

The gardener rested a hand on his carpenter's belt, which was loaded down with half a dozen different types of clippers. Angel was as painstaking as a neurosurgeon when it came to roses: a single wrong cut, he'd explained to me, could take a full year to repair.

'Yes, I gave her Mr Lincoln because next week is Lincoln's birthday. In Santa Barbara he never stops blooming all winter.' His expression grew somber. 'Miss Jaymie? Gabi told me about the baby that is missing. Terrible.'

I'd have to speak with Gabi about talking out of school. Still, I understood. She and Angel were close.

'Terrible is the word. You won't say anything about it, will you?'

'Don't worry, Miss Jaymie. Gabi already said to say nothing. I just . . . can't stop worrying. You know?'

'The best thing is to not think about it.' This was me talking, the one who'd just visited More Mesa against her better judgment. 'I'm afraid there's nothing we can do.'

Angel dropped his eyes and looked at the ground. That was enough to tell me the man didn't agree.

'I gotta go to my next house now, Miss Jaymie. A problem with the irrigation.'

'Angel, wait.' I pulled one of the dragon fruits from my pocket. The soft spines stung my palm, like the bites of a tiny spider. 'You know what this is, right?'

'Yes, a dragon fruit. Where I come from, we call that pitahaya.' He took it from me and cupped it in his callused palm. 'They are so good. You know, I have one growing on my patio. Where did you get this?'

'I found it on the beach. I think it washed in on the tide. Any reason you can think of, as to why it would be in the ocean?'

'In the ocean? No, that is strange. Also, it's not the right time, you know? The pitahaya is ripe in summer and fall, not February. This maybe came from South America.' He gave me a little smile, forgiving me, perhaps, for what I'd said earlier about there being little we could do for Chucha's daughter. 'It's like a puzzle, Miss Jaymie. A mystery for you to solve.'

'This one could be beyond me.'

Angel turned the dragon fruit over and looked at it once more, then shrugged and handed it back. 'Gabi, she says you need a good dinner. We want to cook for you at our house. The citrus is blooming at La Rosaleda, and the air, it smells like lemon perfume.'

As far as I knew, Gabi still lived alone in her tiny apartment, just off Haley. But in Angel's mind, apparently, Gabi had already joined him in the guest house he occupied on a Hope Ranch estate.

'I'd be honored to dine with you both, Angel. Just name the day.'

Mr Lincoln flared forth in the sparkling bud vase on the corner of Gabi's desk. The bright red rose expressed justice and courage.

'Miss Jaymie, is that you?' Gabi called from the kitchenette.

'None other.' I walked in and tossed my messenger bag on the table.

Gabi was scrubbing the coffee pot with baking soda at the sink. She turned and looked at me. 'You're kinda late this morning. Something is wrong?'

'No. I had somewhere to go first.' I didn't mention More Mesa. I didn't want to get her hopes up, about Chucha and the case.

'Somewhere? Oh sure, I forget. I am your office manager and your PA, but it's none of my business.' Her glance fell on the clutch of dragon fruit I'd pulled from my pocket. 'Where did those come from, the Guadalajara grocery store?'

'Believe it or not, I found them on the beach. Any ideas?'

'Ideas, that's your department, Miss Jaymie. My department is to keep all your ideas in one straight line.' She turned back to the sink. 'There's a message for you on the office phone. Very important. But go listen for yourself.'

'First I need some coffee. Was the pot dirty? I hadn't noticed.'

'It is no good to wait till you notice.' Gabi turned on the tap and rinsed the carafe. 'If you notice, then it's too dirty. See what I mean?'

I sighed, walked back into the front office, and punched a button on the phone.

'Please, I have money to pay you. I need you to find my little girl.' Chucha's recorded voice was urgent, strained.

'You know, I am thinking, Miss Jaymie.' Gabi stood in the doorway, wiping her hands on a dish towel. 'Sorry, but I am gonna say it again. You gotta do something.'

'And what if Chucha's daughter was lost at sea?' My heart panged in my chest like a guitar string twisted too tight. 'We could search for a hundred years and never find her. We'd look and look and never come up with an answer.'

'Miss Jaymie? You and me, we don't have no kids.'

I waited, wondering what she was getting at.

'I was a mother for my sisters and brothers, 'cause there was nobody else. And you, you never say it, but I think maybe it was the same for you and your brother?'

'I protected him,' I admitted. 'Or tried to, anyway.'

'Try, that is all we can do. Also I think, 'cause we don't have our own kids, our job is to help other families, you know? The kids, the mothers, and the fathers.' She paused. 'And the mothers that are fathers, those too.'

Gabi had me: my heart was convinced. But my brain ordered me not to give in. 'I'll think about it.'

'Huh.' She raised an eyebrow. 'You know what I always tell you, Miss Jaymie. Don't think about it too much.'

An hour later the sky clouded over. Then raindrops began to tap on the thin old windowpanes. I looked up from the kitchen table and watched the drops palpate the leaves of the bougainvillea sprawling over the wall at the back. A goldfinch hopped from twig to twig, trying to dodge the drops – or maybe to catch them.

The office front door opened. I swiveled in my chair and leaned back to face the open doorway. There, as I'd half-expected, stood Chucha. She wore skinny leg jeans and a raspberry-colored hoodie. She caught my eye as she slipped the bright hood from her long black hair.

'I'm sorry, I had to come back. You know why?' She tried a smile. 'It's like I said – there's nowhere else I can go.'

'No need to apologize. I'd have come back too.' I got up from the chair and walked on through. 'Chucha, I don't think you've met Gabi, my office manager.'

'And I'm also Miss Jaymie's PA.' Gabi walked around her desk and extended her hand. 'I am happy to meet you.'

Chucha inclined her head. 'I think I've seen you before – do you live on Haley?'

'One block away. I see you sometimes in the Guadalajara Market, you know?'

Chucha nodded. 'I live upstairs, above the store.'

'It's raining.' Gabi looked out the window and hugged herself, as if the pitter-patter of warm raindrops threatened to freeze us. 'Do you want some hot chocolate?'

'Sure. That'd be nice.'

I noticed Chucha's wig was askew. I felt bad for her: the pain in her eyes was obvious. But it was nothing compared to the pain I feared she'd soon come to know.

'So, Jaymie. I guess you think it's no use?'

I didn't want to answer Chucha's question. I walked over to the open doorway. The raindrops plopped on the giant bird of paradise leaves, bounced off to the ground. Rain in a dry climate: it was all about life, wasn't it? This was the season of green grass, spring poppies, and lupine. Not the death of a child.

'I wouldn't say "no use," Chucha. But if your daughter wasn't in the boat . . .' I steeled myself. 'It's possible she never made it to shore.' I used the word 'possible' to be kind.

Chucha stared at me. Then she held up a finger. 'Before you say anything else, I have something to show you.'

She reached into her hoodie pocket and pulled out a small note-book with an elastic band. 'They say a picture is worth a thousand words, right?' She snapped off the band, opened the notebook, and took out a photo. She gazed at it for a minute as a ghost of a smile hovered on her lips. 'Here.'

Time stopped as I studied the photograph. For a long moment, even the rain hung motionless in the sky.

'That's my Rosie,' Chucha said in a low voice. 'The picture is from six weeks ago.'

Somehow, I'd imagined an infant. But this bright-eyed child was at least a year old, maybe closer to two. There was no baby chub-biness about her. Like Chucha, her complexion was dark, her features fine. She stared straight into the camera. She met the camera's eye, and yet, at the same time, something in her drew back. The child was hurt and bewildered, you could see that. But you could see something else: little Rosie was a long way from giving up.

I swallowed hard. Then everything started up again: Gabi moving about the kitchenette, clattering cups and saucers, the traffic out on Mission, and the tap-tapping of the rain.

'Your daughter is beautiful.' I held out the photo.

'Thank you. But keep it.' Chucha took half a step back. 'She has a birthmark, you should know that. It's just here—' She slipped her hand under her hair to the base of her neck. 'It's kind of shaped like a dolphin.'

'Chucha—' I began, but then I stopped. It didn't matter if I kept the picture or not. I'd seen it, and I knew I wouldn't be forgetting those black eyes anytime soon.

'You two better sit down,' Gabi counseled from the kitchen doorway. 'I'm gonna bring you the hot chocolate now.'

But neither of us moved. Chucha's chin was tilted, challenging me. Challenging me to say no.

At last, I gave in.

'Let's have Gabi's hot chocolate. Then we'll talk about how we're going to proceed.'

THREE

Mike leaned back in the kitchen chair and tipped up a Firestone Double Barrel ale. 'Jaymie, you're sure about this?' The chair rocked back onto all four legs.

'Mister Mike, she already decided. Miss Jaymie did the right thing. Chucha, she's got no papers. And only a little money. Also, you know, she is a woman but sometimes she looks like a man.' Gabi counted off on her fingers. 'That's three reasons why Chucha cannot come to anybody else. And that's why Miss Jaymie said yes.'

I reached across the kitchen table, picked up the photo of Rosie, and handed it to Mike. 'Try saying no to that face.'

'A sweetie, for sure.' He frowned. 'She looks scared.'

'Right now, if Rosie's alive, I'd say she's more than a little scared.'

Mike handed the photograph back to me. 'Any chance she never left Mexico?'

'It's possible, sure. But Chucha asked around. Her cousin's friend was certain about one thing: Rosie was put on the boat, all safe and sound.'

'Tucked into the marijuana bales, huh?' Mike began to peel the label off his beer bottle. 'Listen. Those drug smugglers don't give a shit about anything.'

'The jefe, yes.' Gabi reached over and swept Mike's label peelings into her hand. 'But the ones in the boat, the pangeros, sometimes they are just kids. Kids who want a ride north and a few American dollars, that's all. I think we gotta try and find those guys. They might talk to us, you know?'

'Too late, Gabi. They're in LA by now, if not farther away. The pangeros don't just hang around town, waiting to get picked up by ICE.' Mike lifted the tiny silver cross from the unfolded handkerchief. 'I'm inclined to agree with Jaymie on this. It doesn't look good.'

'But Chucha thinks her daughter is still alive, Mister Mike. A mother can tell. And a father – I think maybe a father can tell, too.'

Mike shot Gabi a grin. 'Which is she, Gabi? A mother or a father? You're making me confused.'

'Stop teasing me please. Chucha's a lady, that's for sure. Wait till you see her. But the baby needs a father, and that's gonna be Chucha too.'

'I have to commend you, Mike.' I'd decided to do a little teasing of my own. 'You're very cool about Chucha.'

'I don't think about it too much. I figure if she says she's a woman, that's what she is.' He cocked an eyebrow in my direction. 'I'm not saying she's my type.'

'No, your type is Miss Jaymie,' Gabi instructed. 'And Miss Jaymie, her type is you.'

Time to change the subject. Ever since Gabi had fallen for Angel, she was an expert in all matters involving love and romance.

'Until proven otherwise, we'll assume Rosie's alive,' I said. 'It's the only way to proceed.'

'If she's alive, then she was abducted,' Mike replied. 'The question is, why? Chucha was ready to pay the remainder of what she owed the traffickers, right?'

'Right.' I polished off my own beer and set the bottle back into its water ring on the tabletop. 'Maybe somebody else wanted her.'

'But who? Rosamar has a papá already.' Gabi flung a hand in the air. 'And her mother, she's in Mexico and treats her bad.'

'I hear you.' Mike opened his hand. 'But how does this fit in?' The silver cross gleamed in his wide palm.

'Maybe it's just what Chucha thought,' I said. 'One of the pangeros was carrying the cross for his own personal reasons and lost it. It could have belonged to his daughter, something like that.'

Gabi pushed back her chair and got to her feet. 'You know what? Let's not call the baby *MACB*. Let's call her Millie, for Milagros.'

'Milagros – miracle?' Mike shook his head. 'I wouldn't call any of this a miracle, Gabi.'

'No. But we gotta think that way, you know? For Chucha's little girl, we need a miracle. And also for the one we don't know about, *MACB*. Maybe she's OK, but maybe she needs a miracle too.'

'Sure, we can call the missing one Millie,' I replied. 'But I don't believe in miracles, Gabi. I'll do my best by Chucha, but something tells me this won't turn out well.'

Gabi's face fell. 'Miss Jaymie. I hope you are wrong.' She walked over to the kitchen sink and proceeded to wash out the coffee carafe yet again. We had the cleanest damn coffee pot in town.

'I gotta go.' Mike got to his feet and lifted his windbreaker from the back of his chair. 'We're working on a big meth operation way back in Los Padres Forest. I'm driving up tomorrow, hiking in the next morning.'

'What, so soon?' I stood too. 'I thought it was going to be at the end of the month.'

'We moved it up.'

I knew that was all Mike would say about the investigation. When it came to sheriff's department business, he worked on a strict need-to-know basis.

I didn't want to put on a show in front of Gabi, so I resisted stepping into his arms. 'When will you be back?'

'Four or five days – no more than a week. Anything you need me to do before I take off?'

'Just one thing.' I have to admit, I employed my most irresistible smile. 'Can you get me in to take a look at the panga boat? The PD must have it in storage somewhere.'

'Probably in the warehouse downtown, where they keep the confiscated vehicles. Sure, I can't see why not. Let me look into it

– but since I'm taking off, it will have to be tonight or tomorrow.'
He leaned forward and planted a kiss on top of my head. 'See?
When you ask nice, I'm putty in your hands.'

I pedaled through the Westside on my way home. The rain had
stopped, and a soft purple dusk glowed. The seductive scent of the
Victorian box trees hung in the air like a lux perfume.

All the talk about mothers and fathers had me thinking about
my own. As a rule, Paul and Doreen didn't manage to slip into my
thoughts. Years ago, when I was a kid, I'd planted a thorny hedge
in my mind. Over the decades it had grown into an impenetrable
thicket, and my parents seldom passed through.

I never talked about my parents to anyone, not even Gabi or
Mike. Not because Doreen and Paul were evil or cruel: they weren't.
In fact, there was nothing dramatic to tell. And yet, they managed
to hurt the people around them. But even that I couldn't get angry
about, not anymore. I knew my parents damaged others because
they were damaged themselves.

I turned into Loma Alta and leaned forward to pump up the steep
incline. Near the crest of the hill I pulled over, straddled my bike,
and gazed over the city. Already house lights were winking on the
hillsides and hundreds of tail lights pulsed like corpuscles along the
thick artery of 101.

The truth was that Rosie – if she was alive – was a lucky girl.
She had a parent that loved her, loved her deeply.

My own mother had never seen me as anything more than a
competitor or a nuisance. I was adopted as a baby, and her decision
to adopt hadn't been what you'd call mature. As far as I could figure
out, all the other women her age were having kids, and Doreen decided
she wanted one of those, too. But somehow I never filled her needs.

She'd regretted my adoption and had taken pains to make sure I
knew that. I'd grown used to rejection. Neglect had wound its barbed
strands through my mind.

Brodie, on the other hand, had come into the world as Doreen's
surprise natural son, her darling. But in the end he'd let Doreen
down too, because of his mental illness. Even now, three years after
Brodie's death, she still took her son's illness as a personal insult.

Our dad, on the other hand, had worked hard to bestow gifts on
Doreen, gifts she never accepted. She'd never stopped pushing him

away, and he'd never ceased trying to get close. Dad was wounded too, of course, locked in an empty embrace, always too ready to give and never receive. Doreen and Paul: to those who didn't know them well, they'd no doubt seemed like the perfect couple. At least, for a time.

I looked out over the harbor. A giant cruise ship, gleaming white and gold in the last light, was anchored not far out. From here it looked like a floating pleasure palace, an enchanted isle.

The truth is, nothing lasts forever. And one fine day, when my father had made some mistake or other and failed to satisfy the queen, she'd screamed 'off with your head.' Doreen kicked Paul out and told him to go rent an apartment. I'm certain my mother never thought for a minute that he wouldn't return.

A laugh squeezed through my throat. Because I'd just realized my father probably also never imagined he wouldn't go back. But there was a wild card neither of my parents could have foreseen: clever Glenda Barnes.

Glenda, as it happened, rented an apartment in Paul's complex. With impeccable timing, she cha-cha-ed in from the wings. Then she cemented the deal, in short order, by producing two kids, Stephanie and Paul Junior, both now grown. That was clever of Glenda, too: she'd given Paul one kid to replace me and another to replace my brother.

A car sped up Loma Alta, and some smartass leaned out and shouted something. That was good, because I yelled back. My annoyance snapped me out of the funk I was in, and for the moment, broke the link to the past.

Dexter hopped out through the dog door when I pedaled up the hill to the house. He half-barked, half-howled out a scolding. I climbed off my bike and knelt down to embrace the three-legged guy.

'Missed me, huh? Sorry, bud, I had a long day.'

Together we walked to the front door and entered my two-bedroom stucco abode. I fed the heeler, then grabbed a glass of wine and a packet of chips and went out to the narrow patio at the back.

The channel was dark now, the lights on the oil rigs flashing an invitation – or a warning, hard to tell which. I sank down into the aluminum patio chair, then jumped up: the seat was wet with rain-water. I picked up the chair, tipped it over and banged it on the concrete before sitting down again. But my jeans were already soaked.

I rubbed Dexter behind the ears and stared into the dark. As my eyes adjusted, the constellations took shape. High above, Orion climbed the wall of the sky.

Patterns . . . the constellations were nothing more than patterns created by the human mind. But the pattern I was trying to grasp, the pattern of Rosie's disappearance, was real. And the first thing I needed to understand was just how the panga boat fitted into the story.

What did I know for certain? The boat had come to shore in the night, on the beach below More Mesa. It should have carried a little girl named Rosamar Robledo.

What else had the boat carried? Marijuana bales. At least two, perhaps three or four pangeros. A silver cross hidden in a gap. And maybe – I smiled a little – maybe a load of dragon fruit.

Of course, in spite of Chucha's certainty, it was possible Rosie never made it to the boat in the first place. And even if she had, it was also possible she never made it to the beach below More Mesa. But to get anywhere, I had to step around those two possibilities and forge on.

Dexter trotted off to inspect a noise or an odor in the night. Then a great horned owl sang a dirge from the hillside behind the house: *hoo, hoo-hoo* . . .

I jumped up and walked the length of the wall. The wind blowing in off the water was cold, and I hugged my arms to my chest.

My cell rang in my pocket. I glanced at it. *Mike* – his name glowed in the dark.

'Hey.' I dropped down on the low block wall. 'What's up?'

'Missing you, Jaymie. Should have got you to come over and spend the night.'

I didn't much like Mike's apartment. The ceiling and the walls were thin. It felt like a cell in a beehive. 'Come over here. What's stopping you?'

'Nothing. Let me pack up for the job tomorrow and make a phone call or two. I'll be there in an hour. But – Jaymie? That's not the only reason I phoned.'

I was grinning into the dark at the thought of falling asleep in his arms. 'Then what?'

'I called in a favor with a guy downtown. If you can get out of bed at five a.m., we'll go take a look at that panga boat in the morning.'

Now I was alert, all the warm fuzziness gone. I jumped to my feet. 'Absolutely. Thanks for sticking your neck out on this.'

'Yeah, the SBPD wouldn't like the idea of a deputy sheriff looking through their stuff. I could get my knuckles rapped, I suppose. Anything for you, though.'

'Not just for me. It's for a good cause.'

'I know it is. Maybe you'll get somewhere with it.'

His faint optimism was damning. 'Where's your faith?'

'You know me, I'm a realist. See you pretty quick – you better go warm up the sheets.'

Mike switched off the overhead light and raised the bedroom window. Then he unzipped my sweatshirt, tugged it over my shoulders and tossed it on the bed. 'Hold up your arms.' He lifted my T-shirt over my head, snagging it on my elbow.

'It's like undressing a kid. Don't you own anything with buttons?'

'Complaining?' I arched my back as he kissed my neck. His mouth moved down to my breasts.

'Mmm. Never, not me.'

'Kinda chilly, isn't it?' It was nice, though, having the window open. The cold air was fresh and clean, washed by the rain earlier in the day. It carried the smell of the ocean.

'You won't notice in a minute.' He got to his knees.

Later, I lay on the edge of my small double bed and listened to Mike snore. It was a gentle snore, a quiet noise coming from such a big guy. No doubt it would get worse as he aged.

I smiled into the dark, thinking about Mike and I growing old together. He'd always wanted to get married, and now he was beginning to push me again on the subject. If I were honest, it was nice to be wanted. But deep down, I wasn't so sure it was for the best.

The truth was, I preferred things the way they were. Mike and I could get together when it suited us, and stay away when either of us needed space. What we had was good. *If it ain't broke* surely applied.

I heard Dexter scratch himself, then settle down on his blanket in the corner of the room. The little old house creaked in the salt-laden wind. I curled into Mike's back, closed my eyes, and drifted away.

Five a.m. Still black as the middle of the night. I staggered into the shower.

The aroma of eggs, toast, and something fried and delicious reached me as I toweled off. It occurred to me that maybe it wouldn't be such a bad idea to keep the guy around.

'Madam, take a seat.' Mike slid a plate of scrambled eggs, fried hot dogs, and buttered toast along the tabletop. Then he poured a mug of black coffee and set it down in front of me, along with a knife and fork.

I stared at the mound of food. 'Hot dogs? I can't put that in my stomach at this time of night.'

'Not much to choose from in that fridge of yours.' Mike chewed on his toast. 'Anyway, it's the top 'o the morning, and breakfast is the most important meal of the day.'

'If I married you, I'd get a mother and father, not just a husband.'

He smiled back. 'Speaking of mothers and fathers, I've been thinking. When do I get to meet your parents?'

The smile slunk off my face. We'd been over this before. 'What's the hurry? You might turn tail and run.'

He stopped chewing. 'That's bullshit. Is that what you think?'

'Guess not.' But in a way, I did. The truth was, when it came to my parents, the best thing was to just stay away.

I'd never told Mike about the inner workings of my family. I'd never seen a good reason to discuss it. Big deal: I was adopted, my mother was a Class A narcissist, and to this day my dad enabled her, even though they were long-divorced. Who the fuck cared?

I hated to whine about my family. Besides, I'd moved on. But if we traveled over to the San Joaquin Valley, the Zarlin clan was something I would have to explain.

FOUR

It was still as black as the inside of a whale when we pulled up at the warehouse on Indio Muerto Street. I trained Mike's flashlight on the lock while he opened the steel door with a key. The building was at least a hundred years old, but the door was new, fortified with steel bands.

The switch just inside turned on floodlights set high in the rafters, under a corrugated iron roof. The warehouse was large, the size of a basketball court. Three vehicles, a van and two cars, were parked at the far end in front of a roll-up door. Closer to us was an aluminum boat on a trailer.

'Let's not take long, Jaymie. If somebody on patrol drives by and notices the lights, they might decide to investigate.'

The fishing boat was about twenty-two feet long and shallow. The design was simple: cross boards for seats, oars, and a pair of outboard motors hanging off the back.

'Panga boats all look pretty much the same,' Mike explained as he circled the boat. 'They were designed by Yamaha in the 1970s for a World Bank project, did you know that? Now they're used by fishermen all over the world.'

'Interesting.' I peered down into the hull. 'I figured the detectives would remove any evidence. Looks like they've vacuumed it clean.'

'Yeah, somebody's been thorough.'

I bent down and looked under the trailer. 'Mike? Here's something.'

I reached into my pocket and pulled out a latex glove and a plastic baggie. I snapped on the glove, dropped to one knee and retrieved two flattened greenish skins off the concrete floor. Dragon fruit.

'Looks like the detectives thought this was trash. They must have tossed it out of the boat and forgotten about it.'

Mike peered at the skins. 'It *is* trash, isn't it? From somebody's lunch.'

'Dragon fruit.' I dropped the skins into the baggie and sealed it shut. 'I found some whole ones on the beach. Not exactly what you'd choose to take along for sustenance on a sea voyage.'

'Can't see that it means much.' Mike shrugged. 'Anything else?'

I leaned over and looked under the seats again. 'I don't really see anything. Give me your flashlight, would you?' I walked around to the back of the trailer, boosted myself up, and climbed into the boat.

The detectives had been thorough, all right. I examined the floor, inch by inch, and found nothing. Then I ran a hand under the seats, first one, then the other.

'Mike? There is something here.'

I lay down in the boat and flipped onto my back. 'Here, take the flashlight. Shine it up under the seat for me.' Crab-like, I scooted myself under, facing upward.

'Have I got the right angle?'

'To your left a shade. Hold it, that's good.'

Sure enough. The metal thwart was curled under, to ensure no one would run a hand under the seat and slice open a fingertip. But at one end, the flange was bent back. Something, a piece of fabric, maybe, had snagged on the sharp edge. I slipped partway out of the space, then managed to wedge my arm farther in. I gripped the fragment and jerked it back and forth till it came free.

The scrap was maybe an inch by two inches, woven from beige-colored artificial fibers. It hadn't been under the seat long – in fact, the plastic material looked brand new.

'Can I see that?' Mike took it in his hand and shined a light on the fabric. 'I'll tell you what this is.'

I struggled to sit up in the boat. 'You've seen it before?'

'Yeah, and not so long ago. This is the same stuff that was wrapped around the marijuana bales we confiscated six weeks ago, up at Jalama Beach. Those were soaked – the bales fell off a boat in that big storm we had back in January.'

'Doesn't tell us much we didn't already know. But it confirms Chucha's story.'

'Yep.' He rubbed the scrap between his thumb and forefinger. 'You know, Jaymie, you're focusing on Chucha's daughter. But don't forget, the main business was the smuggling. The little girl was an afterthought – just hitching a ride.'

I climbed onto the trailer frame and dropped to the ground. 'Mike? There's something I want to run by you.'

'Let's get out of here. We can talk in the truck.'

'Uh oh. Don't look now, but we've got company.'

Naturally, my head snapped up and I looked. A Santa Barbara cop car, lights off, slinked by. I couldn't make out the driver, but what did it matter who it was? We'd been observed.

'Shit. Now what?'

'Jaymie, just get in the truck.'

For once, I did as I was told. I slammed my door shut and turned to Mike. 'What do we do now?'

'Nothing.' Mike shrugged. 'They know my vehicle. If they want to make a stink about it, fine, let them. When they find out where I got the key from, I bet you they won't.'

We drove over to Shoreline. The tide was high. Dawn was breaking, and weak light seeped into a sullen gray sky.

Mike pulled the Silverado into the parking lot. I lowered the window so I could listen to the surf pounding the cliff face below.

'I'm worried, Mike. I can't see any good outcome for Chucha's daughter, you know?'

'Yeah, it's one hell of a business.' He switched off the engine. 'Listen, Jaymie. You need to take care. If this involves the cartels, you know you're asking for trouble.'

'Let's put that to one side for a moment.' I stared out over the dark navy waters. 'I want to run something by you. But please . . .'

'What?' Mike turned to look at me. 'Come on, spit it out.'

'Please quit telling me I need to be careful. You're treating me like some little kid.'

'Hey.' He slipped his hand behind my head. 'Sometimes you do sound like a girl.'

I refused to bite like a fish at a baited hook. 'I can take care of myself.'

'I know you can. But you seem tense. What's this about?'

'I'm a little edgy, that's all.' I took a deep breath, let it out. 'Frustrated, maybe that's a better word for it. I don't seem to be able to nail anything down.'

Mike removed his hand from my neck, folded his arms, and stared out at the churning sea. 'You don't have enough information, that's all. You know, what they used to call clues in the old days.'

'Clues are good. But how about logic? That's where I'm having a problem. See, if Rosie was in the boat when it landed, and if she was alive, then she was abducted. Correct?'

'Plenty of "ifs".'

'Come on, play along.'

'Yes. Go ahead.'

'What if there *was* a second little girl, the one Gabi calls Millie? Maybe she was also being smuggled in to be reunited with family, just like Rosie. But maybe Millie died, and so somebody took Rosie instead – in Millie's place.'

'Jesus, Jaymie. Your imagination runs like a rabbit with a coyote tight on its tail.' Mike turned to study me. 'Look, you mentioned

logic. A kid isn't a pet dog. If my daughter died, I don't think I'd—'
He stopped. 'What do I know. Sure, it's possible, I suppose.'

'No. No, you're right.' Mike had just yanked the rug out from
under me. 'If a mother and father found out their daughter had died,
the last thing they'd do would be to immediately accept another
child in her place.'

'Hold on.' Mike tapped his fingers on the steering wheel. 'I
can't believe I'm stepping over to your side. But it is possible
somebody didn't think things through. You know, some kid piloting
the boat?'

'I can just about see that. It's crazy and stupid, but one of the
pangeros might have wanted to make up for their loss. Grabbed
Rosie and taken off with her, thinking the parents would accept her.'
I looked eastward in time to catch the first golden gleam. 'But it's
just a wild-ass guess.'

'Yeah, it is that.' Mike started the engine. 'Listen, do me a favor.
Think you can kind of lie low till I get back?'

'There you go again.' I snorted. 'Do I need to have you right
here in town watching over me while I investigate a case?'

'I don't want you attracting attention while I'm away. Not if this
involves the cartels. Odds are, it does.'

I was quiet for a moment, thinking. Not about Mike and his
mother-henning, but about what he'd just said, about the cartels.
'So what happened to Rosie – in your opinion that was some kind
of a sideline.'

'Yeah, a very unfortunate sideline. Not the main show.'

The guy was good looking, in a dark and romantic sort of way. He
wore a nice-fitting pair of jeans and a suede jacket. I'd never seen
him before, and it wasn't till he stepped into the office that I smelled
a cop.

'Del Wasson.' He smiled and stuck out a hand. The guy's smile
broadened as I hesitated. 'Let me guess. You don't like cops?'

So Del was smart and observant too. I shook his hand. 'I make
exceptions.'

He nodded a hello to Gabi, who was peeking around the side of
the computer. 'I get it. There are one or two cops I don't like myself.'

I was being played. I had to remind myself of this, as I was already
warming to Del's bedroom eyes. 'Are you a police detective?'

'You guessed it. That's why I'm here.' He glanced at the couch, to indicate, I supposed, that he wanted to sit down. But my intuition warned me not to let the guy make himself too comfortable.

'So, Del. How can I help you?'

He folded his arms across his chest and slouched in a cowboy kind of way, hips thrust forward. Gabi was also not immune to Del's charms: I heard her clear her throat.

'Well, it's like this. You were observed entering a police facility down on Indio Muerto.' He smiled. 'Mind if I call you Jaymie?'

'Don't mind at all, Del.'

'OK if I sit?'

'Sure.'

He again looked at the couch, but I indicated the hot seat for Officer Wasson.

'Yeah, I went to the warehouse.' I perched on the edge of the desk, which put me on higher ground than my smiling interrogator. 'Is there a problem with that?'

'As a matter of fact, yes. You didn't have authorization. That facility is locked at all times, accessible to PD personnel only. Mind telling me how you got in?'

This was all crap. Wasson knew perfectly well I'd entered the warehouse with Mike. He most likely had pictures and also knew we'd entered with a key. And he knew the last thing I was going to do was to get Mike, a sheriff's deputy, in trouble with the city cops. Was Del Wasson willing to start up a quarrel between the two agencies? I decided to call his bluff.

'Sorry, Detective. I'm not free to tell you.'

'That a fact?' The guy quit smiling. 'I think you're free to tell me whatever you damn well want.'

I figured two could play at Del's game. I emitted a theatrical puff of frustration.

'Look. I heard the PD is going to auction off a few cars, all right? I asked a friend, who will remain nameless, to let me into the warehouse so I could check out the one I'm interested in. It's not playing by the rules, I admit. But is my little infraction worth your valuable time?'

Del crossed one long leg over the other, and leaned back in the chair. 'Which car was that, Jaymie?'

The SOB had me. The truth was, I'd been so focused on the boat that I hadn't paid any attention to the cars at the other end of the warehouse.

'Oh, did I say one? I'm interested in all of them. I'll be bidding for the best deal.'

'Let your friend know we aren't laughing.' Del gave me a hard look. 'I'm telling you for your own good, don't pull a stunt like that again.'

'Miss Jaymie, she don't pull stunts,' Gabi warned from behind the computer. 'You should not talk like that.'

Del tipped back his handsome head and laughed. 'Oh, I don't know. I'd say Miss Jaymie has pulled a fair number of stunts in her time.' He gave me a broad wink, then got to his feet. 'You ladies have a good day.'

The office door closed as quietly as it had opened.

'Ugh! I can still smell his perfume.' Gabi picked up a sheaf of papers and waved them in the air. 'Maybe he is handsome. But I don't like perfume when it's on a man, you know?'

'That had everything to do with the panga boat, Gabi.' I hopped off the corner of the desk. 'The marijuana smuggling. Del thinks I'm poking around.'

'He knows you are, Miss Jaymie. And he don't like it.'

'No. I wonder why not?'

Claudia Molina beamed from the kitchenette doorway. 'We heard you need help. BJ picked me up at school, and we came over right away.'

It was good to see the kid smile again. Over a year had passed since her sister Lili was found murdered in a downtown solstice parade workshop. I knew it was BJ Bonfiglio who had helped Claudia come out of her shell.

BJ stepped up behind her. 'Hey, Jaymie. Hi Gabi.' His smile matched his friend's.

Gabi *hmphed* from behind her desk. 'Claudia came over 'cause I told her we'd pay her to put up flyers, that's why.'

'Fuckin' bullshit.' Claudia tucked her plaid shirt into her twenty-two-inch-waist chinos and grinned. 'If you want, Jaymie, we'll do it for free.'

Claudia Molina was a busy girl. She left her dad's Smith and Wesson knife at home these days, and applied herself at school.

Gone was the partly shaved head. She wore her hair in a short cut, parted to one side. It reminded me of a good little boy's cut, slicked down with his mama's spit, but I'd never dare say that to Ms Molina.

'OK, that is good.' Gabi got to her feet. 'Cause that's how you can pay us back for all the sodas and pastries you take.' She waved a hand in the air. 'I mean her, BJ. Not you.'

Claudia cackled. 'Yeah, BJ. You can have all the pastries you want. Cause mommy likes you better.'

I rolled my eyes to heaven. I knew Claudia hadn't forgotten that Gabi had saved her big time, six months earlier. But even though I was sure the kid was grateful deep down, these two shards of flint couldn't help but strike sparks.

'Nice to see you, BJ. How's college?'

'Pretty good. I don't know what I'm going to major in yet, but I like all my classes so far. I really like computer science, but I'm still nowhere as good as Claudia at all that.' He smiled. 'And she's still in high school and never took a computer class in her life.'

'I keep telling you, you don't need classes for that stuff, BJ. I can teach you whatever you want to know.' Claudia stepped into the front office and BJ followed. 'Anyway, BJ's keeping his options open. Me, I like closure.'

'Uh huh,' Gabi muttered. 'Closure, over and over and over.'

Gabi was referring to the fact that Claudia had changed her mind quite a few times over the past few months. At one point she'd decided to become a detective, and then, most improbably, a cop. The last thing I'd heard, she'd settled on a career in law, all the better to enable her to 'kick all the big fat rich people's butts.'

I plopped down in the hot seat. 'Is it time for afternoon coffee?'

'I'll put it on,' BJ replied. 'And I brought a few slices of pound cake. I made it with the blood orange juice we froze from Claudia's mom's tree.'

'Fuckin' delicious.' Claudia perched her tiny rear on the arm of the Craigslist couch. 'So what's this all about, Jaymie? The flyers, I mean. Can I take a look?'

'They will be ready when they are ready,' Gabi answered. 'Come before school tomorrow morning.'

'Some little kid is missing?'

'No,' Gabi snapped. 'No, she's happy with her mah. We just want to show people what a cute little girl she is.'

'Hey, I'm talkin to Jaymie.'

BJ retreated into the kitchenette. 'Coffee and cake, coming right up.'

'The flyers are a good idea.' Gabi's back was to me as she attacked the blinds with a long-handled duster. The copy machine, meanwhile, was clattering away. 'But I'm gonna tell you what else you should do. You need to go talk to the lady priests.'

'The lady priests. Is that some kind of a cult?'

'Huh?' She looked at me over her shoulder. 'They are Catolica. They used to be sisters, Sister Laura and Sister Bernadette, and then they turned into priests. Now nobody knows what to call them. We can't call them Father Laura and Father Bernadette, you know?'

'No, I suppose not.' I leaned against the kitchen doorframe. 'But the last I heard, the Catholic Church still doesn't let women become priests.'

'Of course, El Papa, he don't agree. If you go to the lady priests' church' – she slid a finger across her throat – '*excomulgar.*'

'Excommunication? They must be dangerous women.'

'Yes, but nice. They help people so much. Especially the people who come in with no papers, who got nowhere to go.'

'I get it. So Laura and Bernadette are a danger to both Washington D.C. *and* Rome.'

Gabi giggled. 'Yes, I guess so. Very dangerous ladies who look like abuelas.'

'Oh, grandmothers can be subversive, all right. If necessary, they can be the most dangerous women in the world.'

Two of the most dangerous women in the world ran their op out of a small mobile home park on De La Vina, where ten to twelve tired old trailers were packed in like sardines.

I had no trouble identifying the women priests' trailers: lined up side-by-side, they were freshly-painted and surrounded by a collection of potted fruit trees and berry bushes. The space between the two single-wides formed a courtyard, where a buff-colored St Francis cradled a dove in his hands.

A pair of little girls sat at an old redwood picnic table in the courtyard, chattering away as they applied themselves to coloring books. I was about to say hi when a young man hurried around the back corner of one of the trailers. The guy gripped a short-handled hoe.

When our eyes met, I tried to quell my reaction. A severe cleft palate and lip split the lower half of the young man's face. He uttered several words, but I couldn't understand what he'd said. He repeated himself, struggling to enunciate.

I pointed at the open door of the mobile home on my right. 'I have an appointment.'

But he took a step forward, blocking me. His message was clear enough: I shouldn't advance.

FIVE

'Roberto, it's fine.' An older woman, tall and slim with long white hair and gray eyes so bright they looked silver, stood framed in the mobile home doorway. She didn't look like a nun or a priest. She looked like an angel.

'I'm Laura. Are you Jaymie Zarlin?'

'Yes.' I found I had no problem beaming back.

'Roberto, this is Jaymie. She is a friend.' Roberto tipped his head in acknowledgement, then disappeared back around the corner.

Laura descended the steps and approached me, extending a hand. 'Roberto is protective of us. Now that he knows you're a friend, he will be protective of you, too.' Her hand was light as a leaf.

'Are you in need of protection?' I asked.

'What is there to be afraid of?' She smiled. 'But it doesn't hurt to have a sharp pair of eyes on the premises.' She motioned me inside. 'Let's go in, shall we? Bernie will be along in a minute.'

The old mobile home was comfortably furnished. A round coffee table stood in the center of a circle of chairs.

'Please, sit down. By the way, I hope Roberto didn't startle you, Jaymie. He's rather fierce-looking, poor man. We're searching for a way to help him.'

'You and Bernadette must do a lot of good.'

'Oh, not just us, not alone. It's the old story of stone soup, you know? We couldn't accomplish anything on our own. We're part of a community, and everyone pitches in. And you, Jaymie. You do good, too.'

'Uh – me?'

Laura smiled her gentle smile. 'We know about your good works. One of our benefactors is Darlene Richter, you see. She told us all about how you helped her with the little boy last year.'

'Darlene has it backwards.' Praise made me uncomfortable, and unearned praise made me break out in a sweat. 'She arranged and paid for Beto's surgery, and she took him and his family under her wing.'

'You gave her the opportunity to step forward. No, those weren't her words. Darlene said you opened her eyes.'

'I don't think—'

'Good morning.' A brisk voice female sounded from the doorway. While Laura wore a washed-denim skirt and pale pink blouse, this woman was dressed in black pants and a long-sleeved white oxford shirt. A pair of reading glasses hung around her neck on a silver chain. 'Jaymie? I'm Bernadette.'

I stood and exchanged a brisk handshake. 'I'm glad to meet you.'

The atmosphere in the trailer had altered. It still felt welcoming. But with Bernadette's arrival, a meeting had been called to order.

'Please excuse me for one moment, Jaymie.' She turned to Laura. 'The Esposito girls, out in the courtyard. Why aren't they in school?'

'Their mother had to go to emergency with their brother early this morning. Nothing too serious, hopefully, but Jorge cut his hand and it needed stitches. Yolanda will be back as soon as she can.'

'The girls should be in school. When we've finished talking, I'll take them myself.' Bernadette sat down in an old harp-back chair. 'It's always something,' she said to me. 'Now. How can we help you?'

How can we help you? A casual phrase people spoke every day. But I had a feeling Bernadette meant it.

So I talked about Rosie and Chucha, and about the silver cross and the phantom child we called Millie. The women listened closely, without asking questions. Laura nodded a few times, and Bernadette fixed me with a sharp unwavering eye.

When I'd finished, Laura shook her head. 'That's such a sad story. I'm so sorry for both little girls, and for their families, too.'

Bernadette nodded. 'Family separation. It's so destructive for the children. We see it again and again.' She leaned forward in her chair. 'But I have to say, what you've described – it is highly unusual.'

'What Bernadette is saying is true,' Laura agreed. 'We know adults arrive in boats from time to time, along with the marijuana. But to send a child on her own in a panga boat?' She looked over to Bernadette for confirmation. 'I don't believe we've ever come across this before.'

'Laura's right. Unaccompanied minors don't travel here in the panga boats. Boats are an unnecessary risk.' Bernadette hooked a stray wisp of gray hair behind her ear and anchored it in place with the stem of her glasses.

'In some ways, you see, a child is not so difficult to bring into the country. The boy or girl can travel in a vehicle, with a family member or acquaintance who has papers and will pretend to be the parent. Now, I do see why your friend Chucha arranged the boat trip. She had no one else to turn to, it seems. But for another little girl to have come into the country in the same way before her?' Bernadette shrugged. 'I suspect there's more to this story than meets the eye.'

Laura turned to me. 'Do you have a picture of the missing child, Jaymie?'

'Yes.' I'd taken a snapshot of the picture of Rosie with my cell. I pulled it up, then handed the phone to her. 'That's Chucha's daughter.'

'Oh . . .' When Laura looked up at me, I saw her eyes had filled with tears. 'Such a beautiful little girl.' She got to her feet and carried the cell phone over to Bernadette.

Bernadette lifted her glasses to her nose, and peered at the photo. 'This is Rosamar? Her looks are distinctive.'

'She looks just like Chucha.'

'Does she have any identifying marks, do you know?' Laura asked.

'A small birthmark at the nape of her neck. According to her mother, it's shaped like a dolphin.'

'Hm. Fanciful, perhaps,' Bernadette replied. She turned to Laura. 'You know, I wonder. What is the name of that attorney, the woman who campaigns against illegal adoption?'

'I think you mean Staffen Brill.' Laura had stopped smiling. 'But, illegal adoption? Bernie, there's nothing to indicate—'

'Jaymie's at a dead end, Laura. You're right, of course: this sad matter most likely has nothing to do with adoption, illegal or otherwise. But talking to Brill might help, and it can't hurt. I seem to recall that the woman knows a fair bit about illegal immigration as well.'

Laura rose from the couch and went over to the counter dividing the living room from the small kitchen. She spun an old-fashioned Rolodex for a few seconds, then opened it to a card. 'All right, here we are: Staffen Brill.'

'Yes, that's it.' Bernadette nodded to me. 'You should go and talk with her, Jaymie. Pick her brain, as they say. With the possibility of two children missing . . . well. Imagine, if you could help either – or even both. You'd be doing God's work.'

'Yes . . . yes, OK.'

'But? I hear hesitation. Do you object to my reference to God, is that it?' Bernadette leaned forward. 'No. No, I do see. It's only the one child you are concerned with. Am I right?'

'Bernadette,' Laura warned. 'Let's not press.'

'No, it's all right.' I looked down at the water-ringed coffee table. 'It's not that I don't care about Millie – if she exists. I do care. But Rosie, I know she's real. And if she's still alive, she's in danger.'

'And business is business, am I right? You have been hired to find only the one little girl.'

Mother Bernadette was pushing a trifle too hard. But I nodded. 'Something like that.'

'Let me put it this way then, Jaymie. If you help the one child, you very well may then be in a position to help the other. Can we agree?'

I smiled in defeat. Not all saints were gentle, I was sure. 'It's possible, yes.'

'Then we *are* agreed.' Bernadette's smile was warm. 'So, did you come in a car? I have a busy schedule today. Those two little Esposito girls are playing hooky, and they need a ride to their school.'

I marched the two little scofflaws into the Franklin School office and handed them over to the school secretary.

'Their mom had to take their brother to emergency,' I explained to the frowning woman. 'That's why they're late.'

'People have to go to emergency all the time. We can't accept that as an excuse.'

'This was a real emergency, not a case of the Monday morning flu. He was badly injured, and the wound required stitches.' I was right in my element now – an old hand at making up excuses for school tardiness. For good measure, I added, 'There was a lot of blood.'

The disapproval on the secretary's face softened to mild skepticism. 'We'll see. Girls, go to your rooms.'

The Esposito girls exchanged conspiratorial grins and scampered off through a side door.

I escaped to the school parking lot and climbed into Blue Boy, the El Camino I'd inherited from my brother. Thanks to an interim owner, Blue Boy was painted a gleaming candy apple red.

I rolled down the windows, then leaned back in the reupholstered seat and closed my eyes. The joyful sounds of kids at play brought back memories of recess: that heady release into freedom, all the sweeter for its brevity.

A few minutes later I opened my eyes and shifted my thoughts back to the here and now. The lady priests had pointed me in a concrete direction. They thought my next step should be to talk to the attorney they'd suggested, Staffen Brill.

But I felt cautious. This investigation, which was growing like a magic beanstalk, wobbled on a thin stem. I knew from experience that going in too many directions often led to disappointment down the road, not to mention wasted time. Was I getting too far ahead of myself?

In spite of Bernadette's sermon, my job was to find Chucha's daughter – not to discover the identity of the phantom Millie. Yes, it was possible the two mysteries were linked. But the truth was, I could be chasing after ghosts: the ghosts of two deceased little girls.

Sobered, I jammed the key in the ignition and the Cam purred to life.

I'd begun my investigation based on an assumption: that Rosie Robledo was still alive. But now, mired in quicksand, I needed firmer footing. Proof. I had to find out for sure if Rosie had survived the ocean journey.

Still I sat there, with the engine rumbling. I sat there because I had no clear idea of where to go next.

Blue Boy got tired of idling. He carried me out of the lot, along Mason to Milpas. I saw I was reverting to my usual fallback destination: the beach.

And I wasn't paying attention. I had to hit the brakes hard to avoid hitting an older woman who was crossing the busy street. Her shopping basket was piled high with all her belongings. She plowed forward into the traffic, head down, back bent.

Sitting there stopped in the middle of the road, I woke up.

I recalled the guy I'd caught sight of in the brush above the beach at More Mesa. Most likely he was homeless, too.

He'd chosen a good place to hang out, I realized. He was less likely to be harassed by the usual assholes than he would be in town. And he had a vantage point at that location: he was hidden and could see trouble coming before it saw him.

Then I wondered something. Something I should have wondered before. That night – what had the guy seen?

The woman crossing the street stumbled and went down on one knee. The jerk in the car behind me leaned on his horn. My blood pressure zinged.

I switched off the engine, got out of the car, and turned to look at the driver behind me. I'd expected some crusty old bastard, but it was a young woman of around twenty-five. I gave her a hard look, and she turned her head the other way.

Meanwhile the woman with the cart was still frozen in position. 'Let me help you,' I said.

Terrified, she moved just her eyes to look at me. I could see she'd been scared stiff for a very long time.

I managed to get her to her feet. Together we pushed the cart across Milpas. She was desperate not to let go of the handle. 'They won't stop,' she said.

'Oh yes they will.'

Five or six cars had pulled up behind little Miss Bossypants by the time I walked back to Blue Boy. As I climbed into the Camino, I gave her a nod. I'd have liked to jump up and down on the hood of her car, but what would that have accomplished, besides making me feel good? The homeless had plenty of enemies already. They didn't need me to generate more.

I decided to take charge of Blue Boy. We bypassed the beach and drove over to Cliff. I stopped off to pick up sandwiches, sodas, and chips, then headed on up the road to More Mesa.

I crossed the meadow on foot, wading through the long luscious grass with my day pack on my back.

Four years had passed since we'd had winter grass so green, thick, and high. The wind off the ocean ran through it like a giant invisible comb, parting it this way and that.

All sorts of birds sang all sorts of songs under the fresh warm sun. It was a symphony, and under the melody ran a rhythm: the rasps, buzzes, and clicks of insects. Rich composty smells welled up from the wet warm earth.

I reached the edge of the mesa and halted. The uplift from the breeze off the ocean was strong here. I shut my eyes and spread my arms like wings. If I jumped off, maybe I would soar.

Something rustled in the brush, below me and to the right. I opened my eyes and peered into the lemonadeberry thicket. I couldn't see a thing.

I made my way down the path. As I descended, a thick layer of damp clay built up on the soles of my running shoes. It wasn't long before I felt as if I were walking on lifts.

The tide was high this morning, the exposed section of beach narrow. When I reached the sand, I turned and looked up. Something moved on the cliff face, but I resisted the urge to take out my field glasses. The last thing a homeless guy would want to see was some jerk searching him out with binocs, as if he were prey.

I climbed back up the path. Halfway up, I stopped. Unless I made a first move, nothing would happen.

'My name's Jaymie,' I called out. 'I've got some food – sandwiches and drinks.'

The guy had to be hungry. There were no shops nearby, and I was pretty sure he didn't venture out often. 'Look, I'll wait up at the top for you.'

I continued on up the cliff, slipped out of my pack and rested it on the polished exposed root of a Monterey cypress. Then I zipped the pack open and removed the sandwiches, chips, and sodas. I waited for several minutes, but no one appeared.

I looked around and noticed a big eucalyptus log lying a few feet back from the edge. I walked over and placed a sandwich, soda, and bag of chips on the log. Then I returned to the cypress root and sat down to await my fellow picnicker.

Before long his head appeared. He hadn't used the path – he must have followed his own trail, and zigzagged across the cliff face. I raised a casual hand and let it fall. Then I opened my own bag of chips and popped one in my mouth. I looked up and saw the guy standing at the edge, in full view.

He was a wisp of a man, of less than average height and very thin. He wore a tattered and sun-faded pair of cargo pants and a threadbare T-shirt. He looked forty, but he was probably no more than twenty-five or twenty-six years old. The wind rising up off the ocean ruffled his light brown hair.

'Hi,' I called over.

He didn't say anything, just stepped up onto the flat mesa and over to the food on the log. He walked on tiptoes, as if he feared that any minute the ground might fall away under his feet.

Without looking my way, the guy picked up the sandwich, studied it, then slipped it into his cargo-pants pocket. He collected the soda can and the chips and turned to go.

'Please,' I called. 'Please, before you go. I want to ask you something.'

He still didn't look at me. But he paused and stared out to sea. I knew he was listening. I also knew I had only one shot.

'Listen, I'm Jaymie. I'm not a cop. I'm trying to help somebody, a lady who's searching for her daughter.'

He half-turned to look at me. I could see in his face how the poor guy struggled: no doubt he heard voices relentlessly, night and day. But he was working hard to push them away now, forcing them into the background.

'I saw you.' His voice was cracked from disuse. 'You went down to the beach.'

'Yes, that's right. I came to have a look. But the boat that landed on the beach was already gone by the time I got here.' I decided to take a risk. 'What's your name? Just your first name, I don't want to get you in any trouble.'

He was quiet for a moment, as if he were trying to remember. 'Darren.'

'Thanks, Darren. Listen, that night the boat landed on the beach. You saw it, right? You saw what happened.'

'Yeah.'

'Good. What were they doing, unloading bales?'

He nodded, then looked back to sea. 'Yeah . . . weed.'

'I thought so. But I'm not interested in that. See, I think there was also a baby in the boat. Maybe even two babies.'

'I gotta go.'

'I know you do. Just a second, OK? It's important.'

'No baby . . . but there was a lady. And a cat.'

'What?'

'A really tall lady, she looked inside the boat. She was crying. But then – the – the lady turned into a man.'

'Yes, I understand.' That would have been Chucha. 'But what did you say about a cat?'

'One of the Mexican guys from the boat. Before the lady got here, he went back down and picked up a cat. I heard it, I—' he stopped, confused.

'What way did he go with the cat?'

Darren pointed eastward, down the south-facing beach. Then he took a step away.

'Darren, how about another sandwich? You can keep it for later if you want. You must get hungry out here.' I took out my own sandwich and placed it out on the far end of the cypress root. 'My brother used to live outside. He was like you, he stayed near the beach.'

Darren walked over and stood looking down at the sandwich. 'It *sounded* like a cat . . .'

I'd assumed he'd been hallucinating. Because why would someone smuggle a goddamned cat? But then I had an idea.

'Darren, do you think you heard a baby, not a cat? A baby can sound like a cat sometimes. When it cries.'

'Maybe. It sounded like it was sick, or . . . or real sad.'

It was a kid, all right. It was Rosie or Millie, one or the other. My throat tightened.

'I need to be someplace now.' Darren looked up at the pristine blue sky. 'Soon as it clears, I've gotta go.'

SIX

I walked back across More Mesa, slid into the Camino, and shut the door. I turned on the engine, then checked my phone. Dammit, I'd missed a call from Mike. I tapped on the voice message.

'Jaymie, we're about to go in. From here on out I'm going to be off the grid. Like I said, it's going to be a few days before I talk to you again.' He paused. 'Be careful, will you? I'm not going to be around, so you're going to have to look after yourself.'

I had to smile. Mike knew just how much his last sentence would rile me. The guy couldn't resist a parting shot.

After a moment I scrolled down through my notes and pulled up the number Laura had given me from her Rolodex.

'Staffen Brill's office,' announced a young, self-assured male voice. 'Eric speaking.'

'This is Jaymie Zarlin. I'd like to talk to Staffen Brill.'

'Concerning?'

I sighed to myself. This was a gatekeeper, if ever there was one. Eric had the power to bestow or deny entrance, and I could tell he'd milk the situation for all it was worth.

I wanted to inform Eric that it was none of his business. But this wasn't the time for self-indulgence. 'Concerning Ms Brill's committed advocacy on behalf of illegally adopted children.' It never hurt to flatter, I figured. 'The women priests, Laura and Bernadette, suggested I talk to her.'

'I see.' Eric sounded disappointed. 'I'll have to consult with Ms Brill first. She's extremely busy this week.'

When I had to, I could manipulate with the worst of them. 'Of course, I do understand. But please be sure to tell her a child's life is at stake. This matter concerns the possible abduction of an unaccompanied minor.'

'What's your name again?'

'Jaymie Zarlin. Here's my number.' I rattled off my cell, then the office number. 'I don't want to push, Eric' – like hell I didn't – 'but time is of the essence. I'm sure Ms Brill will want to talk with me soon.'

I was sitting at Gabi's desk staring out the window when a movement caught my eye. The giant bird of paradise trees were in flower, and something partly hidden was sipping from one of the waxy-white flower cups.

I'd just determined that the creature lapping up nectar was a rat when my cell rang. 'Your message sounded urgent, Ms – I'm sorry, what is it? Zaren?' Steffan Brill's voice was clipped, businesslike.

'Zarlin.' What, was Eric's handwriting messy? I doubted that, somehow. 'The women priests, Laura and Bernadette, suggested I phone you. They said you work to expose illegal adoption.'

'Oh yes, Bernadette and Laura. They're so cute, aren't they?'

'Cute? No, I can't say I – saw them that way.'

'Perhaps you don't know them as well as I do. But yes, illegal adoption is a terrible scourge. We do our best.' She paused. Just as I began to reply, she started up again. 'Eric said something about an abduction. Can you tell me more?'

Time was money for Ms Brill. Did I give a damn? 'I'd find it easier to explain in person.'

'Oh? Yes, all right. I suppose that would be a good idea, if it's an urgent matter. Hold on, will you?' I pictured Staffen Brill consulting a desk calendar, black with appointment notations.

'I can give you fifteen minutes, this afternoon at two. Does that work?'

'Um, yeah. Yeah, sure.'

'Please stay on the line, will you? Eric will give you directions.'

Brill was all business, but she was fitting me in right away. Maybe she wasn't so bad after all.

The name of the estate, *Agua Azul*, was worked into the scrolled wrought-iron gate. I rolled down the window and pushed the button on the intercom.

'What?'

Oh, that Eric. He and I were having just too much fun.

'Jaymie Zarlin.'

'And you are here for . . .'

I'd had enough. 'I am here to deliver the squabs and piglets for the great feast, m'lord's servant.'

There was a long moment of silence. I had the impression Mr Eric was dumbstruck. Then there was a well-oiled whirr, and the massive gate swung open.

'See you soon, Eric.' I stepped on the gas and gunned it.

Blue Boy cruised up Staffen Brill's landscaped drive as if the Cam were to the manor born. Agua Azul boasted a handsome Mediterranean-style mansion perched at the top of the hill. Just below the house, an infinity pool spilled a curtain of water down to a second pool below.

I'd done my homework. Ms Brill was a local divorce attorney, and her husband, Jack Morehead, was a partner in a top-flight Los Angeles firm dealing in corporate law. Judging from their abode, the scales of justice were weighted with gold.

Blue Boy and I tooled past the house, as Eric had instructed over the phone. Fifty yards on, I pulled into a short drive, then parked beside a redwood lattice screen. Beyond the screen I could make out the roof of Staffen Brill's office.

I got out, slammed the door shut, but didn't bother to lock it. Not that there wasn't plenty of thievery going on in this neck of the woods.

I stepped onto a path of sandstone pavers set in black beach stones. Wispy Mexican bamboo arched overhead. The path curved to the right, and the bamboo gave way to ferns and begonias. Now I could see across the rolling hillside. I stopped for a moment to take in the estate.

The big house stood at the top of the hill, facing south. Brill's office, a single-story Spanish-style structure, lay straight ahead and slightly below me. Between the two structures, some hundred yards away, was a large garden shed designed to look like a miniature barn. The barn doors were closed, and a ride-on lawnmower was parked out in front. Separate heaps of mulch and different grades of gravel were piled along the side of the structure. Agua Azul was quite the operation, it seemed.

Just as I was about to turn away, a maid dressed in a black-and-white uniform and carrying a stack of what looked like bed linens approached the barn. She set the linens on an outdoor bench, took a key from her pocket and opened the door. A maid in a white apron with bed linens, sent to a barn? My interest was piqued.

But I didn't see what happened next because at that moment a large canine, some sort of Rottweiler mix, exploded out of the shrubbery.

Let me say this: I love dogs, goofy creatures that they are. I like to think I understand them. And it was pretty hard not to understand the message this snarling beast was sending my way: *lady, I'm going to chew on your ass.*

Options leaped through my brain. Turn tail and run? That would only encourage the Hound of the Baskervilles. Talk sweetly? Stand meekly? He'd relish that too – and me, into the bargain. This was an attack dog, born, bred, and trained up. What kind of a game was Staffen Brill playing, for fuck's sake? And with that thought, I was furious.

'Back off! Back off, you freakin mutt!'

To my complete surprise, Fido fell back. He seemed surprised too, but I didn't count on that to last long.

'Greco, here boy.' No doubt this was Eric who'd opened the door to the office building. The young man had a grin on his face, the junior son-of-a-bitch. Greco lifted a lip, then sidled over to the guy. The two of them disappeared inside, leaving the door ajar.

I wasn't all that keen on approaching the office. On the other hand, I wasn't about to let Eric think I was afraid. So I stepped up to the door and kind of peered in.

Eric was seated at a computer desk. Greco now sported a shiny chain-link leash. On the other end of the leash was Eric's wrist. It was difficult to tell who was restraining whom.

Greco snarled at me, but this time it was a quiet snarl. He was using his inside voice.

I took one eye off Greco and glanced at Eric. Man, he was a white guy. I don't mean that as a racial designation: I mean he had an almost translucent white complexion. His blond hair was nearly colorless. I wondered if he glowed in the dark.

Eric was terribly busy. It took him a full minute to look up and acknowledge me. 'Ms Brill will be down in a few minutes.' He nodded in the direction of an Italian chair, so very moderne, orange leather and chrome.

There was no way I was getting into that chair. It looked like a torture rack, and besides, I wasn't sure I'd be able to climb out in time if Greco got cozy. 'I'll wait outside. In the garden.'

Eric shrugged. 'Suit yourself.'

I stepped out the door and sat down in one of two teak chairs sporting striped cushions. I tipped back my head: a weeping ficus, houseplant gone wild, provided a bright green umbrella high above. I wondered about Eric and his bad attitude. Did Ms Brill keep him around to express her shadow side?

Three or four goldfinches hopped about in the canopy. Their breasts gleamed like gold bubbles caught in the branches of the fig. As I watched I became aware of a repetitive sound – footsteps crunching along gravel, from the general direction of the big house.

I turned just in time to meet the steady gaze of Ms Staffen Brill. It was she, of course: who else could appear so in charge of this opulent world? Of average height, the woman somehow seemed taller. Her rich auburn curls bounced as she strode along in her black leather pumps. She wore gray slacks of a light wool, a gray-blue silk blouse, and a matching cashmere sweater.

'Miss Zarlin? Staffen Brill.' She glanced at her wristwatch. 'I had some personal business to attend to.' She smiled and extended a hand. Her handshake was perfect, like all the rest of her: not too soft, not too hard. But now that Staffen Brill stood in front of me, I couldn't help but notice her face.

She was attractive from a distance, but up close her features looked as if they'd been wired together. She'd had too much plastic surgery: everything was perfect, yet somehow the end result was not pretty. Nose, chin, cheeks: all were a shade too hard, too tight. Except for Staffen Brill's brown eyes: they were soft and vulnerable. Did the attorney realize her eyes betrayed her?

'No problem, Ms Brill. I'm enjoying your garden.'

She inclined her head, and her curly bob swung forward jauntily. 'Yes. It is lovely, isn't it? I'm so busy, you know, I never have time to enjoy it.'

Eric jumped up as we entered the office. Greco began a growl but cut it short when his mistress raised a warning hand.

'Can I do something for you, Staffen?' Eric asked.

'You can take Greco back to the house, Eric, and lock him in his kennel. You know he doesn't belong out at this time of the day.

Then run down to the post office with the mail and check the box.'
She hadn't bothered to look at her assistant.

'Jack wanted Greco out. But sure, I'll put him away.' Eric moved
quickly, with deference. I almost expected him to tug on his forelock.
Yet there was also a hint of something sullen in his voice.

'Come through please, Miss Zarlin.' Brill slipped a small keychain
from her slacks pocket. She walked up to a door in the wall behind
the desk, inserted the key in the lock and pushed the door open. So
she didn't entirely trust the help. I couldn't say I blamed her.

The office was small but not claustrophobic. There were windows
on two walls, and a large skylight poured a wavering rectangle of
light down on the rosewood desk. A matching rosewood credenza
stretched along one wall, and above the credenza hung fifty or sixty
framed portrait photos arranged in three rows. Each photo was of
an infant or a child.

Staffen Brill took the desk chair and offered me the visitor's chair
with a wave. 'I apologize for the dog. Did Greco threaten you?'

'You could say that. Or maybe it's just his way of saying hello.'

It was a weak joke, and Staffen Brill didn't smile. 'Greco belongs
to my husband. He's meant to be kenneled during the day.'

'The dog or your husband?'

To her credit, Staffen Brill smiled a little this time. When she
did so, the invisible wires in her face ratcheted tight. 'My husband
is very security-conscious. I'm afraid both his work, and mine, can
be adversarial at times.'

'In your case, do you mean divorce work?' I nodded at the photos
on the wall. 'You seem to have also arranged many adoptions.'

She hooked an auburn curl behind her ear. Staffen Brill presented
a mixed message: her face was stressed and severe, but her hair
was positively wanton.

'I balance one with the other, I like to think. I counter the destruc-
tion of broken families with the creation of viable new ones.'

Oh my. Staffen Brill seemed to see herself as some kind of
goddess, holding sway over mortal lives.

'And are all those pictures of children you've arranged adoptions
for?'

'Yes.' The wires pulled and she smiled again. 'When I started
my practice, I dealt exclusively with divorce. But frankly, it was
depressing work, day in and day out. Each year now, divorce

comprises a smaller percentage of what I do.' She shook her head. 'I didn't feel I was doing any real *good*, you know?'

'Uh-huh.' I had the feeling this was an oft-repeated recitation.

'I just sort of fell into adoption work. A couple I knew couldn't conceive, and they didn't fit the rigid requirements of the agencies. Thank God, I was able to help them. First they adopted a little boy, and then two years later, a girl. Not every adoption is perfect, you understand. There are just too many variables and unknowns. But that first case, I'd have to say it was ordained.'

'It sounds like satisfying work.' And it did. So why was I feeling provoked? My own problem, maybe. Did I always have to suspect that something was going on behind the painted screen?

'Oh, it is satisfying. But after a number of years, I started to reconsider. You see, I am the first to admit it: a private adoption is not cheap. By and large, my clients are quite well-to-do.' Staffen Brill folded her hands on her desk and leaned forward. 'So, I decided I needed to do more.'

'Ah.'

'The Center to Halt Illegal Adoption – CHIA – was already in existence. But it was poorly run. Frankly, the organization was a disgrace.'

'So you stepped in to help. Very admirable.' I hadn't intended to sound anything but positive, yet somehow a whiff of sarcasm clung to my words. Luckily, Ms Brill didn't seem to notice.

'I've done what I can. Of course it's never enough, just a drop in the bucket. But we try. We have speakers, and an active publicity team. I've been president of CHIA for three years running, but I plan to pass that on next year. I intend to always be active, of course, behind the scenes.' She held up a hand, palm outward.

'I'm sorry. Once I get started on this subject, it's hard for me to stop. How can I help you, Ms Zarlin?'

'To start with, I want you to know I'm a private investigator.' Most often, that confession caused people to clam up. But Staffen Brill inclined her head and nodded. I guessed she already knew.

'And the thing is, I've been hired to locate a little girl who was smuggled in from Mexico.'

'I see. And do I understand you believe this child is part of some illegal adoption arrangement?'

'It's a shot in the dark, I admit.' How much should I say, I wondered, even to the above-reproach Ms Brill? 'Did you read in the paper about the panga boat, the one that was found last week down on the beach below More Mesa?'

'I did read about that. They think the boat was used to transport marijuana. How does that relate to our conversation?'

'It's complicated.' I hesitated, then decided to press on. 'What the newspaper article didn't say is that there are indications a little girl was in the boat, too. And now she's disappeared.'

'Unconscionable.' Staffen Brill's mouth tightened, and she flushed. 'It doesn't sound as if this has anything to do with adoption, but even so, imagine! A child, traveling alone in a drug smuggling boat. Have the police intervened?'

At Brill's mention of the police, I realized I'd made a mistake. I shouldn't have mentioned Rosie. Now, I would have to say more than I liked.

'The police don't know anything about this. In fact, her mother is desperate to find her. But it's best that the authorities aren't involved.'

'I'd be inclined to say the mother has forfeited her rights to the child, wouldn't you?' Staffen Brill tightened her lips and studied the desktop. 'What is the mother's name?'

I'd taken one ill-considered step, and wasn't about to take another. Staffen Brill might decide to take what she saw as the high road and report what I'd just told her to the cops.

'I'm sorry, but I'm not free to divulge her identity. I'm sure you understand.'

'Of course.' Brill rose to her feet and went to a window. Her back was to me when she continued. 'So. You went to the women priests and told them about this, and they suggested you come to me. Did they say why?'

'They said you were an expert in illegal adoption and might have some advice.'

'I see. Well, it's a very sad story, and I can't blame you for coming here. But I've never heard of anything remotely like this. And as I've said, from the scant information you've given me, I can't see what it has to do with illegal adoption. Now, I'm going to say something distasteful, but true.' As she turned to me, Staffen Brill smoothed the collar of her silk blouse.

'In my experience, Hispanic children – as I understand it, that's what we are talking about here – are not so easy to place. Racism is fading, perhaps, but prospective parents still tend to be wealthy and white. They want children who look as if they could be their own. I am afraid there just aren't too many Brangelinas out there, you see.'

'The little girl is a sweetheart. I'm pretty sure—'

'You asked for my opinion.' Brill's voice had taken on a sharp edge. 'I will say it again: I am certain this has nothing to do with adoption. Now, it is true, children are on occasion brought into the U.S. for illegal adoption purposes, most often from Central America. But it's highly unlikely such a child would come into this country in a fishing boat.'

Staffen Brill returned to her chair, sat down, and positioned her manicured hands on the arms. 'I'm sorry to say this, Ms Zarlin. But I suspect your client may not be telling the truth.'

'What do you mean?'

'Have you considered the possibility that she may be attempting to steal the child herself? Perhaps her husband is the sole legal guardian, for example.'

'It's possible, I suppose. But her emotion, her panic and fear, it's all real.'

'Oh, mothers can be terribly emotional, sorrowful. And it's all very touching, until you press them and learn the full truth. Sometimes the mothers that seem the most perfect are in fact child abusers. The worst of the worst.'

The desk phone buzzed like a trapped fly. Brill picked up the receiver and listened.

'No, we're done here, Jack. You can come in.' She got to her feet, and the door opened.

A florid, stocky man in tennis whites entered the room. His glance lasered in on me for a split second. Then he turned away.

'Jack dear, this is Jaymie Zarlin. Ms Zarlin, my husband, Jack Morehead.'

The man nodded in my direction but didn't look at me again. 'Did you take care of that matter we were talking about, Staffen? I'm busy the rest of the afternoon.'

'Lupe took care of it, Jack.' Staffen Brill turned to me. 'Now Ms Zaren, was there anything else?'

'It's Zarlin. And no, that's all I can think of.' My time, apparently, had come to an end. I was about as interesting as yesterday's garbage. Even so, I noticed Jack Morehead took a sharp second look at me as I walked out the door.

Instead of driving straight back out, I decided to indulge my curiosity. I turned left out of the parking area and headed farther north up the private road. On my right I passed a tennis court backed by a tight row of Italian cypresses.

Two men, both in late middle age, were bashing the ball at one another. A third stood in the shade and drank from a fluorescent green bottle.

As I drove past, one of the players lumbered to the net and slammed an air shot against the black-painted cyclone fence at the far end. His opponent roared in triumph or pain – it was hard to know which. He sounded like an arthritic bull.

A hundred yards on, the private road came to a dead end. When I drove back down the road, I saw Eric standing beside the court. He was watching the two men, who were thrashing it out from the baselines now.

Eric turned at the sound of the Camino and stared at me. When I put my hand out the window and waved, the errand boy leaned forward and spat on the ground.

SEVEN

I drove off the estate, then followed Via Tranquila as it wound through rolling hills verdant with green grass and live oaks festooned with fresh growth. At a bend in the road I pulled over and shut off the motor.

'Fuck,' I said aloud. 'What the fuck am I doing?'

I rested my forehead on the steering wheel and shut my eyes. This little jaunt had yielded nothing. I was scampering in a hamster wheel, going through the motions.

I made myself think about Rosie. A bright little button. I could not imagine the fear she must be feeling. I understood Chucha's panic, though, and knew I was avoiding her, trying to stay away from her scalding pain.

What was I accomplishing? Nothing. I was wandering on a whim because I couldn't figure out any of it, for the life of me. In spite of—

'License, Miss.'

I lifted my head. A private security guard looked down at me through the open window. The guy looked as if he hit the bottle hard every night after work, but he was sober now.

'My *what*? You're no cop.'

His eyes wandered over the Camino's interior, in which I'd mounted an assemblage of empty water bottles, back copies of the *Independent*, and a layer of Dexter's hair. Hey, art is in the eye of the beholder.

'You're trespassing.' The security guy's face was blank. 'Only Las Palmas Drive is public. This here is a private road, and you aren't a resident of Hope Ranch.'

I was ripe for a fight. My frustration required venting. 'But I am a citizen of California. And the last I heard, we hadn't instituted pass laws. At least, not yet.'

'Your license, lady. Or I make a citizen's arrest.'

I stared at the guy in disbelief. 'I'm a private investigator, bud. And I'm here on business.' I decided I'd better pull strings. 'I'm here in this neck of the woods because I have an appointment with Staffen Brill. Ms Brill is the owner of Agua Azul, by the way. I've got her number – feel free to give her a call.'

His chin had a stubborn set to it, and he seemed very sure of himself. 'You *have* an appointment – or you *had* an appointment?'

Had an appointment? How would this guy know that? Had someone at Agua Azul phoned him and told him to escort me off the premises? Of course they had.

'Have or had. Does it matter? I'm here on business. I've been here plenty of times, and this is the first time anybody's ever taken the slightest interest in me.' I thought I had him backing up, just a little. 'Did somebody call you, make a complaint? What, I don't look rich enough? Not driving a Lexus, is that the deal?'

He batted a hand, as if my words were pesky flies. 'Look, lady. Do us both a favor, all right? Don't argue. Move on.'

I drove out of Hope Ranch and pulled over at the top of Marina Drive. My little confrontation with the security guy had me feeling much better. Now I just needed to quit feeling so defeated about the case.

I switched off the engine, relaxed down in the seat, and gazed out to the islands. I needed to cogitate. There was a way into this investigation – I was certain of it. I just had to discover the open sesame. Once I'd found my way in, I was sure I'd find a way out.

'I asked you to come in, Chucha, because I want to prepare you for what we're going to do next.'

She leaned forward in the garden chair and looked at me in alarm. 'What are you thinking about?'

'Nothing bad.' I rested my hand on her wrist for a moment. 'Gabi's made flyers with Rosie's picture on them. They're going up around town, especially in the Hispanic neighborhoods along Milpas and the west side. I wanted you to know.'

'Whatever you think's the best thing to do. But I'm getting scared, Jaymie. I'm worried that too much time's passed.'

'Hang in there, Chucha. I know it's tough.' I'd decided not to tell Chucha about Darren and what he'd observed. I felt cruel, withholding hopeful information from her, but it was just too tenuous. After all, Darren had schizophrenia, and he hallucinated. I couldn't raise Chucha's hopes based on what he may or may not have heard in the middle of the night.

The sun shone down on us, but there was a chill in the air. Chucha wrapped her black sweater close over her chest. 'Rosie's out there somewhere. I know it. But that's . . . that's scary too, in a different way.' Her gold-brown eyes met my own. 'I can't even think about it.'

'Don't. It won't help to worry.' I didn't want her to start focusing on all the ugly things that could be happening to her daughter. That would drive her to distraction for sure. I would try to put a positive spin on the situation.

'Let's concentrate on moving forward, Chucha. This may seem random, putting out flyers, but it makes sense. It's possible one of the pangeros ran off with Rosie, thinking he was saving her from something. So there's a chance somebody in town has seen her or has even been taking care of her.' This sounded logical. I'd almost convinced myself.

'Yeah, I can see that. I'm glad you told me about the flyers. I guess I would of freaked if I saw one and you hadn't warned me. Is your phone number on it?'

'The office number, and our address. They're going up this afternoon.'

'Can you give me a stack? I could help.'

'I'd rather not. I want you to stay out of sight, in case the cops are watching.' Which I figured they'd be doing soon, if they weren't already.

She nodded, then rubbed her forehead. 'What else can we do?'

It was decent of Chucha to say 'we.' This was my job, and so far I hadn't accomplished a thing. 'Stay optimistic. It's hard, but can you do that?'

'I'll try.' Chucha got to her feet and walked over to the bougain-villea draping the block wall. A few radiant pink flowers had opened their papery bracts. She picked one and began to peel off the bracts, dropping them to the ground.

'You wonder, right?' She glanced back at me. 'I mean, you wonder how somebody like me got in this situation.'

Chucha loved her daughter with a passion. But the six-foot-plus woman with a five o'clock shadow did not fit the image of the motherly sort. 'You told me you hooked up with a girl in your village. Unless it's pertinent to the case, Chucha, that's all I need to know.'

'I don't know what's pertinent. I don't know anything anymore. But I want you to understand.' Chucha reached to her head, pushed her fingertips back at the hairline, and lifted.

I tried not to gape. Chucha sat down in the lawn chair and placed the wig in her lap.

Before me sat a handsome young man in his mid-twenties. His black hair was shaved close to his skull. Without the wig, Chucha's high cheekbones and curved nose stood out.

'Your daughter looks like you, all right.'

Chucha gave a shadow of a smile.

'How did it happen, then? Only if you want to tell me.'

'I haven't had the operation on the bottom, not yet. Only the top.' Chucha shrugged. 'But that's not what you mean, right?'

'Correct.' But that was part of what I'd wondered, yes. This was new territory for me. I felt I was on a risky path and needed to choose my words with care. I didn't want to hurt Chucha, or to shut her up if she wanted to talk.

'I'm not the first one. When you're a trannie like me, it can be lonely, see?' She traced a pattern in the dust on the glass tabletop. 'No, not *can* be. It *is* lonely. Some people are just plain mean, and that's almost better. Because the other ones, the ones that *use* you – to them you're just an object, a thing.'

'I'm sorry.' I saw how it hurt, I saw it in the twist of her mouth. And I also saw how exhausting it must be for Chucha, to always be hiding a secret. Hiding, yet wanting to reveal at the same time – it was a bewildering sleight of hand, and no doubt very few people were cut out for it.

'So . . . when somebody acts nice to you and wants to be close, you kind of want to respond. You know? I went down to Mexico over two years ago, to see my grandma. I really loved her. She was dying, and I was kind of messed up at the time. Leticia was nice to me, like she wanted to be my friend. Now I think maybe she was, you know, curious. Nosy. Anyway, one night it just happened.' Chucha laughed a little.

'We were drinking tequila. I don't know, I must have been thinking about her brother or something. He was cute.'

'And nine months later, you had a baby girl.'

'Yes. Like I already told you, at first I thought everything was OK. I sent Leticia money, for her and the baby. When Rosamar was three months old, I went down and saw her. She's such a little doll, I fell in love with her right away, you know? But a few months after I got back, that's when I heard from my cousin that Leticia was with some guy. A real asshole. They were living off what I was sending them. I figured, OK, I can afford it if this is what I have to do for my baby. But then, later on, I heard something else.'

'Something worse.'

'Way worse, worse than I told you. My cousin sent me a letter. She said I needed to get Rosie out of there, fast. Leticia and her boyfriend, they were neglecting Rosie. They weren't beating her, but they were treating her real bad. She was dirty all the time and they were making her sleep on a towel in the corner. They gave her hardly any food. My cousin was trying to feed Rosie, but Leticia, she was all the time standing in the way. She didn't want anybody on my side of the family to get involved.'

'She wanted the money all to herself?'

'Yeah, the money. That's what it was.'

As I started to respond, I heard a sharp rap from inside the office, on the front door. I walked in through the back and opened it.

'What a dump.' Deirdre Krause wrinkled her nose and shook her curly blond head. 'I didn't think it would be *this* bad. You can smell the mold from here.'

'Deirdre. What can I do for you?' I didn't step aside. But the PD detective leaned to the left and looked past me.

'The mold – or maybe something else. Got a visitor, Zarlin?'

I turned my head to follow her gaze. Deirdre Krause was looking straight through the kitchenette doorway, directly at Chucha.

'I'm busy, Deirdre. Do you want to make an appointment?'

'What, you don't have time to talk about a missing kid?' She said it with aggression, as if a missing kid was somehow a bludgeon. 'I thought you'd be interested – you're plastering up flyers all over town.'

This surprised me. Claudia and BJ must be moving fast, and so, it seemed, was Deirdre.

'I have time. Just not right now.'

'We're gonna talk now, Zarlin. I've got something to tell you.' Her voice had hardened, and the result was like the shrill whine of a drill in hardwood. 'Get rid of the tranny ho.'

My blood boiled, the way it will do from time to time. 'You're slandering a member of the public, Krause. Come back in thirty minutes if you have something to say, but get off my doorstep.'

'Jaymie, it's OK. I'll call you later.' Chucha had walked through the kitchenette into the office and now stood behind me. She was a good foot taller than Deirdre, but even so, she looked a little afraid.

I started to protest, but then I stopped. This wasn't about Chucha, it was about Rosie. And Chucha was begging me with her eyes.

'So now you work for hos. That's a new low, Zarlin, even for you.' Deirdre had pushed past me into the office. 'Where's the short fat one that works for you? Couldn't stand the stink from your clientele?'

My blood pressure zinged and rang the bell.

'Still pissed about Mike, Deirdre?' I knew this was low and unworthy of me. Even so, I barely refrained from pumping a fist.

'What, Dawson? As far as I'm concerned, he's a pain in the ass.'

She didn't mean it, of course. Deirdre's crush on Mike went back years. I knew she'd been overjoyed when Mike and I had split up last year, and now she was no doubt seething because we were back together.

'You think you're hot shit, don't you, Zarlin.' She completed her surveillance of the room and turned to face me. 'I got a question to ask you. Do you have any idea what you're getting yourself into?'

'What the hell are you talking about?' I had to admit, my behavior was at its most foul around this woman.

She pulled a folded square of paper from her pants pocket, opened it, and dangled Gabi's flyer in front of my nose. 'This wouldn't have anything to do with the panga boat at More Mesa, would it?'

'What if it does?' I said with exaggerated nonchalance. 'It's my job, it's what I do. All within the law, by the way. You're thinking too hard, Deirdre. You could fry your brain that way.'

Deirdre was very fair, and I watched as a dark flush crept up from her neck, millimeter by millimeter, to her hairline.

'Don't ask me why, Zarlin, but I came here to do you a favor. To warn you, all right?'

'But now you're going to say screw it,' I prompted.

I saw her hesitate. She wanted to tell me to go fuck myself, and who could blame her? But I suspected she'd been told to deliver a message. The woman was caught in a bind.

'Go on, Deirdre. What did they tell you to say to me? You know, the ones who jerk your strings.'

By the time Deirdre got the words out, she was snarling like a trapped bobcat. 'Forget about the kid. If you know what's good for you, you'll forget about More Mesa and anything and anyone connected to it. I'm telling you, Zarlin, you have no idea what's going on.'

'Forget about the kid? I know you hate dogs, but I didn't know you felt that way about kids, too.'

'You idiot.' Deirdre Krause choked. 'You can go to hell for all I care. You don't have a fucking clue.'

The weekend storm had driven the surf across Leadbetter beach and up onto the tarmac, where it left behind heaps of yellow sand. I rode my Schwinn into the parking lot and slowed. The beach itself was blanketed in swathes of brown and green kelp steaming in the sun.

The Great American Novel was parked at the far end of the lot. I pedaled up to the driver's side window. The tattered hopsack curtain, which may or may not have been orange back in 1968, was drawn across the open window. It swayed in and out with the breath of the sea.

I tapped on the rusted frame of the VW van. 'Charlie, you home?' Of course he was home. But maybe my old friend wasn't inclined to talk.

A full minute passed. 'That you, Jaymie?'

'It's me. Sorry – are you taking a nap?'

I heard some rustling and grunting. After a moment, the curtain drew back. 'I was.'

'Sorry, mate. But it's eleven a.m.' I grinned at my old friend. His eyes blinked through the holes in the gauze sack he wore over his head, to hide his burn-scarred face. The sack was newish, one a nurse had sewn for him when he was in the hospital with pneumonia six months earlier. I was sure she'd sewn it out of self-preservation: the original sack was so dirty it stood up by itself.

'Yeah, well. When you get to my age, you'll sleep when you damn well want to, too. Plus the young ones, they make so much noise down in the Funk Zone these days, they keep me awake all night. Sippin' wine and spittin it out. What kinda nonsense is that? How about some coffee, Jaymie girl?'

I leaned my bike against the once-white van, now inscribed from the driver's door around the back to the passenger door with Charlie's novel. It was currently titled *Life's A Be-ach*.

'No thanks, Charlie. I've seen that rusty thermos of yours. I want to live a little longer.'

'Iron supplement, Jaymie. Puts hair on your chest.'

'Chest hair. Just what I need.' I pulled the newly printed flyer from my pocket and unfolded it. 'For once this isn't a social call, Charlie. Here, take a look.'

Charlie put out a hand banded with scar tissue and took the flyer. '*She*-it. This little one here, somebody took her?' A rough growl sounded deep inside my friend's corrugated lungs.

'Somebody took her, all right. From a panga boat. Her mother was supposed to collect her off the boat, but it looks like someone else grabbed her first.'

'Jesus, there's some evil bastards in this world.' His hand shook a little. 'You talkin' about the panga boat that landed up More Mesa way, couple a days back?'

'That's the one. Smuggling pot.'

'I heard about that. OK, I'll talk it up. You might want to get me some more a these papers. Plenty a people stick their heads in this window. Say, where's Mike? You put your boyfriend on the case, too?'

'Mike's on a meth bust in the back country. He should be home in a few days.'

'Hmm. You two married yet?'

'Charlie, you know we're not.' Here it came, the third degree.

'Why not?'

'I'm like you, I guess. I like my freedom.'

'Don't you go dragging me into it. Me and Annie, we lived together for more'n thirty years before the hell fire took her.'

'Sorry. I know.' Charlie was referring to the campfire that had badly burned him and taken the life of his beloved partner. I gazed out to the ocean, where silver waves danced arabesques under the late winter sun.

'When I mentioned freedom just now, I was talking about how you refuse to park the van up at my place at night. Seems a lot better than that restaurant parking lot you like to call home.'

Charlie grunted. 'You still pissed about that, Jaymie? I told you, I don't like to be beholden, that's all. Plus it's too quiet up at your place. Too peaceful for an old coot like me. I'd wake up and think I was already dead and gone to heaven, what with that view you got, and all those damn birds singin' their heads off.'

'Bullshit. You just do what you feel like, that's all there is to it.'

'And I ain't apologizin' for it, so don't hold yer breath.'

I picked up my bike. 'I'll check back in a day or so, see if you've heard anything.'

'Right-o. By the way, how's my buddy Dex?'

'Dexter misses you. He wants to know why you abandoned him.'

'Misses the snacks I give him, you mean. Don't you ever feed that pooch?' He reached up to draw the hopsacking across the open window.

'Charlie, wait. I almost forgot.' I slid my hands off the grips to the cold handlebars.

'I know you forgot. I don't see no horehounds.'

'Sorry. Next time, I promise.'

'You better. I'm pretty sour these days. I need sweetnin' up. So what was it you forgot?'

'Something I meant to ask. You know some of the folks who sleep out near the beaches, right?'

'Sure. I know most of 'em, and they know me.'

'I wonder if you know this guy I met the other day. He hangs out at More Mesa.'

'Not many go out there. It's a good place, the cops pretty much leave you alone. But it's too far away from food, water too. What's this fella look like?'

'He's real thin, not too tall, maybe five-seven, five-eight. His hair is light brown, he's, it's hard to say, maybe twenty-five.'

'You just described about half a the people I know, Jaymie. This guy, he got any tats?'

'No tats. He's mentally ill. Hears things, I think, but he works hard to live in both worlds.' I thought for a moment. 'You know, there is something different about his looks. One of his eyes drifts out a little.'

'Oh, hell. You're talking about Sideview. Sure, I know Sideview. Don't know his real name, but he's been around for a while.'

'What can you tell me about him?'

'Sideview's all right. He didn't used to be so confused, I think the outdoor life's been tough on him. He's real shy, tries to stay out of sight. You know, I think maybe he grew up right here in Santa Barbara, but I ain't ever seen any family try to help him. Is he in trouble, that why you're asking?'

'He's not in trouble, not exactly. But he saw what happened out at More Mesa the other night. I've tried to talk to him, but he doesn't trust me much.' I shrugged. 'Can't say I blame him.'

'Wanna know how to get him to trust you? Talk to him about Brodie. Tell him Brodie was your brother.'

'He knew Brodie?'

'Yeah. Brodie tried to look after Sideview, helped him out of a jam once or twice. Your brother was like that, Jaymie. Not so different from somebody else I know.'

EIGHT

'Hi, Jaymie. Listen, I'm here to talk to you about the brat. The one you've got on the poster.'

I heard Gabi, who'd hunkered down behind the computer screen, suck in her breath.

Del Wasson had slipped. He'd just revealed his less attractive side, namely, his character.

'The little girl, you mean.'

'Yes, the little girl.' Dark Eyes corrected himself and smiled prettily. At least he was sharp enough to know he'd taken a misstep. 'If you don't mind, I'd like to ask you some questions.'

'So – Deirdre's not in charge of the case?' I loved to play dumb.

Del looked surprised. 'Officer Krause? What's she got to do with it?'

'She dropped by yesterday. Wanted to talk about the same thing as you. It sounded like she was in charge.' I shrugged. 'I'm curious – how come I get two visits from the PD within twenty-four hours, both about the same non-issue?'

And I *was* curious. Very.

'We – me and Deirdre – we're working this together, OK? And it's not what I'd call a non-issue, not if it involves a missing child. Do you see a problem with that?'

His reply was lame. No. It sounded like a flat-out lie. 'No problem at all, officer. Fire away.'

Del still looked confused. But he'd assumed his usual fallback position: spreading charm like manure. 'Mind if I sit down, Jaymie?'

'Fine.' I indicated the hot seat for Officer Wasson, as I had on his previous visit. Del didn't want to sit – he just wanted to get cozy. Best to avoid the couch.

He sat in the chair and I perched on the edge of the desk. I could smell his musky cologne.

'So, Jaymie. I assume somebody hired you to find their kid. Am I right?'

'Dead on the money, Del.'

He leaned back in the hot seat and crossed his legs. 'Who was it?'

'Oh, come off it. You know that's confidential.'

'Mmhmm.' Del looked over at the desk, where Gabi was still trying to hide behind the computer screen. 'Excuse me, miss?'

Gabi's head popped up over the top of the screen. 'Me?'

'Yes, you.' Del smiled. 'What's your name?'

'Rufina Martinez.' This wasn't a lie. Rufina and Martinez were two of Gabi's names, just not the main ones.

'Rufina, unlike your boss here, you seem like a woman who has respect for the law.'

Gabi's eyes slid over to mine. 'Yes, I respect all the laws. And so does Miss Jaymie.'

'Very good. You respect all the laws, plus *The Law*, right?' Del pointed a casual finger at his chest. 'The Law. Meaning me.'

'Oh. Uh huh.' Like a frog sinking below the surface, Gabi had dropped so low again behind the screen that only her eyebrows showed.

'So if I ask you who the client is, who wants to find that poor missing girl, you'll tell me, right?'

'There are lots of laws,' Gabi muttered. 'Like about not telling stuff you don't want to.'

'Yes, there are lots of laws, aren't there.' Del got to his feet and walked around the desk to stand behind Gabi. 'For example, there are laws about not remaining in the US without a visa.'

'Harassment,' I snapped. 'You asked your question and got your answer. Now cease and desist.'

By this time I'd stepped over behind the desk, too. The frog was hunkering down between Del and me like a stone.

'Unless there's something else, Wasson, you need to move on.'

'Know what? Plenty of my co-workers wouldn't put up with your lip. Lucky for you, Zarlin, I'm an easygoing kind of guy.'

Late that afternoon I was still imprisoned in the kitchenette, attempting to tackle a stack of papers my PA had slid under my nose, when the office phone rang. I heard Gabi answer in English, then switch over to Spanish.

I possess a modicum of Español. But as the conversation progressed, Gabi's words grew more staccato and incomprehensible, till they rat-tat-tatted like machine gun fire.

At last the phone banged down and the office was quiet – for a moment.

'What a stupid man! Did you hear that, Miss Jaymie?'

'Yep. But I didn't understand a word.'

I heard her shove back her chair. 'It was very strange!' She appeared in the doorway. 'Some guy, he called about the flyer.'

'But that's good.' I tossed down my pen. 'What did he say?'

'Waita minute, OK? I don't know it's so good.' She smoothed the hem of her fuzzy velour sweatshirt. 'He talked Spanish. So in the beginning I thought, maybe this is the one we are looking for. The one from the panga boat that maybe took Rosie.'

'But?'

'There are two buts. First, his Spanish was wrong.'

'Wrong? What, you mean he made mistakes?'

'No, no mistakes. But I could tell, Miss Jaymie, he wasn't from Mexico. That accent, it was Tejano. And I got the idea the guy speaks English good, maybe it's his first language even. But he don't want me to know that.'

'A Texan pretending to be from Mexico? Odd.' I propped my heels up on the table. 'Why would he do that?'

'Miss Jaymie. I do not like to tell you what to do. But please take your shoes off the table. You eat on that table sometimes.'

She had a point. I lowered my feet to the floor.

'Now. You ask me why somebody would do it? Because' – Gabi pointed a finger upwards – 'because he does not want me to know, but I know anyway: he is a cop.'

'The man who called was a cop?' I stared at her. 'How could you tell?'

'I been paying attention, that's how. I been paying attention to the way you figure things out. This guy? He had nothing to *tell*. No, he only had things to *ask*, you know? Like, who is the little girl? Where does she come from and why is she missing? Who wants to find her?'

'The third damn cop in less than twenty-four hours. What the hell is this all about?' I got up and slid my chair under the table. 'How much did you tell him?'

'Me?' Gabi widened her eyes. 'If you talked Spanish better, Miss Jaymie, you would know. I told the cop guy to mind his own business.'

'Very good. Because it's also possible he was a criminal, Gabi, somebody trying to get his hands on Rosie. A crim, not a cop.'

'Miss Jaymie, please, what are you talking about? Of course he is a crim.' She narrowed her eyes. 'Like I said, he is a cop.'

Gabi left at five. But I stayed on, till dusk began to collect in the corners of the little rooms. Then I dropped the blinds, stepped out onto the front porch and locked the door. As I bent to uncouple my Schwinn from the bannister, something made me stop and listen.

The birds had broken off their evening roosting songs, and the only sound I could hear was the swoosh of traffic out on the street. I straightened and glanced to my right.

Standing just inside the cluster of giant bird of paradise trees was a man.

He was Hispanic, slight, and young – no more than nineteen or twenty years old. He wore jeans and a T-shirt, inadequate in the evening chill. The guy didn't look threatening, but he didn't look friendly, either. Wary, maybe even afraid.

'Buenas noches.' I kept my voice low. Then I waited. The guy seemed to be debating: run, or stay?

'Buenas . . . noches.' The fellow seemed awkward with the words. He had an odd voice, lilting and high. Like that of a tropical bird.

He trilled a few more words, and I realized he wasn't speaking Spanish. An indigenous language of Mexico, maybe. 'Sorry.' I spread my hands in apology.

He tried a few halting words in Spanish. Then he reached into the breast pocket of his thin cotton shirt and pulled out a piece of paper folded many times over. Keeping his eyes on me, he opened it and held it up.

Rosie gazed back at me from the flyer. My breath caught.

This guy was the one we were after, I was sure of it.

'Si.' I patted my chest. 'My flyer.' God, how stupid was it, not speaking Spanish in this place and time?

My eyes on him, I tugged my phone from my pants pocket. But when he saw the phone, his face closed. Quickly, before he could take off, I held up a hand.

'Mi amiga,' I pleaded. 'Mi amiga habla español. OK?' I was pretty sure he knew some Spanish. Gabi would be able to bridge the gap.

He relaxed a little and nodded. He'd understood.

'Gabi Gutierrez, she works with me.' Again I patted my chest. 'Jaymie, Jaymie Zarlin. And you?'

Again, the shutters came down. He shrugged. 'Chino.' I was pretty sure that wasn't his real name.

But he pointed at the phone and nodded. 'Is OK.'

Just as I began to dial, the repo woman next door stepped out on her porch. She looked over, and Chino faded back into the shrubbery.

'Everything good over there?'

'Everything's good,' I called back. 'How about you?'

'Couldn't be better.' The woman descended her steps, reached into her shirt to adjust a bra strap, then walked on.

I thought about asking this Chino guy to step inside the office, but I was pretty sure he wouldn't want that. So instead I moved toward the back garden, motioning him to follow. He complied.

I sat down at the round garden table. The small space was dark now. The heady tropical scent of the tobira bushes filled the night air.

After a moment's hesitation, the young man sat down opposite me. I noticed he had little hair on his face, just a downy mustache on his upper lip. His eyelids had an Asian fold. Maybe his nickname really was Chino, who knew.

He looked away from my direct gaze, out of politeness. That told me he hadn't been in this country for long.

I dialed the phone, and Gabi answered on the first ring. 'Miss Jaymie, what, did I forget something?'

'No. Gabi, I'm sitting here with a young man who says his name's Chino. He's come with the flyer, and he wants to tell me something.'

'But he don't speak no English, right? Maybe he really is the one.'

'Right. But his Spanish isn't that good either. I think he might speak an Indian language. Gabi, he's spooked. I need you to translate, but don't go scaring him off, OK?'

'I'm gonna talk straight.'

'Straight is OK. Mean is not. Remember, we don't know that he's had anything to do with Rosie's abduction.'

'Miss Jaymie, please trust me. Give him the phone.'

I watched as the young man spoke, hesitantly at first, then with gathering force and directness. He and Gabi talked for two or three minutes. Then he looked over at me and handed me the cell.

'Miss Jaymie, OK. Listen to me. This guy, yes, his nickname is Chino. He's too scared to tell us the rest of his name. And he speaks Spanish, but you are right, his first language is an Indian one that I never heard of.' Gabi's words merged together in a turbulent stream.

'Now here it is. Chino was on the panga boat with two other guys. Some other people in Mexico, some people he don't wanna talk about, they made him get on the boat. They said they would hurt Chino's family if he didn't help take the marijuana up to California. Now listen, Miss Jaymie. One of those two other guys on the boat was the boss. The other one, he didn't want to go, just like Chino. But guess what else he said, Miss Jaymie. In the beginning, there were two little girls in the boat.'

'My God.' I turned and stared at Chino.

'It is terrible, yes. Terrible. One little girl died. She was three, maybe four years old. He says nobody hurt her, she just got sick and then died. And the other one, she was sick too, but not so much, and she didn't die.'

'And that was Rosie.'

'Yes. The one on the flyer, he said.'

'Gabi. Are you certain that's what he told you? That one child died?'

Chino got to his feet. His eyes were fixed on me, and he looked ready to bolt. I put out a hand, pleading with him to stay.

'Yes, he said that. I think maybe—'

'Gabi, quick. Just the main points.'

'OK. He don't know why the little girls were in the boat. And the other guy like him, he knows nothing too. But he thinks maybe the leader, the third pangero, a guy named Flaco, he knows it all. And that is the end.'

'Gabi, we need more. Chino has to know more than that. Did you push it?'

'Yes, I pushed it and pushed it. He thinks maybe that guy Flaco, he went back down to the beach and got Rosie after they unloaded the marijuana. But he don't know why, and he don't even know that for sure. Because right after Flaco left, Chino took off. And now he's scared, Miss Jaymie. Real scared.'

I looked up. Chino had fluttered a hand in farewell. 'Gabi, I gotta go.'

'Lo siento,' Chino said.

He was sorry. And so was I.

'Wait. Dinero.' I made the sign for cash with my fingers and thumb.

I walked back around to the office door, let myself in, and switched on the light. Because I still wasn't one hundred percent sure about Chino, I shut the door.

I managed to locate the key that unlocked the bottom drawer in Gabi's desk, slid it open and lifted the cash box lid. I hesitated: how much would it take to make sure Chino returned if he received more information?

When I stepped outside, Chino was waiting, once again concealed within the massive leaves of the giant bird of paradise.

'Muchas gracias.' I held out the money.

Chino stepped forward, then stopped. I could see him hesitating. He stared down at the five twenty-dollar bills in my hand.

'Lo siento,' he said again in his awkward Spanish. He held up the flyer.

He was telling me he'd come forward to help Rosie, not for the reward. I understood. It was blood money, after all.

'Yes. But I want you to have the money. If you learn more, please come back and tell me.' I tried to mime out my words.

His eyes met my own. Then he ran a swift finger across his throat. 'Tengo miedo.' He was afraid.

'*Narcos*?'

'*Narcos*, si. Y . . . El policía.'

'*The* cop?' Had I understood right? He'd said 'cop', singular. Not 'cops'. 'Chino, who—'

But he'd moved away. I stepped forward to stop him, but in the blink of an eye, he was gone.

NINE

'Where's Blanca?' I asked Dexter the following morning. This set off an urgent howl. Dex rocketed out through the door as I opened it.

Dex was still the same cocky little punk he'd always been. He seemed to have forgotten he'd ever had four legs. He couldn't go on long runs with me anymore, but other than that, three legs served him just fine.

Together we climbed into Blue Boy. I backed my brother's Camino out of the old redwood car shed and pointed it down the steep drive. Dex hopped up from the floor to the passenger seat. We weren't moving fast enough: he threatened me with his herding dog stare and a low throaty growl.

We coasted down the drive and turned into El Balcon. At the corner of El Balcon and Cliff, I pulled over and applied my parking brake.

'Wait here, OK?' Dexter didn't deal with orders, but he did listen to offers, suggestions, and tips.

Blanca was out in her backyard, rounding up imaginary sheep. Deaf and blind since birth, the lethal-white border collie dwelt in a silent yet vibrant world of her own making.

Mrs McMenamin peered out from her breakfast nook table and gave me a wave, but she didn't stand up. At eighty-five, her arthritis could be nearly unbearable at times, especially first thing in the morning. I waved back and drew the gate shut behind me.

I lifted Blanca's leash from its hook on the porch post and walked up to the collie, holding out my hand for her to smell me. She escalated into a paroxysm of pleasure, twisting in circles and leaping at me. Blanca was still young, around two, and her energy was irrepressible once uncorked.

Mrs McMenamin did her best by Blanca. Her granddaughter had rescued the white collie pup from a tote bag left beside a freeway on-ramp. Four months later the young woman was locked up in Chowchilla, thanks to her heroin addiction.

I waved goodbye to Blanca's mistress and led the dog back out through the gate.

'Here's your girlfriend!' I announced as I opened the car door. Blanca scrambled in. Much wagging of tails and nose pressing commenced. Then we were off, up the road to the gully.

The Hondo Gully was ideal for these two misfits. Unless they flushed a coyote, there wasn't much trouble they could get into. And even if they did come across a coyote, Dex had a way of disarming his cousins.

I parked at the lower entrance, opened the passenger door and stepped back as the two blithe spirits bolted off up the slope. I followed at a more relaxed pace.

The gully, an old creek bed, was lined with a steep series of benches cut by long-ago water surges. The path meandered along one of these benches. Live oaks arched overhead, creating a dappled shade when the sun was out. This morning, though, a breeze off the ocean sailed straight up the gully, trailing a lacey mantilla of fog in its wake. I zipped up my sweatshirt against the chill.

As I ambled along, the fog thickened. Even in the fog the air bubbled with birdsong.

Blanca raced ahead in loops of joy, surging ahead and then circling back to Dexter and I. There wasn't much she could bump into on the path, and besides, by now she knew it by heart.

I let my mind wander. I thought about Chino and his visit the evening before.

Chino was no criminal. He was just an impoverished young guy who was struggling to survive. He'd felt guilty, all right, and wanted to help. Even so, he hadn't told me much. He was afraid of the traffickers – and a cop.

So there'd been a cop, or somebody who'd seemed like a cop, at More Mesa that night. This wasn't looking like a simple case, not anymore.

The dogs and I were closer to the ocean now, and the fog was dense. I could hear the fog horn bleating a warning off the marina below. I couldn't see Blanca, though. I stopped and listened.

Without warning, the white collie burst out of the underbrush at the side of the trail. Head down, low to the ground, she raced over to Dex. Dex halted, sniffed the breeze, and let out a warning growl.

A runner loped out of the fog. He was tall, dressed in a navy warm-up outfit. Dexter let out a serious snarl, and Blanca cowered against my legs.

'Jaymie!' Del Wasson halted mid-stride. 'So, you walk down in here?'

I studied Del's lean handsome face. Nothing seemed awry, and yet something wasn't quite right. Was this encounter by chance?

'Yeah, me and the dogs.' Dex had stopped barking, but every ten seconds or so, he let out a growl. Blanca, confused, roved from me to Dex and back again.

'I can see what's wrong with that one.' Del laughed and pointed at the three-legged heeler. 'What about the white one? He looks psycho.'

Now, if there's one word that sets my teeth on edge, it's the word psycho. I'd heard people say it to my brother, and I knew how it could hurt. Blanca didn't care, but I damn well did. Del Wasson, forever more, would be nothing but toast.

'He's a she. And she's blind and deaf.' I would have moved on, but I was curious to see what Wasson was up to and decided to stay put.

'Huh. You had any tips yet about the missing kid?'

'Nothing yet.' I assumed an innocent expression. 'How about the drug smuggling?'

Del smiled, a sexy lazy smile that no doubt worked for him ninety-nine percent of the time. 'You know I can't talk about that, Jaymie.'

Now I saw what wasn't quite right about Del. He looked as if he'd just scrunched Wowie Maui into his hair and stepped from his vehicle. He wasn't out for a run – that was a lie.

'Is that your jogging outfit? I'd have pegged you for a tennis player, Detective.'

'I play tennis, yeah.' He grinned. 'But I like to keep in shape, you know?'

'Sure.' I realized I was sick of bantering with Del. I took a step to move on around him.

'Jaymie, hold on a minute, will you?' The man had the nerve to put a hand on my arm. I looked down at it, then met his eyes with a hard look. Wasson lifted his hand.

'Something I wanted to ask you.'

'Oh yeah?'

I watched as Wasson unzipped the side pocket of his warm-up jacket and removed the flyer. Rosie's pixie face looked up at me.

'Come on, Wasson. We've been over this before. Or do you have some new info for me?' What was the guy playing at?

'No, I don't. But my boss is putting pressure on me. I'd like to know what all this is about.' He took a step closer, and Dexter bared his teeth. Wasson stepped back.

'Help me out here, Jaymie. You know how it works. Scratch my back, and—'

God damn. Had the guy learned nothing? He'd actually winked.

'Like I told you, it's just a case I'm working on. A missing kid.' The man's persistence was beginning to worry me. I needed to redirect his attention. 'We think it's her father who's taken her, and she's not in any immediate danger. The girl just needs to be back where she belongs, with her mom.'

'That so? It still needs to be reported.' But Del looked skeptical. I hadn't quite sold him on what I thought was a most excellent lie. I could make it better, though.

'The mother did report it, down in Los Angeles. But they stuck it in the bottom of the stack.' Plausible, I thought. Anyone could get lost in the labyrinth called LA. It was a miracle anything, or anyone, was ever found.

'So, what – the mother came to you about this, out of the blue?'

'That's right. I wouldn't call it out of the blue, though. People know what I do, Del. Word of mouth.'

'That's good. Means your business is taking off, right?'

'Uh huh.' My mind was working overtime trying to figure out what the guy was after. I was sure the barrage of false signals was hiding a hard-edged purpose.

'Anyway. Shouldn't be too hard to find her, with a weird birth-mark like she's got.'

Interesting. I'd read through Gabi's text for the flyer, and I didn't remember seeing the word 'birthmark'.

'Birthmark? What are you talking about?'

Now Del's mask slipped. He looked concerned, almost, and I watched his expression change as he struggled to regroup.

'What? The flyer said something . . .' He scanned the paper and read aloud. 'OK, here it is: *Distinguishing mark.*'

'Distinguishing mark can mean a scar,' I replied. 'Right?'

Wasson smiled, a touch too brightly this time. 'OK, it just said "mark." So shoot me for ass-suming.'

'No,' I answered, playing along. Best to let old Del think he got away with it. 'No, I won't shoot you for that.' I shrugged and turned to go. 'Know your way out of here, Wasson?' Maybe I shouldn't have said that, but I couldn't resist.

He forced a laugh. 'I told you, I run through here all the time.' He started off.

But Dex wanted the last word. He bounded after on his three legs, caught up with Del and nipped him on the achilles.

'Fucking mutt!' Wasson pulled back his leg to kick the little cow dog.

'Don't you dare touch him, you jerk!'

The gloves were off. Wasson glared, and I glared back. Blanca whined and circled in fear.

Alas. Del and I would now never be friends.

When the dogs and I had returned to the Camino and settled in, I switched on my cell and phoned Mike.

I knew he wouldn't pick up. He was on the assignment now, hiking into the backcountry to bust up the meth op. By this time he'd have moved into a different mindset, one that was focused, uncomplicated. One that didn't involve me and my messy life.

'Mike, there's no need to call me back. I just want to let you know Rosie is alive, we're sure of that now. There's more, a lot more I want to talk to you about . . .'

I stopped. I wanted to tell him everything, about Darren, Chino, Del Wasson, and most of all, about the little one who'd died at sea. But Mike had enough on his plate, and I could tell him when he returned.

I also wanted to say, 'Please be careful. You are so important to me. Take care of yourself.' But instead I just signed off with 'love ya', and left it at that.

I guess I hoped 'love ya' would cover it all.

Blue Boy was too convenient, his newly upholstered seats so cushy. If I kept opting for the Camino over my Schwinn my own seat would soon become cushy too. Even though it was a long ride out to More Mesa, that afternoon I cowgirled up.

I checked my back more than once as I pedaled along. Del Wasson seemed to be taking an interest in me, and the last thing I needed was a cop on my tail. But today, it seemed, I was on my own. Maybe my suitor was losing interest.

When I arrived at the mesa, I bumped my way across the weedy meadow, heading for the ocean cliff. I chained my Schwinn to a muscular eucalyptus trunk and paused for a moment at the top of the path that led down to the beach. The morning was cool, but a current of heated air rose up the cliff, caressing my face.

Santa Cruz Island was only just rising from her bed, and the night's mist swaddled her feet like a discarded nightgown. The channel waters effervesced like champagne.

I made my way down the narrow path, through thick stands of lemonadeberry. I could hear rats or rabbits bustling in the under-growth, and the coo-cooing of doves. It was that delicate season in California for which there is no name, the lush weeks of late winter and early spring when the grass glows with the green of stained glass and wild flowers swell with tight buds.

Halfway down the slope, at a switchback, I halted. From there I could see the beach below. The tide was in, and the teasing waves lapped at dry sand.

Not far out from the water's edge, a thin dark figure splashed in the surf. A man was playing in the chilly water like a child, carving wide arcs of spray with the flats of his hands.

I stepped off the path so I was hidden from the beach by the scrub. Then I pulled out my binoculars and trained them on the reveler.

As I'd guessed, it was Darren. I watched him for a few moments, my heart hurting a little. Even from here I could see he was happy. It was midweek in winter, and the beach was empty of visitors. For once, Darren could let down his guard.

I lowered the field glasses. I was about to intrude, and it didn't feel right.

But I couldn't stand there all day. After a few minutes I continued making my way down, keeping my eyes on the path. I didn't look out at Darren again till I was crossing the crusty sand. He must have caught sight of me, because he'd sunk down in the cold water. Only his head and the tops of his shoulders were visible.

To give Darren time, I waved at him, then continued walking westward. Sand hoppers popped around my ankles. I passed by his clothing, folded and stacked. When I came to an old driftwood log, I sat down to wait.

It wasn't long before Darren walked out of the ocean. I was glad to see that, because the water was frigid enough to kill a person, given time. People with schizophrenia aren't always aware of temperature, and I wasn't sure Darren would know if he was heading into hypothermia.

He struggled into his sweatshirt and pants, his back to me. Then he tugged the hood of his sweatshirt over his head and started to walk away.

'Darren, wait,' I called out. I hated to hound the guy, but I couldn't afford to let him get away.

He stopped and looked out to sea. I took it as an acknowledgment – as much of one as I was likely to get.

I trudged toward him, trying not to break into a trot. When I got to within speaking distance, I halted. 'Hey, Darren. I'm Jaymie, remember?' As I reached toward my messenger bag, he froze.

'It's OK. Just thought you might like a little lunch.' I snapped open the bag, took out a wrapped sandwich and a bottle of water, and held them out to him. When he didn't respond I ventured into the no-man's land between us, knelt down and brushed the sand clean, and put down the water and food. Then I retraced my steps.

Darren hesitated, but not for long. He walked forward, reached down and grabbed the sandwich. He took a few steps away, turned his back on me again, and began to eat fast. I could see the poor guy was famished. When he was done, he folded the paper

wrapping again and again, then slipped the small square into his
sweatshirt pocket.

'Darren, remember? You and I talked the other day. I'm trying
to find the little girl that came in on the boat.'

'Yeah . . .'

'Listen, we have the same friend. Charlie, the old guy who lives
in a van and always parks down at Leadbetter.'

Darren glanced at me, then away. 'The guy in – in the sack?'

'Yes, that's Charlie all right. He asked me if you're OK.'

'I'm OK. It's just – it's just—'

He didn't seem as well as he had the first time we'd spoken.
Maybe Darren was just having a bad day, or maybe something scary
had happened, something that had pushed him deeper into himself.

'Darren, there's one question I forgot to ask you. That night, the
night they unloaded the bales of dope off the boat? I heard that one
of the guys was a cop.'

He began to hum – not a tune, but a single long extended note.
Brodie used to do that too sometimes, to block out the voices.

'I'm sorry I have to ask. Nobody will know you told me, I
promise. Was there a cop here that night?' To Darren's ears, I was
sure my promise had a hollow ring. People with schizophrenia learn
the hard way to never trust anyone – they're let down all the time,
especially by the ones who bleat 'trust me'.

He cleared his throat. 'A cop, yeah. One of the bad ones.'

'Someone you know?'

'He – he's – downtown. He comes around at night, under the fig
tree.'

Of course I knew the tree he meant. The fig tree down near the
train station. The largest Moreton Bay fig in the world, it had shel-
tered homeless people for decades. At night men and women curl
into the curves of its roots, grabbing snatches of sleep. And some
nights the most malicious cops, those with time on their hands and
an itch in their brains, storm through and jostle the sleepers awake,
harassing and tormenting them.

'So he's one of the mean ones. Do you know his name?'

Darren began to shake his head back and forth, like a metronome.
I was pushing him too hard, throwing shit at him, shit he didn't
want to remember. But I needed to know one more thing.

After my tête-a-tête with Wasson in the gully, I'd taken the time to download Del's photo from the internet. No surprise, the guy wasn't camera shy. He especially liked to be snapped when he held a tennis racquet in one hand and a super-sized trophy in the other.

'Darren, I need you to look at a picture, that's all.' I took my phone from my pocket and pulled up Wasson's photo. 'Is this the cop you saw that night?' I held out my hand.

He didn't take the phone from me. Instead he stepped closer, then leaned forward and peered at the phone. I saw him relax a little.

'No. That's . . . that's not him.'

I didn't have to ask again. Del Wasson wasn't the guy.

'Thanks, Darren. I owe you.' I slipped the phone back in my pocket and shouldered my bag. 'You know Charlie. I wonder if you knew my brother, Brodie Zarlin? He used to hang out around Leadbetter. He was a surfer, and he had a Camino. Back then it was painted blue.'

'I know Brodie, man. He's, he's all right.' Darren met my eyes for the first time. 'Brodie died, man. That was – that was—'

'Yeah. That was sad.' I kicked a little sand over a glistening lump of oil. 'Darren, I don't want to pry. But is there some way I can help you? Find your family, maybe, or help you get a place to stay?'

'I don't need nothin'.'

I looked at him: one of his eyes was infected, and a bead of yellow pus leaked at the inside corner. 'Darren, you sure?'

'Yeah, man. I got everything I need.'

Del Wasson slouched when he walked. I recognized that walk when I caught sight of a figure at the far end of the More Mesa meadow.

He must have followed me after all. Damn it to hell. I'd been careful, but not careful enough. Now I'd put Darren at risk.

I pedaled harder, determined to catch up with the creep. But he moved rapidly, and the rough meadow path was pocked with stones and pitted with gopher holes. The going was slow, and by the time I'd crossed the meadow and reached the road, the guy had disappeared.

I cruised to a halt. 'Come on,' I muttered aloud. 'Think this through.'

The cop Darren had seen that night wasn't Wasson. Yet Wasson had made it his business to follow me, first to the gully, now here. I'd stepped into a maze I couldn't comprehend.

One thing I did comprehend: if Wasson had spotted me with Darren, the homeless guy wasn't safe. I needed to tell Darren to get the hell out.

I turned my Schwinn around and pedaled back. I called and called Darren's name along the cliff edge. Then I climbed halfway down and scanned the beach. He was nowhere to be seen. I yelled some more, but no one answered or showed.

No doubt Darren had had enough of me for one day. I'd have to come back again later to alert him, to let him know he'd better move on.

TEN

'**N**ice place you have here, Angel.' I relaxed in the aluminum lawn chair and took a long slow sip of a Gabi-rita, the saltiest, tangiest margarita this side of Mexicali.

Angel chuckled, and his laugh made me laugh. He was the most modest of men, and yet his chuckle had a hint of throaty seduction about it. Not for the first time I thought, *Gabi, you are one lucky girl.*

'It is true, sometimes I think all this belongs to me. Mrs Fleischman, she lives in New York. She don't want to come here no more. The last time she came for a visit was two years ago.'

'Her son, he died over there.' Gabi pointed into the dusk, across the wide rose bed to a gazebo. 'He shot his own self in the head with a gun.'

'I'm sorry to hear that.' I set my margarita down on the small table.

'It was terrible. Mr Chris, he was a nice man.' Angel rested his hands on his knees. 'Because he died here, Mrs Fleischman will never sell this house. But she cannot stay here. For her it is too hard.'

I thought of Brodie's studio. All his belongings were stored there, going back to elementary school days. It was still difficult for me to enter the space, even though my brother had never managed to move in.

'Believe me, Angel, I understand.'

The three of us sat in a semicircle facing the roses. Dusk had filtered into the garden, and all the color had pooled in the blossoms: glowing mauves and reds, gleaming splashes of white.

'It is sad,' Gabi murmured. 'But still the night is beautiful, you know?'

I watched a large pale moth weave its way through the rose bushes. 'I can't help thinking about Rosie. Where is she right now? What is—' I stopped. I'd been about to say, 'What is happening to her?' But some of the possibilities were unthinkable. A sudden chill passed through me, and I shivered.

'Miss Jaymie, I will go get a sweatshirt for you.' Gabi got to her feet.

'No.' I reached up and put a hand on her arm. 'A sweatshirt's not going to help.'

'Then drink your margarita.' She dropped back into her chair. 'That will warm you up, I can promise.'

'It's a damn good margarita.' I complied and took a few more sips. Gabi had not stinted on the tequila. 'Now's the time for your positively-positive approach. Rosie is out there, alive. We've got to find her.'

'OK, Miss Jaymie.' Gabi sat up straight. 'But what's the next thing to do? I don't think you got any, you know, what they call leads.'

Both Gabi and Angel had turned to me. I could just make out their expressions in the dark: expectant, hopeful.

'Maybe not leads. But there's at least one loose thread I can pull. I've got an appointment to visit Darlene Richter in the morning. Remember her?'

'Miss Richter?' Gabi looked at me in surprise. 'The one who paid so, so much money for you to find her dog?'

'The very one, Gabi. The one who arranged and paid for Beto's plastic surgery.'

'That is a very good lady,' Angel observed. 'Gabi told me about her. She is like another mother for those children, you know?' For some reason, he looked away.

'That lady,' Angel added after a moment, 'she is the way all mothers should be.'

'Jaymie, it's so good to see you.' Darlene Richter narrowed her green eyes against the morning sun. 'It's been what, eight or nine months since we've seen one another?'

'Something like that.' I returned her smile. 'How's everything going?'

'Wonderful. Never perfect these days, but perfectly wonderful. Let's go sit outside, shall we? The garden is just waking up with the spring.' She took me by the arm and led me along a flagstone path. 'It will be nice to sit down and relax for a bit. Coffee?'

'No thanks, Darlene. Gabi made a pot in the office.'

'Gabi, how is she? Still keeping Santa Barbara on the straight and narrow?'

'Doing her best.' I grinned. 'You've got her number.'

We turned a corner and entered the enormous garden at the back of Darlene's estate. A King Charles Spaniel was digging furiously in a bed of lavender, spraying dirt in all directions.

'Chica,' Darlene called out. 'Come see who's visiting us.'

The pooch looked up, then scampered over. I knelt down and ruffled her ears. 'So Minuet is called Chica now?'

Darlene pushed her hair off her face. The auburn was streaked with gray, and she wore no make-up this morning. Even so, she was a beautiful woman.

'Yes, I gave in. Beto and Alicia call her Chica, and she seems to prefer it. Besides, I think it suits the rascal more than Minuet. The children indulge her, and of course she's not as well-behaved as she used to be.'

I followed Darlene to a patio overlooking the grounds. And no, the yard wasn't perfect: it looked like Chica had spent the entire morning excavating.

'How are the kids? Are you still babysitting them after school, when their mom's at work?'

'Oh yes, though I wouldn't call it babysitting. Alicia's a young lady now, you know. She loves to bake, and I give her free rein in the kitchen. And Beto, he's very responsible for his age. He brushes Chica and takes her for a walk every day.'

'Beto – I know he came through his plastic surgery OK. But what were the results?'

'Oh . . . good, I'd have to say.' Darlene gave me a quirky smile. 'I don't know, Jaymie. Maybe I'm too much of a perfectionist . . . I'd hoped for more.'

Chica raked my leg with her tiny claws. I reached down and patted her again. 'So Beto's birthmark is still pretty obvious?' Most of the little boy's face had been covered with a dark wine-colored stain.

'More obvious than I'd like. But it's much better. People still notice, but they don't stare the way they used to.' Darlene led me over to a white-painted wrought-iron table and chairs. We sat down facing one another.

'What matters most,' she continued, 'is that other children don't make fun of Beto anymore. And the doctors say he can have another operation in a few years, so that's something too.'

'Sounds like a success to me. Beto can play with kids his own age, go to school. He doesn't have to hide at home. That was no life for a little boy.' I thought about how he'd been tortured by a group of schoolmates, how they'd held him down and rubbed the skin on his face with gravel, till it bled.

'No, it wasn't. Though I have to tell you, I'm not so sure the school staff members are thrilled to have him back.' Darlene laughed her silvery laugh. 'He's a delight here with me, but at school he can be quite the little troublemaker.'

'Good for him.'

'Yes. Yes, indeed.' Darlene smoothed her mint green twinset over her arms and leaned forward in her chair. 'Well. You helped me so much, Jaymie. And now it sounds like I can begin to return the favor – is that right?'

'You don't owe me a thing, Darlene. But yes, I have a question I want to ask you.' My gaze followed an orange and black hooded oriole as it dipped into a fan palm. 'I understand you attend the women priests' church, is that right?'

Darlene raised an eyebrow. 'That's the last question I'd have expected you to ask. How did you know?'

'I visited Laura and Bernadette. They mentioned you because you'd told them about me.'

'Yes, I suppose I did. Back when you were investigating the solstice murders. You helped me, Jaymie. You helped me face up to my past.'

'You did the heavy work, Darlene.' I ran a hand over the bumpy wrought-iron tabletop. 'What do you think of them? You must know Laura and Bernadette pretty well.'

'You'd think so, by now.' Darlene got to her feet again. She wrapped her arms over her chest, as if she were cold. 'You know, the Magdalen community is important to me. I was raised Catholic, and after the Solstice Murders, I wanted to start going to church again. But because of my . . . *background* . . . well, I was not going to go to a church run by a male priest. Period. I'm sorry, I won't do that, not anymore.'

My first case: the Solstice Murders. That's what Santa Barbarians were calling them now. I'd put the perp away in Pelican Bay State Prison up in Crescent City, but I couldn't take much satisfaction in that. To me, the murders of Lili Molina and her friend were still too painful to think about. And then there were the murders in the Santa Barbara Aquarium. The conclusion of that heartrending case had brought me nothing but sorrow.

'I understand, Darlene.' I waited. I knew how it hurt her just to remember the abuse she'd endured.

'Anyway, there's no need for me to revisit all that.' Darlene walked to the edge of the flagstone patio and back again. 'Laura and Bernadette are fine women. And the Magdalen congregation is caring, nonjudgmental. I can't make even *one* negative comment about them, Jaymie. The priests and the members – they've all welcomed me.'

Even so, I was pretty sure I heard a reservation in her voice. 'But there's something, if I'm hearing you?'

She turned and faced me with her hands open, palms up. 'The thing is, I can't say I truly *know* Laura and Bernadette. No, wait. That's not quite right.' Her arms fell to her sides. 'I think I do know Bernadette. While she hasn't told me much of her history, I feel she would if I asked.'

'But you're less sure about Laura.' I stopped petting Chica and stood too. 'You've surprised me. Bernadette is the one I'd have wondered about.'

'Oh, believe me, I understand that.' Darlene laughed. 'Bernadette can be a bit snippy. But think about Mother Teresa – she could be snippy, too!'

'On the other hand, Laura—' I stopped. I didn't want to put words in my friend's mouth.

'Laura is sweet. Very gentle, children love her. And you know what good instincts children have. She's just very private, I suppose. I asked her once about her prior work experience, and she changed the subject. Of course, I just left it at that.'

The oriole swooped through the air again. It made me think of an orange and black note of jazz, flying along a staff.

'And what did they do before they were ordained, do you know?'

'Bernadette was a nun. An order based in San Francisco, I think, one that serves the poor. She may still be a member of that order.'

'And Laura?'

'As I said, I know so little about her. I believe she worked with children. I think she may have worked for an adoption agency, something like that.'

An adoption agency? I felt myself flush, and it must have showed.

'Jaymie, what is it?'

I bit the inside of my cheek, to keep from saying too much.

'Jaymie? It's Paul here.'

I was on my way from Darlene's to the office when I stopped my bike to answer the ring. And it was just as well I stopped, because I'd been cruising down Mountain Drive at a good rate of speed. I was so surprised by the caller's identity that I might have sailed off into thin air.

'Dad – is something wrong?' When he'd married Glenda, Dad had insisted that Brodie and I switch to calling him Paul. In a way he'd always been a stranger, so it wasn't that hard.

'Nope. Well, yes. I guess there is.'

I heard from my father about once a year. We had a tradition: I sent him a card on his birthday, and he followed up a week later with a phone call. But his birthday was in November, and this was February.

'It's your mother.' He cleared his throat. 'Doreen's got cancer. I guess you better get in touch with her.'

My stomach dropped. It wasn't just the word 'cancer' that did it. It was the three phrases together: 'your mother' plus 'cancer' plus 'get in touch'.

'What? When did you hear?'

'She called last week and told me. I figured Doreen would call you next. But then she called me again, three more times as a matter of fact. She told me she wasn't going to tell you because – ah – you don't care.' He cleared his throat again. 'You know how she is.'

'Yeah. I know how she is.' *A full-blown narcissist, that's how she is.*

I looked over the edge of the road to the neighborhoods spread out below. The little city was bordered by a scallop of yellow sand and the bluest of seas.

'I'm not telling you what to do, Jaymie,' Paul said.

'How's Glenda?' I replied in an attempt to change the subject. The plump little woman controlled my dad with one finger, and unlike Doreen, Glenda had the smarts to do it in a way that seemed to make Paul happy.

'Glenda's just fine. You need to come and see us sometime.' It was nice of him to say that. To the untrained ear, it would have sounded like he meant it. 'Jaymie, your mother's—'

'Stephanie and Paul Junior?'

'Doing good, both of them. But your mother, she's—'

I gave in. 'I know, she's hounding you to death. Paul, listen. I'll get in touch with Doreen. But don't lay a guilt trip on me, OK? It doesn't work, not anymore.'

'You always were a tough little nut. I saw that from day one. I remember when they brought you around to the house that first day . . .'

Dear Jesus. One phone call, and I was already up to my chin in shit soup. 'I'll get in touch with her. All right? Soon as I can.'

After we said goodbye, I got back in the saddle and coasted on down the steep road. When I arrived at the Mission I dismounted, parked my bicycle, and climbed the wide steps. I let the heavy door thud closed behind me, and the noisy world was immediately shut away.

The sanctuary was dark and still and smelled of wax, incense, old plaster and wood. When my eyes had adjusted to the light, I crossed the worn concave tiles as I walked down the aisle toward the altar. Halfway along, I took a seat in a hard-backed pew.

Santa Barbara Mission is a tourist attraction. I have no idea how many people tromp through it each year. But even so, there's a sacredness about the place that cannot be spoiled.

I'd spent time at the Mission in the months after my brother died. I'd prayed and lighted a candle or two. I don't believe in much anymore, but I do have faith. Faith that something big is out there, something I'll never comprehend.

A woman entered from a side door and passed through the pews, swishing a feather duster. She was old and bent, Chumash, maybe.

The Chumash maintained a presence at the Mission, though the Catholic Church owned the property. In the end, perhaps the European church would relinquish the Mission, as it had other California missions. But the descendants of the original inhabitants of the land would remain.

The old woman glanced at me as she passed by, skipping my pew. I nodded, and she returned my nod without a smile. When you'd seen as much of life as she had, I guessed there was little left to smile about. Life was a solemn business, after all.

So, Doreen had cancer. She hadn't phoned, but she'd put out the message: she was waiting for my call.

Paul, lucky guy, was out of the picture. I thought about my dad for a moment. He never would have managed his great escape if it hadn't been for Glenda. She'd hooked him and reeled him in. But to be fair, he'd leaped at the baited hook.

I shut my eyes. I could sense my mother's centrifugal force dragging me in. I knew I had the usual choice: I could succumb to the pull and enter the funhouse, or do the smart thing: switch on the afterburners and blast away.

I got to my feet and approached the bank of flickering flames near the altar. I emptied my pockets into the box, lit my own candle, and placed it in the rack. Was it for Doreen? No. I knew I couldn't quite manage that level of good will. It took all my generosity just to accept her for what she was.

Maybe the candle was for Brodie – or Rosie. Or maybe, if I were honest, it was for myself.

I stood there for what seemed like a long time, losing myself in the wavering light.

I stood on the steps outside the sanctuary, warming myself like a lizard in the weak sun. Inside the church time had slowed to a stop, but out here in the world time raced on at a blistering pace. I prepared myself to dive back into the stream.

I switched on my phone and pushed the button on a familiar number. One I hadn't pushed for awhile.

'Zave? It's me, Jaymie. I need to come and talk to you, OK?'

'Sure.' Zave's voice was uptown, smooth. The way he sounded when he talked to other people – not to me. 'Feel free to come by the office.'

Zave's cool tone hurt, I had to admit. As did the fact that he hadn't invited me to visit him at home. But I understood.

We'd been close, at times so close you couldn't have slipped a sheet of paper between us. And now that was done.

'OK, consigliere. When?'

'Come when you want.'

In the old days, meaning a few months ago, I'd have cracked a cheap and smutty joke in reply. But that was the old days. Now everything had changed.

ELEVEN

To attain the summit of Zave Carbonel's office at the top of the Granada Building, I took a ride in an elevator so fast it could give you a nosebleed, then battled my way through a phalanx of skinny female assistants. One of them, a strawberry blonde not old enough to buy a beer, looked down her snub nose at me as she cracked open the door to Zave's suite.

'Mr Carbonel, I want to remind you that you have an appointment coming up at two.' Could you believe it? The child dimpled when she smiled.

'Thanks, Kayley. I won't be long.'

'So you're down to the Kayleys now,' I said as the door closed on the girl's perky rear end. 'The average age of your staff is younger every time I come by.'

Zave narrowed his eyes and leaned back in his power chair. His desk looked bigger than my office.

'Your observation is incorrect, Jaymie. The mean age of my staff remains the same. You, on the other hand, are getting older.'

'Ouch.' His jab stung. Not the jab itself, but the fact that my friend had aimed it at me. I walked over to the plate-glass window and looked out over the city. 'I don't mind getting older, Zave. How about you?'

He shrugged. 'It doesn't matter so much in a man. Not if you have power.'

I turned to look at him. This was painful. What did I have to do to get the guy to lighten up?

'If the size of that desk is anything to go by, you must be the most powerful man in Santa Barbara.'

'Not even close. The most powerful black man, maybe.'

'But there aren't that many black—' I stopped. I'd never seen Zave Carbonel like this. I almost wanted to use the word 'grim'.

'Look, Jaymie.' He glared at me. 'What do you want?'

I would not accept this. God damn it, Zave was my friend.

'Hey, come on. What happened between us, it doesn't feel good. But you and I, we were friends way before we were . . .' I'd almost said the word 'lovers'. But I stopped myself once more, because now I was beginning to feel grim too.

'Bull shit. We were never friends, OK? Even before we fucked.' He shoved back his chair and got to his feet. I stared at him, amazed.

I'd never seen Zave show anger before, not even once. He was always cool and collected. In control.

'Jaymie? Knock it off. Don't look so damned surprised.'

'Surprised?' Now I was a little warm under the collar myself. 'I'll tell you what I'm surprised about. All those times we were together, Zave? Somehow you never felt it was necessary to tell me you had a wife.'

He stuffed his hands in his pockets and rocked back on his heels. 'I'm *slightly* married, all right?'

'Bullshit. It's like being pregnant: you are or you aren't. And what's more, your wife is beautiful, which I admit I deeply resent.'

Zave laughed. I guess he just couldn't stop himself. 'OK, OK. I'll give you round one.'

Zave sat on the corner of his desk and folded his arms across his chest. Then he smiled that wicked smile, the one I knew and – to be honest – still adored.

'Tell me how can I help, sweetheart.'

'Don't call me sweetheart. Here's how.' I was grinning back at him. It felt good, so good to be back in Zave's arms. Metaphorically speaking, of course. Thank God Mike was many miles away.

So I started to talk. I told Zave everything and didn't hold back. Ten minutes later, I shut up at last. I'd emptied my mind of every single detail I could think of, everything even remotely connected to Rosie's case.

Zave rubbed his chin, cleared his throat. He began to look

uncomfortable, then worried. And for the first time, it occurred to me that Zave Carbonel wasn't one hundred percent invulnerable.

On the other hand, the guy was pretty damn close.

'I've got one thing to say to you, Jaymie. So listen up.' He got to his feet and walked over to the window. His back was to me. 'Get yourself the hell out of this case.'

'Zave, there's no way I can do that. A child's involved.'

'You can and you will. You're not going to be able to find the kid anyway. Can't you see what you've stumbled into? The girl's a side issue. Who the hell knows what that's all about? No. This is a drug operation, a fucking big one. And in case it hasn't registered with you just yet, the Santa Barbara PD is involved.'

'Zave, please. I'll stay out of the PD's hair. Just answer a few questions for me. Help me out.'

My friend and former lover was quiet for a time. When he turned to look at me, I could see how much he still cared. I wanted to hug him, but I didn't dare get that close. I knew it would feel too damn good.

'OK, Jaymie. What do you want to ask?'

'Staffen Brill and her husband. You know them, right?'

'Sure. Ballbreakers, both of them. Jack Morehead is a partner in Fisk, Morehead and Brach, down in LA. Corporate lawyers, but he'll take on anything that smells of money. Doesn't practice up here in Santa Barbara, though. Keeps the nest clean. Brill, she has her lily-white hands in every money-spinning divorce that rolls down the pike. She wins for her clients, too. That crap she spouts about being an adoption attorney – that's just window dressing. Something to burnish the image.'

'Ah. I wondered about that. She doesn't seem like the altruistic type.'

Zave gave out a laugh. 'That palace they've got. Neither of them was born into money. You don't think they bought that with clean cash, do you? That's not how the system works.'

'So her nonprofit org – CHIA, she calls it – you think that's just a scam.'

'Sure. Or we could be generous and call it a smokescreen. And one more thing, while we're dishing the dirt on Morehead and Brill. That errand boy they've got working for them?'

'Eric?'

'He was in law school when he was convicted on drug dealing charges. His paper chase came to a halt.'

'I guess I'm not surprised. Eric looks like a choir boy, but he's mean underneath.'

'If you want my advice, Jaymie, you'll stay away from Brill. She has nothing to offer you.'

Were all my potential informants going to whither away under Zave's searing gaze? If he kept this up, I'd get nowhere with the case. But Zave was seldom wrong, and I knew I'd do well to take heed.

'All right, I hear you. Now, about the woman priest, Laura. Darlene Richter thought she might have done adoption work in the past.'

Zave raised a skeptical eyebrow. 'You're suspicious of someone just because they once worked for an adoption agency, is that it? I'll never understand the workings of the PI mind.'

'It's not just that, Zave. She's hiding something. And the woman's too nice.'

'Too nice. I get it. OK, I'll look into it. Got a last name?'

'No, but I can get it.'

'Don't bother, I'll figure it out. Mother Laura. Now you've got me digging into the past life of a lady priest, a modern-day saint. Who's next, the pope?'

'I don't know who's next, Zave.' My instinct whispered he was holding back on something. 'How about you tell me?'

Zave walked over to me and reached out his hands. I hesitated. If he pulled me into an embrace, I was done for.

He waited, hands outstretched. After a moment's hesitation, I slipped mine into his. Zave didn't pull me any closer, but his warmth flowed up my arms, then down to . . . somewhere below.

'Jaymie? About Chucha Robledo.'

'Chucha?' I shook my head. 'Oh no you don't. She's a good person.'

'Chucha has a record. Not an extensive one, but she's been arrested a couple of times.'

'Why would you know that? She's – she's not wealthy or powerful. Why do you have info about Chucha on the tip of your tongue?' A suspicion crept into my brain. 'You've been having me watched, haven't you?'

'Don't be so goddamned dramatic.' He squeezed my hands, hard. 'I put two and two together, that's all. Nobody's spying on you, Jaymie. At least, I'm not.'

The man had put two and two together. Sure. Zave never gave me the whole story, I knew that by now. Yet somehow I trusted the guy. Don't ask me to explain it, but I trusted Zave Carbonel with my life.

'I don't want to hear it, but I have to, I guess. So Chucha's been arrested. For what?'

'Solicitation. She's not only a make-up artist, like you think. She's a sex worker. I thought you should know.'

'That – that doesn't make any difference. Chucha's lost her daughter, and she loves her. I admit I'm surprised, but if you think this is going to stop me, you're wrong, dead wrong. I have to find Rosie, Zave. No matter what.'

'I know you do. But be prepared for failure, OK?' He released my hands, then slid his own hands up to my elbows.

'And stay away from the drug smuggling angle. Promise me that, sweetie. You know? For old times' sake.'

'Sure. I'm not interested in the maryjane trade. Eyes on the prize and all that.' I heard a husky edge in my voice and took three steps back.

'Where you going, girl?' His voice had changed, too.

'Know what? I love you, Zave. But from now on it's going to have to be in another kind of way.'

'Yeah? What way is that?'

'What do they call it? Cerebral. You're the genius, you work it out.' I turned and made a beeline for the door.

'I don't think I've ever been in this restaurant before.' Chucha slid into the booth opposite me. I looked at her and wondered if she was keeping up with her hormones. A rash of razor bumps covered her chin.

'The locals don't come here, only tourists. That's why I picked it.' I looked out the plate-glass window, across the water to the marina. 'I think it's getting risky, Chucha. I don't want people to see us together. Someone might guess you're the missing girl's mom.'

'I don't really care.' She frowned and stared down at the white tablecloth. Her wig was askew. 'I just don't give a fuck about who guesses what.'

'I understand. But we need to be careful.' I reached across the table and covered her hand with my own.

'Ahem.'

I looked up. A waiter stared down at us. For a moment his expression revealed his bald-faced curiosity. Then his face grew opaque. Good. As far as I was concerned, he could keep it that way.

'What can I get you . . . ladies . . . to drink?'

'A tequila sunrise,' Chucha replied, ignoring the waiter's hesitation. She looked over at me. 'I know it's early, Jaymie, but I need a drink.'

'Bring me a Firestone Pale Ale.'

'He's nosey,' I said once the server had moved on.

'Who isn't?' Chucha looked around the restaurant and shrugged. 'Everybody stares. I don't pay that much attention to it, not anymore.'

I knew that wasn't true. I'd observed her registering every slight, every stare.

'Still, it can't feel good. Like being a goldfish in a bowl.'

She let the act of bravado go. 'Yeah. Yeah, what I just said just now, it isn't true.' Chucha met my eyes. 'I've never gotten used to it. I wish I could.'

I glanced at her cleavage and thought about the platform shoes and super-tight skirt. 'But at the same time, you want to be noticed, right?'

Where was I going with this? I knew I should mind my own business. But what Zave had told me . . . I'd said it didn't matter that Chucha was a sex worker. And it didn't. But maybe somewhere in the back of my mind, it did.

'I guess so. Yes. I want people to look at me as a woman, you know?'

I started to say something more, then focused on realigning the fork and knife on the tabletop.

'Jaymie? You said – I thought you wanted to talk to me about the case. What's going on?'

I had to say it, to get it off my chest. 'You told me you're a make-up artist. An aesthetician. But someone told me you've been arrested.' I made myself meet her eyes. 'I don't want to demean you, Chucha. I just want to know.'

'You heard.' She looked like I'd slapped her. Her face dissolved. 'So you heard, and you didn't bother to ask me about it before you decided it was true.'

Now I wished I'd kept my mouth shut. But I hadn't, and I could only keep plowing on. 'I *am* asking you, Chucha. That's what I'm doing.'

'No, that's not what you're doing.' Her eyes had welled with tears, but even so, I saw her tough side shining through. 'I can tell you've already made up your mind. And I thought you were a friend!'

'I'm sorry, Chucha. The person who told me – honestly, he's pretty much never wrong.'

'Guess what. This time he is.' She grabbed the corner of the folded linen napkin and gave it a hard shake.

'Here you are!' The waiter, overly jolly now, set Chucha's frothy orange drink down in front of her. I got the bottle of beer, wet with dew.

'Are we ladies ready to order?'

'No.' I glared at the grinning guy. He seemed to think he was in on some kind of joke.

'No problemo. I'll be back in a couple of minutes.'

'Make that five.'

For some reason his smile widened. 'Sure. Five it is.'

'What a pain in the ass. What's with him, I wonder?'

'Yeah, well.' Chucha took a long sip of her drink and shut her eyes. 'Sometimes it's better not to wonder, believe me.'

A moment of silence filled the space between us.

'Chucha, I'm sorry. Forgive me.'

She opened her eyes and looked at me. 'I accept.' Another long minute passed. Chucha adjusted the silky magenta scarf to cover her plunging neckline. Her fuzzy pale blue sweater clung to her curves.

'Actually, Jaymie, I *was* arrested. Twice. The charges were dropped.'

'I don't need to know about it, Chucha. It's none of my business.'

'No. But I want you to know. Now that you've heard about it, I mean.' She leaned back in the bench seat.

'I had a boyfriend. And then I met somebody else, somebody who treated me better. We would meet in a bar on the west side of town, just to talk. My boyfriend, he knew about that, and he used it against me. Twice, he reported me to the cops. Claimed I was a ho.' She shrugged and sipped her tequila. 'Some of the cops are OK. But a few of them, they've got real issues with somebody like me.'

'I'm not surprised.'

'No. But I was lucky. I got a good lawyer, and in the end the DA dropped the charges. I went down to LA for five months and the cops forgot all about me. Too much trouble to bother with, I guess. So it turned out OK, pretty much. Cost me a lot of money though. I'm still paying off the legal fees.'

'Your ex, he doesn't bother you anymore?'

'Naw.' She grinned. 'I beat him up real good. He didn't want to tell anyone about that.'

I laughed too. 'And your current boyfriend?'

Her face fell. 'Oh, he dumped me. After the – you know, the novelty – wears off, they usually do.'

'Ready now ladies?' Howdy Doody was a real smoothie.

'Look, friend. We are women, not ladies. All right with you?' I enjoyed the disconcerted look on his face. 'Chucha, what are you having?'

She ordered a sensible seafood salad. The aroma of fish and chips had reached me from the kitchen, and I opted for that.

'How do you stay so skinny, Jaymie? If I ate like you do I'd put on ten pounds overnight.'

'I guess I don't eat all that often. Food bores me until it's right under my chin.'

'Don't tell me that. I'm going to hate you.' Chucha smiled.

'You'd have a good reason.'

'Jaymie, come on. I said forget it.' Chucha drained her drink. 'Listen, plenty of trannies are sex workers. It's an easy lifestyle to fall into, especially when they won't hire you anywhere else. But it's a hard life. Lots of suicides, you know?'

'I'm learning. That's about all I can say for myself.'

'Oh stop it. So now, what did you want to see me about? Any good news?'

'There's news. And on balance it's good.' I settled back in the bench seat and took a long swallow of my pale ale just to gain time. 'We had a response to the flyer.'

'When? I wish you'd told me right away!' Her face lit up with a mixture of joy and hope that made my heart ache. 'Rosie's OK, right? Tell me, who was it? What did they say?'

'Rosie's alive. We're sure as we can be. It was one of the pangeros who came forward, a kid. He refused to give us his name. But he said Rosie was on the boat and pretty much OK when it landed. She—'

'Jaymie, stop. "Pretty much OK?" What are you saying exactly?'

Out of the corner of my eye, I saw the waiter heading for us with our food.

'Let's eat, Chucha. Then we'll talk in private, down on the beach.'

'So you're telling me somebody grabbed Rosie. And she wasn't well?' Chucha and I stood at the water's edge. The surf hissed like steam as it pulled back off the sand.

'She was OK by the time the boat landed.' I hadn't told Chucha about Millie, the little girl who had died.

Chucha looked down at me. Only now, as we stood side by side, did I realize just how tall she was.

'This is all good, Jaymie, I'm sure of it. The guy who grabbed her, maybe he thought he was saving her. Somebody's taking care of my baby, I know it. We just have to find her, that's all.'

'That's pretty much it, Chucha. Somebody has her, and we have to locate them.' I dug into the wet sand with the toe of my shoe.

'So?' Chucha angled her head to meet my eyes. 'Why do I get the feeling something's not right?'

A wave rippled up and licked at my shoe. 'Two things. And both of them are going to be hard to hear.'

'OK.' She folded her arms over her chest. 'I'm ready. Tell me now.'

'First. According to the pangero, there was another little girl on the boat.'

'What?'

'And . . . she didn't make it.'

'Didn't – what? What, she *died*?'

'We only have the guy's word for it. But he seems honest, for what it's worth.'

'But – that's awful. Awful! Maybe it was her cross I found. *MACB*!'

'It's possible, yes. Anyway, according to Chino—'

'Hold on. Who's Chino, the pangero? I thought you said he didn't have a name.'

I felt the ocean water roll over my foot, into my shoe, and stepped back. 'It's just a nickname, Chucha. It's nothing we can use.'

'Chino. Believe me, I'll remember that.'

'He said both of the little girls were sick on the trip. The other little girl died. I showed him the picture of Rosie. She was definitely the one who survived.'

'It's scary. I don't know whether to be happy or sad.' Chucha took a deep breath, then hunkered down on the wet hard-packed sand. 'What's the other thing?'

I reached down, took her by the elbow, and raised her up. 'We know Rosie's alive. But we don't know why she was taken.' I waited for Chucha to accept what I'd said.

'You think – so you think—' Chucha didn't sound like a woman, not now. Her voice had deepened and turned hard as flint. 'You think somebody's hurting my baby. Right?'

'Like I said, we don't know why somebody grabbed her from the boat. Most likely it concerns money. Or it could just be like you said, somebody thinks they're protecting her. Chances are, Rosie's OK.'

The cold breeze blew Chucha's long hair across her face. She reached up and yanked off her wig. 'Sometimes I get so tired of wearing this thing on my head.'

It was only the second time I'd seen Chucha without the wig. I noticed again that her features seemed sculptured – beautiful, even. But her looks wouldn't appeal to just anyone, female *or* male. There was something unyielding about them, as if they were carved in stone.

'I know what you're talking about, Jaymie. Maybe better than you do. And yeah, people are fucked up. I have to do something about this as fast as I can.'

'Let me handle it, Chucha.' I grabbed her hand and squeezed it hard. 'Please trust me.'

'I do trust you. But I can't sit back and do nothing.'

'We're making headway,' I pleaded.

'This is my baby you're talking about.' Chucha looked away. 'I'm sorry, it's not fast enough.'

TWELVE

'Jaymie Zarlin? The Black Widow.'

I was about to hang up the phone. But as so often happens curiosity got the better of my good judgment. 'The who?'

The Black Widow laughed. Her voice was pleasant but her laugh was kind of snickery. 'My other name is Pam Spaulding but it's the Black Widow to you. And your other name is La Macheesma.'

'Is this some kind of hate call?'

The Black Widow snickered again. 'You could say so. I'd say it's a call to fame. A friend of yours told me you'd be willing, and are more than able, to fill her spot on the Mission City Brawlers this coming Saturday night.'

'The what?'

'Roller derby, babe. I've got three women, including your friend, down with injuries, two down with the flu.'

'A friend of mine gave you my name? Sounds more like an enemy. Who was it?'

'Her name is La Diablita. Claudia Molina to you. She's injured her ankle, the chicken. Says you owe her a favor, you're good for it.'

'Ah shit.' I did owe the girl a favor. Yes, I remembered voicing that idiocy.

'Look, haven't you got subs? I like wearing my original teeth in my mouth.'

'All the subs have the flu. Listen, La Macheesma, all you gotta do is wear a mouth guard. And don't forget the fishnets – they'll save a couple layers of skin on your legs.'

'*All* the subs have the flu? Maybe I should ask, just who are you playing against on Saturday night?'

'Stanford. They're not too shabby, I admit. And if we don't win this match we get demoted to the D League.'

'Ech. I don't know about this.'

'Come on. This is your chance to whip the skinny asses off a bunch of smart girls.'

'Hmm.'

'All former high school valedictorians, guaranteed.'

'You're tempting me, I admit. Let me talk to that so-called friend of mine. One thing though: If I play, no fishnets. Agreed?'

'Sure. Skin grows back. La Macheesma, whatever you say.'

Claudia Molina was wearing her Junior Lawyer outfit: black pants suit, maroon collared button-down shirt, black lace-up shoes. Only her hair hinted at the real Ms Molina: the good-little-boy cut had morphed back into an alarming sheared-up-the-sides look.

'A guy came in about the flyer? That's so fucking bitchin' fuckin' cool!'

'Words are failing you, huh?'

'No words are badass enough. I don't wanna sound soft, but I'm happy for that little kid.'

'Rosie's not safe yet, not by a long shot.'

'No, but she's alive.' Claudia pitched her backpack onto the desk and her body onto the craigslist couch.

'I gotta rest. Take a nap. Going to school full time, it's a bitch. Where's the Gabster?'

'Gabi's working for Sparkleberry today.'

'Exploitation of the fuckin' masses.' Claudia yawned. 'Why the does she do it, clean up other fuckers' shit?'

'She supports herself by running her own business, in case you hadn't noticed. And she runs this one too.' On occasion Claudia could rile me. Today she was getting close.

'Don't get your tits in a tangle.'

'*What*?'

'Don't get your knickers in a knot.' She rolled her head on the couch arm and grinned at me. 'Cool, huh? That's vintage British slang. There's all kindsa weird crap on the internet.'

'You have too much time on your hands.'

'The fuck I do.' She sat bolt upright. 'Anyways, I came by to tell you something important.'

'Does this have anything to do with the call I received from the Black Widow? As it happens, she and I just got off the phone. By the way, your ankle looks just fine to me.'

'Huh? The Black Widow called quick. I guess it shows how desperate she is. You already knew I do roller derby, right?'

'I've heard you knock yourself silly most Saturday nights.'

'No, I'm the knocker. Not the one who gets knocked.'

'Sure, La Diablita, you're tough. But you're little. I'll bet there are some who hurt you right back.'

Claudia hopped to her feet. 'Fuh. Nobody out-hurts La Diablita.'

'No, 'course not.'

Claudia made a sour expression. 'You wanna know or not?'

'Know what?' I teased.

'Jay-mie!' she wailed. 'Why are you picking on me?'

I laughed. 'Sorry. Just having a little fun.'

'Know what I came here to tell you. You're right. It's connected to the roller derby.'

'Tell me, La Diablita.'

'You better listen and stop joking around. I think this is important.'

'I'm sorry. Shoot.'

'Got this ho on our team named Hot Wheels, OK? She and me, we don't talk. I don't know, we don't get along.'

'Mmm.'

'Anyway, last night I saw something weird. She got picked up by this guy, you could see it was her boyfriend. Yeah, they were like all over each other, you know?'

'Uh huh.'

'Know who he was?'

'I give up.'

'You don't sound very interested. But I think you're gonna be when I tell you. The guy, the guy Hot Wheels is fuckin' is Del Wasson, that cop you told me about.'

The kid was right: she now had my attention one hundred percent.

'Are you sure it was him, Claudia?'

'Sure I'm sure. One of the other Betties told me his name. But that's not the main thing.' She gave me a sly look. 'Are you listening now?'

'You know I am.'

'Bitch's name, her *real* name is Sylvia Sanchez. Know where she's from? South Texas, down near the border. She's got this funky accent. And that's not all she's got.'

'Texas?' Now I was wide awake. 'You're going to tell me she's got a brother, right? A brother who's also a cop.'

A spray of rain, fine as water forced through the mesh of a silk screen, misted the Camino's windshield as I drove into the nearly empty oceanfront lot.

At the far end the Great American Novel was parked nose-in to a heap of seaweed. I pulled up nearby, leaned back and looked out over the channel. The sky gleamed with the pearly-violet sheen of the inside of a mussel shell. Silver sunlight leaked through gaps in the low clouds.

After a few minutes I got out and slammed my door, to let Charlie know I'd come to call.

A stiff scarred hand parted the hopsack curtain. 'Jaymie,' Charlie croaked. 'Seems like I saw ya just yesterday. Somethin botherin ya, gal?'

I pulled the small sack of horehound candy from my sweatshirt pocket. 'Didn't I tell you I'd drop this by?'

'Whoa. Just what I need. My lungs is actin up. The medicines ain't workin lately.'

'Just the horehound, huh?'

'You got that right.'

I handed the horehounds to him. 'Sorry you're not feeling so good, Charlie.'

'Just old age. That 'n a few other things. But I don't complain, since there's only one cure for old age, and I don't like the sounda *that* medicine.'

'Hah. Neither do I.' I heard the sound of unwrapping candy and several loud sucks.

'But, Jaymie? I know you pretty good. This candy ain't the only reason you came by.'

Sometimes I didn't want Charlie to know how much I depended on him. No, that wasn't it – I didn't care if he knew. I just didn't want to dwell on that fact myself.

'I've got one or two things I want to run by you.'

'Run 'em by.'

'The little girl in the flyer? We found out she's alive.'

'Hooray! Gimme five!' The hand reappeared.

I gave his scarred paw a gentle slap. 'But that's not all.'

'No, course not. You gotta find her now, get her back to her mom.'

I rested an elbow on the ledge outside Charlie's window and gazed out to sea. The waves were agitated, fringed in white foam.

'I don't think I told you about Rosie's mom. Her name is Chucha Robledo. She's transgendered, Charlie.'

'What's that in plain English?'

Charlie was an old guy, of the old school. I wasn't sure how he was going to take this.

'Chucha started life off as a boy. She feels in her heart she's a woman, though. So now she's in the process of changing sides.'

'Oh, I got ya. Hell, nothin new about that. It was just the fancy lingo that stopped me. Hm. So this Chucha, she's the mother *and* the father, I guess?'

'Pretty much.'

'I'm kinda surprised at you, Jaymie. It's interesting, won't say it's not, but that don't change nothin', does it? What's holdin' you up with solvin' the case?'

'No, it doesn't change a thing.' I smiled to myself. I should have known Charlie would understand. 'Rosie's alive. But we don't have a clue where she is.'

'Not good. Not good,' Charlie muttered. 'I'm telling ya, there's some bastards out there in the world.'

'That's what I'm worried about. That and a few other things.'

'Lay 'em out. Now's the time.'

'The panga boat carried two children, Charlie. Two little girls. One . . . died on the trip.'

The smack of the waves seemed to grow louder, as if a giant hand were whipping them to the shore. I never thought the sound of waves could be ugly. But now it was: under the slap was a rasping sound, like the panting of a pack of hounds.

'I'm sad, Jaymie. Sad to hear it.'

'We may never know who she was.'

'Most likely not. And when you think there's people that love her out there . . .'

I watched a homeless woman, wrapped in a dirty pink blanket, as she combed through a trash can. 'Maybe there are. Or maybe not.'

'That's true. Maybe not.'

'I have something else to tell you, Charlie.'

'Shoot.'

'There's no question about it anymore. This business has something to do with the cops.'

Charlie cleared his throat. 'Let me get this straight. The dope smuggling, that's what you're talkin' about now, am I right?'

'They're involved in the drug smuggling. And the children, maybe that too. It's human trafficking anyway you look at it.'

'Now wait a minute. I know plenty a cops. And maybe I like about a quarter of 'em. But I can't buy it, Jaymie. Cops, they don't deal in kids.'

'Cops don't, as a rule. But maybe there's a rule-breaker out there, a rogue cop, you know? I can't ignore the facts of the case, Charlie. There's too much at stake.'

'Let's work it through. You'll have to convince me. Go through it point by point if you want.'

For the first time since I'd met Charlie Corrigan, I hesitated.

Usually, I told my friend everything. I trusted him as much as I trusted Gabi or Mike. And I had no reason in the world not to trust him now.

I looked out to the turbulent water. I wanted to tell Charlie all about Chucha, and about Darren and what he'd seen that night. I wanted to tell him about Del Wasson and the shadowy Tejano. But for the first time ever, I didn't dare.

'I wish I could, Charlie. But I can't.'

'That means one thing, Jaymie. Can't believe I'm sayin' this. You don't trust me.'

'I trust you as much as I trust anyone.' The waves reared back, then roared, filling my ears with noise. 'I have to protect Rosie, you know? Chucha's little girl.'

My cell jangled as I drove out of the lot. *Gabi*, it said.

'Miss Jaymie. I got some bad news.'

She sounded as if she'd been crying. It took a lot to make Gabi cry, and I prepared myself for the worst.

'Chucha, she's in the hospital. Intensive care.'

I slammed on the brakes and jammed the gear into park. 'She's *what*? What are you talking about? I had lunch with her yesterday—'

'It's true. I called Cottage Hospital and they told me it's true. She got attacked. Some guys, they beat her up real bad. Her head, Miss Jaymie, they hit her on her head . . .'

I wanted to pound the steering wheel. 'How did you hear?'

'There was this message on the phone. A funny voice, like some-body, they had a cold. It said, "Chucha Robledo, she's gone to emergency. I think Jaymie should know."

'Man? Woman?'

'A woman for sure. Kind of a high voice. Who, I don't know. Miss Jaymie, it don't matter who called. The way the hospital lady sounded, I think you better go over there right away.'

I wanted to ram into somebody, anybody, all the way there.

Fucking assholes! They had to destroy her, just because she was different. Or maybe Chucha provoked fear in some men. I was no damn psychologist. But just by being who she was, Chucha made some people afraid of themselves.

By the time I got to the Cottage Hospital parking lot I still hadn't calmed down. To the contrary: I was now primed to kill.

I took a deep breath before I entered in through the large plate-glass doors. I knew they were strict here in Cottage these days. Two weeks earlier a woman had entered the maternity ward and helped herself to someone else's baby. Fortunately the infant had been located a few hours later in nearby Oak Park, curled up in a picnic basket, unharmed.

'Good morning. How are you?' I managed to beam at the elderly candy striper seated behind the reception desk.

'Oh, hello. I remember *you*, dear. Last time you were here I think you caused quite a stir.'

'I remember you, too. If you hadn't broken one or two rules, I wouldn't have been able to find Uncle Charlie.'

'Yes, Charlie. Now I certainly do remember. He wasn't your uncle though, was he dear? Tell me, who are you here to see today?'

'My sister. Chucha Robledo.'

'Your sister, hmm? Well, I'm not seeing it. We have a Jesus Robledo. But that would be a man.'

'That's her. Chucha is just her nickname. Her full name is Jesus Maria.'

'Oh.' The lady looked at me over the top of her reading glasses. 'I'd like to believe you, but you're confusing me. Jesus is a man's name. But you said you're here to see your sister.'

I opened my mouth. I couldn't think of anything to say but the truth. 'She's transgendered. Her name is Jesus Maria Robledo. She's in intensive care, and I need to see her right away.'

'You have quite a few unusual relatives, don't you dear?' She peered at me. 'But I can see you're sincere. Tell me your name again.'

'Jaymie Zarlin.'

She pressed a button on her computer, and a visitor's name badge scrolled from a printer at her left hand. 'I'm so sorry about your relative, dear. I hope you have some quality time.'

There was to be no quality time. In fact, time ceased to exist.

I stared through the glass window at Chucha. She was

motionless, lying on her right side. Her wig was gone, and a gleaming white dressing covered her skull. I looked away, then made myself look back again.

Chucha was hooked up to four machines. Tubes sprouted from her chest, wrist, from lower down on the bed, and ominously, from the side of her head.

'May I help you?' a male nurse said at my elbow.

'My sister. I want to talk to her.'

'Your sister?' I saw the nurse take in the color of my skin. Then he apparently decided that anything was possible. 'We've been wondering what to call Jesus – he or she.'

'It's Jesus Maria – we call her Chucha. And she's very much a she – just in transition.'

The nurse was young, but he looked as if he'd already witnessed a fair amount of suffering. He nodded. 'I can let you in for a minute or two.'

My eyes filled with tears, maybe because of the guy's decency. But then I felt frightened. 'She's not good, is she?'

He rubbed the side of his face. I noticed he had dark circles under his eyes. The guy was exhausted, maybe at the end of his shift. 'It's not good, no. Critical. But she's strong. Hanging in there for sure.'

I studied his expression and read the truth. He didn't have to say it aloud. Chucha had sustained irreversible brain damage. 'I understand.'

'Your sister is heavily medicated. We've placed her in a light coma. Don't stay long. I shouldn't be doing this, but—' He gave me a wry smile and shrugged.

'Thank you.'

Chucha's left hand rested on a starchy white pillow. Two of her fingers were broken, twisted at odd angles. A needle was inserted into a vein. I placed my hand on her wrist. She didn't stir.

Chucha's mouth was open a little, and a trickle of saliva ran down from the corner of her lips.

'Chucha . . . who did this to you?'

I made myself look at her beautiful face. It was a mess. Her nose was pushed sideways, her lips split and swollen. A dark purple bruise spread from the socket of her left eye.

But none of that mattered so much. What mattered was the head wound. The bright white bandage couldn't hide the fact that Chucha's skull was smashed. Just above the left temple, it looked concave.

'Chucha, I promise I'll get who ever did this—' I fell silent. Somehow this wasn't what she needed to hear.

I stroked her strong forearm. Then I bent down and placed my lips near her ear.

'I will find Rosie,' I whispered. 'I promise you, Chucha. If it's the last thing I do, I'll find your little girl.'

THIRTEEN

'**D**eirdre Krause,' I demanded. '*Now*.'

The frog-mouthed woman behind the plate-glass window leaned into her microphone. 'Quiet down and back off! Or I will have you escorted out.'

I took a breath. *Long and slow, Jaymie. In and out*. Then I spoke into the grill. 'I apologize.' Like fucking hell I did.

'So?'

'My name is Jaymie Zarlin. Please tell Detective Krause I'd like to speak with her.' I thought I might choke on my words.

'Go sit.'

The police department lobby was Spanishy and cute. Colorful old tiles decorated most of the surfaces, and the floor was covered in Saltillo tiles buried under hundreds of layers of wax. Even so, a whiff of vomit and despair, the stink you'll smell in all PD lobbies, lurked in the air.

I didn't 'go sit' – I had a little self-respect, I wasn't a dog. But I did back off to a far corner.

I watched the receptionist as she poked at a keyboard and peered into a screen. This dragged on for ten long minutes. I knew I was paying my penance.

At last the woman picked up a phone. As she spoke her expression changed. I couldn't hear her words, but she seemed to simper. After she hung up she looked over at me. To see how the little doggy was behaving, I supposed.

No more than a minute later, a side door jumped open and Deirdre appeared. She wore her usual: gray blousy pleated slacks and a silk shirt unbuttoned to the navel. What wasn't so usual was that she looked flustered. If I didn't know her better I'd have called her upset.

I took a step forward but Deirdre held up a hand. She walked over to me instead.

'Zarlin. You shouldn't be here.'

'What the hell. I'm a citizen. This is *my* police department, don't forget.'

'Cut the crap will you? I'm telling you for your own good.' Her words were sharp, but her round blue eyes seemed almost to plead. Something unprecedented was happening here.

'Bullshit, Deirdre. For my own good, or for yours?'

Her face scrunched and her tiny bow of a mouth pursed. 'I'll meet you . . . somewhere. Just go.'

'Meet me where?'

'Where nobody will see us. I don't know. The far end of East Beach, I suppose.'

'All right. At the beach past the volleyball courts. Fifteen minutes?'

'What?' Her eyes slid over to check on the receptionist. 'Yes. Yes, all right. But keep your mouth shut about this. I mean totally shut, Zarlin. Do you hear?'

I parked in the easternmost lot. As I crossed the asphalt to the sand I looked back: the bright red Camino stood out like a shout, an exclamation. So much for undercover. Blue Boy needed a paint job.

The sea was still rough after the storm, but the tide was way out. I trudged through the dry sand, then stepped onto the wet strip bordering the water. Here the sand was packed hard as concrete. Piles of kelp lay scattered about, simmering under clouds of tiny black flies.

When I reached the water's edge I took a moment to gaze westward, toward Stearns Wharf. I could see the spot where Danny Armenta's body had been cast up by the waves some nine months ago.

Without wanting to, I pictured Chucha lying in the hospital bed with her skull bashed in. As I stood there thinking about Chucha, something hardened within me. I welcomed the change.

I turned and looked back in the direction of the old Bath House. A woman was crossing the sand, wading into the stiff breeze. After

a minute I realized it was Deirdre. She was short and had an unmis-
takable overblown hourglass figure, which her lime-green jacket
couldn't hide.

'All right, Zarlin. What do you want?' Deirdre shoved her hands
in her jacket and glared at me. Her hair swirled about in the wind
like a big yellow halo. She looked like an angry cherubic demon.

'Don't give me that, Deirdre. What do I want? You wouldn't be
here if you didn't already know.'

Her pout collapsed like a tired soufflé. I'd called her bluff.

'What, the trannie? Don't talk to me about her. Him, her, it. Not
my concern.'

I looked past the police detective to the cemetery bluff. The old
funereal cypresses, high above the beach and black against the gray
sky, reminded me of what mattered.

'Deirdre, let's walk.' It would be better to be positioned shoulder-
to-shoulder, I figured. Otherwise Deirdre and I would be glaring at
one another as we spoke, watching for the chance to peck out an eye.

I didn't wait for her answer. I put one foot in front of the other.
After a moment's hesitation she followed.

'So speak up, Zarlin. 'Cause like I just said, none of this is my
problem.'

I zipped my old sweatshirt up to my chin before I replied. 'You
haven't been to see Chucha, have you?'

'Why would I want to be in the same room as that trannie?'

I ignored the mean-spirited question. 'I went to Cottage this
morning. Somebody tried to kill her and pretty much succeeded.
She was beaten to within an inch of her life.' I glanced at Deirdre,
then away. 'Brain damage. Her skull's bashed in.'

'OK, it's bad. Is that what you want to hear?'

'What *I* want to hear?' I halted and faced the woman. 'I want to
hear what you have to say. I know something's on your mind.'

The woman tightened her mouth and gazed out to sea.

'Listen, Deirdre. I know you were the one who called my office
and left the message. You tried to disguise your voice but you didn't
bother to lower it. You called to let me know about Chucha. If you
don't give a shit, then why did you do that?'

The detective was looking right at me now. I had her full attention, but she wasn't going to open her mouth to answer.

'Fine, I get it. You don't give a damn about Chucha. But maybe you care about the little girl who's missing. By the way, her name is Rosie, did you know that?'

Two tiny tension lines, sharp as knife cuts, appeared between Deirdre's eyes. I knew I'd touched a nerve. 'Rosie is Chucha's daughter. And you know that's why Chucha got beat up, don't you? Not because she's transgender. Because she was looking for her little girl.'

The tension lines deepened. 'Actually, Zarlin, for once you're making some sense.'

'Yeah? So I guess we agree on one thing: somebody out there put two and two together. Figured out who Chucha was, noticed she was attracting attention. Decided to take her out in case she started talking about the human trafficking. Know what? I think that somebody was a cop.'

Deirdre's cheeks flared red. Then the blood was sucked back like an undertow, leaving her face paper-white. 'Cops don't hurt kids, you dumb bitch.'

'So everybody tells me.' I ignored the name calling. I had to, in order to persevere. 'Listen, Deirdre. How this all fits together, I honestly don't know. But like I said, Chucha was beginning to cause trouble, and she wasn't going to stop. And that's where I think your fellow officers come in. They were already smuggling dope. Why not kids?'

'You're full of shit.'

'Deirdre, tell me something. Why did you agree to meet me here?'

'Leave me the fuck alone!' She stomped off. After a few yards she halted and spun back around.

'For the kid, you idiot,' she screamed in her ultra-high voice. 'Get it? You're not the only one in the world who gives a damn!'

I walked on down the beach to cool off. The wind picked up and a few spits of rain grazed my cheek.

Mike. I needed him to help me unravel this snarl. And I needed him to hold me and tell me everything would be OK.

Yet the thought that I needed him irritated the heck out of me. I started back to the parking lot, kicking at the loose sand.

I missed the guy, that was all. Why exaggerate? I quickened my pace. Maybe I missed Mike Dawson, but goddamn it, I could take care of this on my own.

My head was down and my thoughts were churning as I crossed

the beach. I didn't look up till I'd nearly reached the parking lot. When I did look up, the lime-green jacket was the first thing I saw.

Deirdre sat on the low concrete wall surrounding the lot. Our eyes locked.

'About the little girl,' she said when I'd reached her. 'Otherwise, understand, I don't give a shit.'

I kept my voice neutral. 'Fair enough.' *Don't blow it*, I ordered myself.

She opened her mouth to speak, then shut it again. I didn't see any tears but Deirdre looked as if she'd been crying. Her eyes were puffy, her face splotched.

'I was a foster kid, all right? I know what the world's like, Zarlin.' Her chin jutted out. 'I know firsthand what some people will do to little girls.'

I stared at the woman. This prickly cactus had just shown me her vulnerable inside. 'Deirdre, I—'

'Shut up,' she snapped. 'If you haven't been there, you don't have a clue.'

I nodded. And then I did shut up, because of what happened next.

Two seagulls flapped into the parking lot. They didn't make a sound. That was because they couldn't: each had swallowed one end of a string. One tried to land, but the other took off. Tied together for evermore, they beat the air as they struggled on.

'Human beings are disgusting, you know?' Deirdre shrugged. 'People are sick. They tie food scraps to both ends of a string, then toss it to the gulls.'

'People can be cruel,' I agreed.

She looked at me hard. 'That's pretty much how it is, Zarlin. Once *it* happens to you. Like you've swallowed a string. You never ever escape from the memory, not for the rest of your life.'

'I'm sorry, Deirdre.' And I was.

'Yeah, well. Shit happens. Anyway, listen up. Sure, I know all about the weed. And that's all I'm going to say about that. But the trannie, see, what happened to her had nothing to do with the drugs or the PD. Like you said, she was drawing too much attention. Walking up and down Milpas, saying too much.'

'I don't get it, Deirdre. Saying too much about what?'

The policewoman drew a strand of hair from her mouth. 'About her missing daughter. Are you thick?'

I held on to my temper. 'You're saying it was the kidnappers who beat Chucha up.'

'Damn right. And I'm telling you straight: the kidnappers weren't cops. You're crazy to think that. Cops don't kidnap kids. Not even the worst of them. Damn it, Zarlin, you've got such a twisted attitude about the police! It's because of your brother, I suppose. The problem is you can't see things for what they are.'

I sank down into the Camino's seat and shut my eyes. Mike was two days overdue. I'd never known that to happen before. I opened my eyes and reached for my phone.

I knew Mike's sister had little free time. Trudy was a wonder woman, raising three wild kids, teaching fifth grade, and helping to run the family ranch up in Panoche from her home in San Luis Obispo. I knew I shouldn't bother her on her thirty-minute-long lunch hour.

But I was worried, maybe even a little scared, and my mind was going places it shouldn't. I needed to know if she'd heard from Mike.

'Trudy, hi. It's Jaymie. Sorry to bother you.'

'No problem, Jaymie. I'm outside on yard duty. Eating my lunch with one hand, in between blows on the whistle. What's up?'

I could just picture the tall, willowy dark-haired woman, laying down the law up in SLO. I was pretty sure she didn't take any guff.

'I just need to know if you've heard from Mike. He's been working up in the Los Padres Forest, and he should have been out two days ago.'

'Two days? Jaymie, it sounds like you guys are an old married couple already. I haven't heard from him, and no, you shouldn't worry. Is he on a dangerous job?'

An old married couple? Ouch. 'Could be. I guess I shouldn't talk about it. Anyway, he didn't tell me much.'

'Sounds like drugs. Jaymie, you know my brother. Mike can take care of himself.'

'Yeah. Yeah, you're right. How are the kids?'

'Great. Oh, you'll laugh. I caught the twins the other day pretending to be bridesmaids. In your wedding, Jaymie.'

'Trudy. You have to set them straight. We aren't about to get married. Mike and I, we're just . . .' Just what? I stopped, drawing a blank on how to finish my sentence.

'You're what, just friends?' Trudy laughed. Her laugh reminded me of Mike's. 'Listen, we're all thrilled you guys are back together. Just do us a favor – don't you dare go and elope. I'm not sure the girls would forgive you for that.'

Marriage. Elopement. Where was all this coming from, anyway? Nope, you'd never catch me dragging a ball and chain down the aisle.

I went to see Chucha again in the evening. I had to keep going back. I guess I was afraid that if I didn't go she'd drift away.

They'd turned her onto her left side. Now I could hear the guttural sound of her breathing.

A different nurse was on the shift, a young Filipino woman. Her English was heavily accented but good. 'You can talk to her. You never know, she might hear you. And use these if you want. Her mouth is so dry.'

She drew a moistened tissue from a plastic dispenser sitting on the bed stand and dabbed Chucha's lips.

I've never been comfortable in the nursing role. Feeling as if I were intruding on Chucha's personal space, I tugged at one of the tissues, then patted her chin.

'You're doing fine.' The nurse smiled, encouraging me.

I dropped the tissue in the trash and looked around for a chair. There was one shoved into a corner. I carried it around to the right side of the bed and sat down.

My face was on the same level as Chucha's. I saw glimmers of light just under her eyelids.

'I'm working on it, Chucha. Like I told you this morning, I'm going to find Rosie. The cops are involved, I just can't figure out how.' I placed an index finger on her dark creamy cheek and stroked it. 'At first I thought it was just some random punks who attacked you. Homophobes. Now I'm pretty sure that's not how it was.'

Chucha grimaced and made a sound like a low moan. I held my breath. But the sound wasn't repeated, and her face relaxed.

'Deirdre says I'm not objective because of what happened to Brodie. Damn right I'm biased. But that doesn't mean I don't have my eyes open.' I straightened in the chair.

'It's all tied together. But so far, I don't have a fucking clue how.'

* * *

Outside Cottage Hospital the night was dark and still. Too still.
When a rat scuffled in the ivy at the side of the walk, I jumped.

Rats were rampant these days in Santa Barbara. Warfarin was
flying off the shelves, and owls and hawks were quaffing down the
poisoned rodents. Toxins, like evil, were passing right up the line.

When my cell phone rang in my pocket I jumped again.

'There was a tip-off.' Deirdre's voice was high and squeaky, like
a mechanical toy's. She said a few more words but I couldn't catch
them.

'Speak slower, Deirdre. What did you say?'

'Listen harder. I said before the trannie was beat up, there was
a tip-off. An anonymous call about her to our tip hotline.'

Did I believe this? It sounded like crapola. 'What was the tip-off
about?'

'The caller said your client was trying to kidnap a baby. I mean,
Zarlin, did you ever stop to make sure the missing kid is really hers?'

An image of Chucha sobbing for her daughter passed before my
eyes.

'The kid is hers, Deirdre. The tip-off was bogus. So what are
you saying, that the cops beat her senseless because of a false lead?'

There was a long silence. Inches away from my toe, the noisy
rat emerged from the bed of ivy. 'Ugh!' I hopped back and the rat
retreated.

'What did you say?'

I shuddered. 'Never mind.'

'It's like I told you, Zarlin. Cops take care of kids. Can you
blame them for that?'

FOURTEEN

Gabi looked chic. She wore a slinky black cardigan and black
tapered pants, along with a hot pink silky top. 'I had a
dresser,' she explained as she arranged chocolate-oozing
pastries on the pink Fiestaware plates. 'At Nordstrom.'

I breathed in the rich aroma rising off my first cup of the day, then
took a delectable sip. 'Fancy that. I'm sorry your rich uncle died.'

'Huh?' She turned and looked at me, plate poised. 'I got three uncles, two dead and one is alive. But nobody is rich.'

'I'm kidding. Nordstrom's is expensive and working with a dresser, well. They aren't going to show you stuff off the sales rack.' I shrugged. 'Just guessing. What would I know?'

'No you are right, Miss Jaymie.' Gabi turned back to the counter. 'Nordstrom is too much money for me. I buy Ross, or secondhand. Santa Barbara, this is a great town for consignment you know.'

'OK. So how did you work it?'

'Norma Ventura, my brother's wife's sister, she is the dresser. She told me, just come up after five. So I did. To a little room with no windows. Very hot, very bright lights. It's like you are a movie star, OK? You stand up on a little stage. Norma had all the clothes ready for me, you know, what fits my body and also my personality. I tried on almost everything on the third floor, Miss Jaymie. It took more than three hours.'

I eyed the flagrant pink top. As far as personality went, Norma had hit the nail on the head.

'Of course, I did not buy anything there. After, I went with Norma over to Second Time Around and bought almost all the same stuff.'

'I'm impressed. So Norma did all that for free?'

'For free? Miss Jaymie, Norma works hard, she has two jobs. Why would she do it for free?' Gabi set one of the pink dishes in front of me on the kitchenette table, then set down her own and took the chair opposite me.

'Last Christmas I made her six dozen tamales, OK? Three dozen pork, two dozen turkey, one dozen vegetarian. Six dozen, Miss Jaymie. That is seventy-two.' She took a nibble of her pastry and looked reflective.

'Norma, she still owes me. But she is a good person, she won't forget. Some people, they—' Gabi stopped. 'What is wrong with me, Miss Jaymie. All I talk about is me. Tell me more about Chucha, how was she last night? Is she better now?'

'She's had brain damage, Gabi.' I put down my cup. 'Maybe Chucha will get better, but even if she does . . .'

Gabi wagged a finger. 'Positively positive, Miss Jaymie. I heard about this man, he was not related to me—'

'Now there's a miracle right there.'

'OK never mind.' She clanged her teaspoon against the cup as she stirred. 'Maybe you want me to go away now, Miss Jaymie? Maybe you gotta *think* some more.'

She said the word 'think' with a heavy negative emphasis. I knew Gabi was of the opinion that I thought too damn much.

'I need to run something by you, Gabi. Something I heard from Deirdre Krause.'

'Oh, the little police lady with the big, you know, the boobs? The one that is always making eyes at Mr Mike.'

'Yeah, the very one. She told me that somebody contacted the police about Chucha. Someone betrayed her.'

'What?' Gabi jumped up from her chair. 'Are you saying what I think? Did somebody call the cops, and then the cops went and beat Chucha up?'

'It looks like it, yes. According to Deirdre, somebody left a message on the tips line and said that Chucha was trying to kidnap the little girl on the poster.'

'I am so angry, Miss Jaymie! If I ever, ever find out who did that – never mind! But . . . but why?'

'I don't know why, not yet. But it could have been the same guy who grabbed Rosie from the boat. He'd want to throw suspicion on another person. And Chucha, she was the ideal target.'

'I am so angry. I am sorry, I cannot sit still. I'm gonna go clean a very, very dirty house. Mr Petersen's, I think. I'm gonna go do that right now.'

'May I have your attention! Ladies, gents, and bi's! We got a virgin with us tonight. Put your paws together for the Mission City Bettie who is also a real live private eye: *La Macheesma!*'

I finished tying a double knot on the heavy skates and swayed to my feet. The crowd didn't roar, but a few people did clap, and Claudia and BJ stomped and yelled.

'Go, La Macheesma! Jaymie, kill em dead!'

I wobbled into the circular concrete rink. My teammates swept past, strutting their stuff before the crowd. Two or three gave me friendly pats on the ass.

I was dressed in black tights and my old gray and black running outfit. At the last minute I'd added a pair of kneepads just in case, though I didn't plan on taking a spill.

Back home, this had seemed like an appropriate outfit. But now I saw I was appallingly underdressed.

For one thing, my hair was its natural color. I sported no streaks of purple, blue, or chartreuse. That alone labeled me as a plain Jane, frumpy, no fun. Then, there was my tracksuit. Most of the women wore fishnets, tutus, swimsuits, and black merry widows. They all looked like hookers on skates.

Very tough hookers, I hasten to add. Some of the girls were real bruisers. Big and mean with yards of tats and evil twinkles in their eyes. The little ones were even scarier: they looked like wasps or centipedes, and no doubt knew how to stab where it hurt.

By the way, these were my own team members I'm talking about. I couldn't wait to lay eyes on the enemy.

One of the girls bumped me hard from behind, passed me, and looked back over her shoulder. 'Friend of that Molina bitch, huh?' I caught the accent straight off: south Texas.

I felt a jolt of angry adrenalin, then counteracted the emotion with reason. This was my quarry, after all: Sylvia Sanchez, aka Hot Wheels.

'Friends? Sometimes.' I shrugged and kept skating. 'Sometimes not so much.'

Sanchez lifted a sculptured eyebrow, then spun around and skated backwards, keeping me in view. 'So why are you filling in for her?'

'Paying off a debt.'

Hot Wheels curled her lip, spun back around, and powered on.

'Ladies, gents, bi's, and all you curious pervs! Please welcome our visitors, the baddest bunch of four-eyed girls in the league – put your hands together for Leland Stanford JUNIOR University!'

The crowd had swollen in size and was winding up. They stomped and cheered. Our opponents swept in from the wings. They didn't look so different from my own teammates, except that there were more tall blondes, and their merry widows looked like they'd been purchased at Abercrombie & Fitch.

The mayhem commenced straight away. It didn't require a four-year degree at a private university to understand the rules, but who cared about stinkin' rules? My only aim was to stay on my feet.

I failed two minutes in when a willowy coed stuck out a skate and tripped me. I sailed ass over kite and landed in a heap on the asphalt.

'Sorry,' she cooed as she swept by on her next circuit.

Like hell she was sorry. I managed to struggle back to my feet. My tights were torn and when I touched my sore knee, my hand came away wet. With blood.

'I'll protect you, lil bitch,' a Texas-accented voice crooned in my ear.

'I'm not your bitch and I don't need protection,' I growled.

Hot Wheels released a long peal of laughter. 'Whatever, Grandma.'

Looking back on it thirty minutes later, I realized I kind of lost perspective at that point.

I forged into the churning river of competitors. Elbows out, I figured I was giving better than I got. Grinning into the wind, I dealt jabs left and right.

Then a tiny Stanford coed darted up beside me. 'What's an old lady like you doing out here?' She looked about twelve.

'What are you majoring in, sweetie?' I retorted. 'Art history, I suppose?'

'PhD candidate in English Literature, sweetie yourself. My topic is vaginal imagery in Katherine Mansfield.'

'Huh?' I turned my head to look at her. The candidate head-butted me in the thigh. Expertly. I dropped like a downed cow.

At least three skaters fell on top of me. It felt like a dozen. I heard a sharp crack, and when the associated neuron finally delivered its message to my brain, I screamed.

There was a lot of huffing and puffing on top of me. Then, I was clear. But all I could do was whimper with the pain.

A nasty-looking Stanford dolly knelt down beside me. She looked like a member of Kiss who'd ODed on estrogen. 'Get some ice!' she screamed over her shoulder. Then, to my face: 'Don't worry, I'm a doctor. Don't move.'

No way was I going to move. The pain in my shoulder was so strong I feared I'd pass out. But mainly, Doc had me scared shitless.

'It's a dislocation. I'm going to fix a sling for you. You need to go to emergency, girl. Just hang in there. I know it hurts, but you're going to be fine.'

I spotted Claudia and BJ hovering at the outer edge of the circle of bystanders. They looked stricken. With my good hand, I motioned them over. 'Don't get involved,' I managed to hiss. 'Maybe Hot Wheels and I can bond over this.'

It fucking hurt, all right. But the show had to go on.

Sure enough, I managed to finagle Hot Wheels into driving me to the emergency entrance at the back of Cottage. 'I saw that Molina bitch trying to glom on to you,' Sylvia observed. 'She's a lesbo, you know that, right?'

'Unh.' Luckily, I didn't have to pretend to be fuzzy headed. I was so dizzy with pain that I felt like I dwelled in a world stuffed with gauze.

'And that kid she hangs out with – is he gay? I don't get it. What's that all about?'

Jesus. I couldn't decide how to respond, but luckily the answer was provided for me. 'Pull over—'

I shoved open the door with my good arm, but even so, the pain made me squeal. Then I vomited up everything I'd eaten in the last twenty-four hours, a surprisingly large amount.

When I'd finished, I continued to drool into the dirt at the side of the road.

'Here.' Hot Wheels reached over and handed me a Kleenex. 'Must hurt like fuck.'

'I think we better get to the hos – the hos—' I managed to pull the door closed, and leaned back against the seat. 'I don't feel so good.'

Hot Wheels and I became close very fast. That's what happens when you're lying on a gurney, your brain swirling with medication and pain, and someone at least a little sympathetic is holding your hand.

'My boyfriend, Del, he's a detective,' she said in a conversational tone. 'We're tight, know what I mean?'

I stifled a giggle. Damn drugs. 'Uh huh.'

'We're going to get married, we just haven't decided when.'

It wasn't hard to understand what Del Wasson saw in her, the more sober part of my brain remarked to itself. Sylvia was pretty, but more than that, she had the body of a Greek goddess. Del didn't seem like the marrying kind, but what heterosexual male wouldn't lead Sylvia Sanchez on, in any way he could think of, just to keep her around?

'You have a cute accent, Sylvia. Where are you from?'

'Zapata Texas. You don't wanna go there, believe me. My mom and her boyfriend moved out here about five years ago, and all of us kids followed.'

'I've never heard of Zapata.'

'No?' Sylvia laughed. 'I don't know why not. It's famous for the white-collared seedeaters.'

'Huh?'

'I'm not shitting you. It's this dumb little bird.' She patted my wrist. 'Personally I wouldn't cross the street to look at it. But thousands of people come to Zapata just for that. Can you believe it? They come from all over the world.'

'Wow. So you got brothers and sisters?' I was thinking more clearly now, on track, rowing toward my objective with a steadier stroke.

'One sister and one brother. My sister and me, we don't get along.'

'How about your brother?'

'My brother? Steve, he's a cop too.' Sylvia gathered her long black hair at the nape of her neck. 'Steve's all right I guess. He introduced me to Del.'

The nurse, a woman in her fifties who looked like she wanted to go home, sit down with a cup of decaf tea and switch on PBS, walked into the curtained-off space. 'Yes, it's a dislocation,' she announced. 'The doctor will be here soon.'

'Oh man,' Sylvia said. 'When they fix it, that's gonna hurt.'

Hot Wheels stayed long enough to enjoy the mayhem. Then she took off, after I told her I had someone coming to get me. Sylvia was Steve Sanchez's sister, and I didn't need her to drive me home and find out where I lived.

'Miss Jaymie?' Gabi parted the blue-flecked gray curtain with two hands and peered into the space. 'You don't look so good.'

She walked up to the bed and eyed my arm in its brand new sling. Then she turned her attention to what I guessed was a class-A shiner, as my right eye was squeezed shut. Finally she took in my outfit, right down to the shredded tights.

'The bobcat attacked you, right? You told me you saw one last week in your yard.'

I grunted. I wasn't in a talking mood.

Florence Nightingale reappeared. 'Good to go?' She didn't wait for my reply.

'Fill these prescriptions on the way home. You'll want the pain meds, believe me, when the sedative wears off. The doctor has prescribed an antibiotic too. Those scrapes on your legs look nasty, and he didn't want to take a chance with infection.'

I nodded and swung my legs over the edge of the bed as I rose to a sitting position. 'When can I get back on skates, nurse?'

Gabi gasped. 'Probably never.'

'Gallows humor. I like that.' The nurse smiled. 'Didn't the doctor explain it to you? Once you've dislocated your shoulder, it's far more likely to happen again.'

'And anyway you are too old.' Gabi snorted. 'I wonder when you are going to grow up, Miss Jaymie.'

I groaned as I got to my feet. 'I just did. I feel like I'm ninety-two.'

'Where are we going?' The smell of ammonia inside Gabi's station wagon was as bracing as a dose of smelling salts, and my druggy haze was clearing.

'To my apartment and do not say no. I am not gonna drop you off at your place, not tonight.'

'But Dexter—'

'You want me to go get your dog? That one is OK, for a dog. He can stay at my place tonight, if it makes you feel better.'

'Dex has the dog door. I guess he'll be all right. But I need my own bed.'

'No and that is final.'

I rolled my head to look over at her. The set of Gabi's chin, profiled in the dark, told me there was no point in protesting. 'I get up early,' I warned.

'Huh. Not as early as me.'

I let out a long breath and gave in. The truth was, my shoulder was beginning to throb like a sonofabitch, as Mike would have said. *Mike . . . I need you*, I thought. *Please, give me a call.*

'My cell's in my bag, Gabi. Check it for messages, would you?'

'Sure. Let me do that while I drive the car. Then the police will have a good excuse to pull me over. Then they will find out I got no driver's license 'cause I got no papers, just like they thought. Then they will impound this car and I will have to let them keep it, 'cause it will cost more money than it is worth to get it outta the pound. That is what already happened to four people I know in Santa Barbara, Miss Jaymie.'

'It's an injustice,' I mumbled. 'Tomorrow, I'll fix it.'

FIFTEEN

Maybe the drugs had worn off. Whatever the reason, I woke up at two in the morning and found myself staring at Gabi's shadowy bedroom ceiling. Against all my arguments she'd insisted on sleeping on the couch and giving me her king-size bed.

'A big bed for a small person,' I'd said as I'd edged into the tiny bedroom.

'Sometimes I like to sleep sideways. You don't always wanna sleep in the same direction, you know?'

'Not really.' But I'd been happy to stretch out between the fresh lavender-scented sheets.

I'd dropped off in seconds. That was back around ten p.m. Now I was wide awake. But not because of the drugs, I realized. Because of Gabi. Something was wrong.

She hadn't smiled once. And there was pain in her eyes.

I knew my personal assistant/office manager pretty damn well. She was almost always positively positive. Not last night.

I rolled my head in the direction of the window. Gabi had installed black-out drapes. But the glare from car headlights – bright for a moment, then fading away – seeped in around the edges.

There was a constant thrum downtown, even in the middle of the night. I could hear a soft rumble from the freeway. Somewhere nearby, a car door slammed.

Then I heard another sound: a soft beep-beep. I listened and heard a faint clatter. Gabi was up, moving about in her kitchen.

I rose up on my good elbow and sucked in my breath as a dagger of pain pierced my opposite shoulder. I swung my feet to the floor.

Gabi had left a voluminous housecoat for me at the end of the bed. I slipped it on and managed to tug up the zip with my good hand.

'Miss Jaymie, did I wake you up?' Gabi was seated at the small kitchen table. She also wore a big puffy robe. Hers was covered in candy canes. The two of us looked like a pair of overstuffed teddy bears.

A cup of cocoa sat on the table before her, and she'd wrapped both her small hands around it. 'Miss Jaymie, is something wrong?'

'You didn't wake me up.' I slid into the plastic-covered kitchen chair opposite her. 'But yeah, something's wrong.'

'What? Do you need to go back to Emergency?'

The alarm on my friend's face and her concern touched me. I knew she'd do anything for me. Anything as long as it made good sense, of course.

'Gabi. Tell me what's wrong. I haven't seen you smile once.'

She tried a smile. It was ghastly. 'OK. Maybe I can't smile.'

'Why not?'

'Why not what?' But her face fell. 'You are injured, Miss Jaymie. This is a bad time to talk about it.'

'No, this is a good time. Because pretty soon I'm going to have to take another pill.'

'I am gonna fix you some cocoa in the microwave.' She pushed back her chair, got up and busied herself at the kitchen counter.

'Look,' I said as she placed the steaming mug before me. 'If you don't want to tell me tonight, fine. But you know you'll tell me sooner or later.'

I picked up the cup in both hands. 'Mmm. My god, that tastes good.'

'Abuelita, from Costco. And I put some other things in it too.' She cleared her throat. 'OK. Are you sure you are ready to hear?'

I put down the cup. This was a first: I'd never once seen Gabi reluctant to speak. 'I'm ready. Don't worry about me.'

'Angel.' She stared down at the table top. 'It is about Angel, Miss Jaymie.'

'Angel? Did something bad happen to him?'

She shook her head back and forth, her eyes still on the table before her. 'No. Nothing bad happened to him. He did something bad.'

The bastard must have cheated on her. I couldn't believe it: Angel had seemed like such a loyal guy.

'I'm so sorry, Gabi. What are you going to do?'

'Do?' At last she looked up at me. I saw a mixture of anger and sadness in her eyes. 'I am not gonna see him again. Never. Because if I see him, I maybe will kill him.'

I nodded. 'I'd do the same in your shoes. A man who cheats so soon in the relationship, he—'

'Cheats?' Her eyes blazed. 'That would be easy! I would just go and tell the woman she has to leave town.'

'Well then, what are we talking—'

'Miss Jaymie!' Gabi jumped up from the table and swung out her right hand for emphasis. Her hand collided with her mug, and hot chocolate splashed in an arc across the room. 'Miss Jaymie, Angel – he told the cops about Chucha! He was the one!'

I stared at her. I tried to stop the words that came to my mouth, but there was no way. 'The fucking bastard! Why the hell did he do that?'

Then I jumped to my feet too. I suppose my shoulder hurt, but I didn't feel a thing. 'I need an explanation, and I need it now.' I knew I was transferring my fury to Gabi, and that wasn't fair.

Tears streamed down her face. 'Yes it is my fault 'cause I told him all about Chucha. I never shoulda done that, I am so sorry!'

I had to do something, anything, to remove Chucha's image from my mind: her slack face and that gleaming white bandage covering her skull. I went to the sink and turned on the cold tap. Again and again, I splashed the frigid water onto my face.

'Miss Jaymie.' She handed me a clean dish towel. 'Miss Jaymie I'm gonna retire.'

'Retire?' The cold water had calmed me down a little. 'You're fifty-one years old.'

'OK, not retire. What do they call it? Resign.'

I made a disgusted sound and tossed the towel on the counter. 'Like hell you will. I need you too much. Now, explain it to me. Why did Angel do that? He seemed like such a good guy!'

'He wanted to get Chucha deported, that is why. Miss Jaymie, he knew Chucha didn't have no papers, but he did not think they would hurt her. He feels so, so bad about that.'

'And so he fucking should.' I spread my hands. 'I still don't get it, Gabi – why?'

'I do not wanna make excuses for him, OK? All I can say is

what he said to me. Angel said he did not want Chucha to find the little girl.'

'But Chucha is Rosie's mother!' Again I felt my temperature soar.

'Angel, he had a very bad mother, very mean. She would hit him with a big stick. He thought Chucha, 'cause she's a man and a woman too, she would be a bad mother. He thought the people who will adopt Rosie, they will be much better for her. And he says the little girl, she is the most important one.'

'Of all the damn stupid—' I halted. There was no point in expending any more energy on Angel, I knew.

'Miss Jaymie. Angel, he told me he wants to come and talk to you.'

'Don't let that man near me.' I stabbed a finger at her. 'I mean it, Gabi. I don't want to see his goddamn face.'

I couldn't fall back to sleep. My mind churned like a slot machine. At five I got up and dressed.

'Miss Jaymie, what can I do?' Gabi knotted her robe around her waist.

'I'm going to walk home.'

'No you can't. The nurse, I heard her say keep quiet for three days. If you have to go I will give you a ride.'

'I need to walk off this anger, Gabi. I'm not going to be good for anything till I do.'

She raised her arms and let them fall at her sides, kind of like a penguin trying to fly. 'OK. But you have your phone, right? I'm gonna sit here. Call me when you get home, I am not gonna move from this chair till you do.'

It was pitch black outside. I walked west along Gutierrez, then turned up State. A police car cruised past me and slowed.

'You OK?'

I was about to snap back. But then I met the officer's eyes. I recognized him: Cranston. He was one of the cops working the restorative program for the homeless, a guy who actually gave a rat's ass. 'Yeah. Just going for a walk.'

'All right. Take care.'

Was the world turning upside down? A cop who cared, and a friend – Angel – who'd let me down.

Let *me* down? What did this have to do with me? It was Chucha who lay in ICU with a broken brain.

I needed to center myself. Or rather, get myself out of the center. And again, I thought about Mike. I needed to talk to him.

I stopped near the train station and pulled out my cell. A reflexive action: after all, if Mike had returned to civilization by now, he'd have seen my one-hundred-and-one messages and called me back right away. Instead of leaving message #102, I tapped off the phone.

The night was cloudy and a three-quarter moon rocked through the rough waves of the sky. Rain spattered my face, but I knew it wouldn't amount to much. A real rain would have been a blessing, and tonight Santa Barbara was cursed, not blessed.

I continued on, passing by the Moreton Bay Fig. I heard a series of long racking coughs. In the cold light of the street lamp, I could make out a dozen or more forms huddled into the buttressing roots.

The largest individual of its species, the fig tree had boasted its own zip code back in the sixties. That's when the hippies lived there. Now the fig provided an island of refuge to those without homes. At least, it provided a refuge on the nights the cops didn't raid it, jostling the exhausted people awake just for the fun of it all.

My mood continued to plunge. I knew I had to halt the freefall. I'd spiraled into depression once before, after Brodie had died. I couldn't allow it to happen again, not with Rosie out there.

I checked the time as I walked on up Montecito Street, towards Castillo. Five thirty-four. Only one person I knew would be up at this hour in the month of February. Zave slept five hours a night, and by now he'd be wide awake, busy strategizing the day's nefarious moves.

Yeah, Zave was pissed off with me. But he was a friend, wasn't he? What were friends for?

'Jaymie. What a surprise. Where are you?'

'Castillo and Montecito, half a block from the freeway. It's a long story, Zave.'

'Is it? I'm not sure I have the time.' His voice was reserved. 'Besides, you and I don't have that kind of relationship anymore, remember?'

'What kind do you mean?'

'The kind that accommodates long stories.'

'We do. I say we do, Zave.' My voice sounded desperate.

There was a lull in the traffic on the overpass. I thought I heard him sigh.

'Are you in real trouble, Jaymie? The life-threatening kind?

Because if you are, then yes. Our connection covers that. Even so, the one you should be calling is the deputy. Right?'

'I'm sorry, Zave. Maybe I shouldn't have called. I'm OK, all right? Just out for a walk.'

'Funny time for a walk. Funny place, too. See the Seven Eleven? I'll pick you up there.'

The sleek black Jag slid up to the sidewalk in front of the 7-11. I said goodbye to the old homeless guy keeping himself warm with a fifth. 'I'll drop off a blanket tomorrow,' I promised.

I slid down in the Jag's bucket seat. I glanced once at Zave, then shut my eyes. 'Thanks,' I said in a small voice. 'You're a prince.'

'And you're a goddamn princess.' He stepped on the gas and the car powered out of the lot.

'A princess? That would be nice. I'd wave my scepter and the world would be just the way I want it to be.'

'Queens have scepters. Not princesses. Princesses wear starchy dresses and lots of pink. For some unknown reason, people fall all over themselves to do what they ask.'

'That's not me for sure. *Nobody* does what I want.' Good grief. It must have been the pain meds. My eyes stung with self-pitying tears.

Zave reached over and stroked my hair. 'What's with the sling, Jaymie? And that eye. Christ.' His voice was a touch softer now.

'I dislocated my shoulder last night. Playing roller derby.' A tear rolled down my cheek, then another. It was maudlin. I turned my face to the side window, so Zave wouldn't see.

'Roller derby. Right. What, you think you're sixteen?'

'Why do people keep saying that to me? I'm as fit as I ever was. Fitter, in fact.' Annoyed, I quit blubbering. 'Where are we going?'

'I'm taking you to your place. You're a menace to yourself. You're going to get in bed, and you're going to stay there. If I could, I'd lock you in and throw away the key.'

I was quiet as we gunned up El Balcon and turned up my drive. 'Sorry I'm acting like an idiot. Something bad's happened. I need to talk.'

'I know.' He pulled to a stop in front of my door. 'Think that man-eater will let me in?'

I looked out the window: Dexter had barreled out through the pet door. A ball of indignant fury, he snarled and snapped, racing back and forth in front of the Jag.

I knew Zave secretly wanted to baby me. But instead he sat down in one of my two kitchen chairs and folded his arms across his chest.

'I'm going to make coffee, fully-leaded. Want a cup?'

'Why not. Just don't offer to cook.'

It hurt to laugh, but still, it felt good. It was an old joke between us: Zave was a superlative cook, and I was one of the worst.

I set up my old drip coffeemaker, then sat down opposite him. 'You know what happened to Chucha, right?' I knew there was zero chance Zave hadn't heard.

'Yeah. Ugly business. Is she going to make it?'

I shook my head. I didn't want to go into it, not now. 'Brain damage. Severe.'

'Shit. Sorry, Jaymie. I know you liked her.'

'*Like* her, you mean. Yeah, I do. Zave, here's the thing. I just found out it was Angel. Gabi's boyfriend, you know? Angel tipped off the cops about Chucha.'

Zave's expression turned hard, and a corner of his mouth lifted. 'Asshole. Why the fuck did he do that?'

'Prejudice. Ignorance. He thought Chucha would be a bad parent, that Rosie would be better off being adopted. So he went to the cops to get Chucha deported.' I puffed out a stream of air. 'According to Gabi, Angel had no idea she'd be beaten to within an inch of her life.'

'He had no idea.' Zave gave a short laugh. 'They never do, the snitches.'

'Gabi's finished with him. I hope to God I never see the man again. I'd be tempted to rip him to bits.'

'Speaking of people who aren't what they seem. There's someone I didn't tell you about when you came to the office the other day.'

I studied my former lover. 'Great, just great. Another fucking surprise.'

'I had an urge to protect you.' He looked away. 'Though why the hell I'd want to do that is a mystery.'

I adjusted the sling. It was biting into my neck, and my shoulder throbbed. 'Because we're friends?'

He smiled a little. 'Yeah, all right. Put it that way if you want. We're friends.'

'So who is this about?'

'Laura Marie Brautigan.'

'Who?'

'The nun. The priest. Whatever she is. Brautigan's her last name, Jaymie.'

'Oh.' I was quiet. It was still dark outside, and I could hear a barn owl calling from the top of the Monterey cypress. 'Laura's very nice. And she seems genuine.'

'Nice, maybe so. But genuine? Not entirely.' Zave splayed his hands on the gray Formica tabletop. 'It's like this. A buddy of mine represented her, nine or ten years ago. I remember because the case was unusual. He told me all about it at the time, as a matter of fact.'

'Should he have done that?'

Zave dismissed my question with a brusque wave of his hand. 'Brautigan was employed by the county – I think she was based up in Lompoc. She was a social worker, dealing with foster kids. What happened was this: she helped some fourteen-year-old run away from his foster parents. Initially she was charged with kidnapping, but that was dropped for lesser charges.'

'Laura must have had a reason for doing that, Zave. She doesn't seem like the type to break the law.'

'Brautigan argued that the law of God was superior to the law of man. Something like that. The boy was being abused. The foster parents denied it, of course. The kid was in a bad spot, and the wheels of bureaucracy were jammed. Laura took matters into her own hands.'

'What happened to her?'

'She was convicted of a felony. Didn't spend long in jail, though. The judge had a record of being tough on abusers. He was sympathetic to her.'

'So when she got out, that's when she must have decided to become a priest.'

'Yeah. Maybe because she wouldn't have been able to get a job in the public sector again, that's for sure.'

'And the boy? What happened to him?'

'He was removed from the home. Other than that, I've got no idea.'

The coffeemaker let out a long, pent-up hiss. 'So – why would you think I'd need protection from that information? No, let me guess.' I got up and switched off the coffee, then reached for a couple of mugs. 'Staffen Brill. She was part of the picture, am I right?'

'On the money. Brill and her partner, Morehead, were going to adopt the kid, take him off Laura Brautigan's hands. That was the plan. They let him hide out at that estate of theirs, as a matter of fact. When Brautigan was arrested, Morehead and Brill came close to being charged. Real close. But they wriggled out of it.'

'Claimed ignorance, I suppose. As if.'

Zave accepted the mug I offered him – chipped, but my best. My best, except for the mug Brodie had given me. That one I kept for myself.

'Sure. They were in the dark, or so they claimed. But that was a joke. One thing about that pair you can count on, is that they always know what's going on.' He laughed. 'You think *I* can pull strings?'

'So let me understand this. You want me to stay away from Brill and Morehead. I wasn't interested in them before, Zave. But you're right: now that I know about the past they share with Laura, I'm curious. I have to wonder why they wanted to help.'

'We'll never know. But there was something in it for them, you can be sure of that.' Zave squinted as the steam off the coffee hit his eyes. 'Listen, Brill and Morehead are poisonous. The less you have to do with them the better off you'll be.'

'Control freak.'

'I try. But you can be a slippery little salamander.'

'Look. I want to know that boy's name.'

'What for?'

'Call me a pack rat. I'm attracted to odd bits of information, that's all. Who knows, I might need it some time.'

'No. What you *need* is to let it go.' Zave set down the cup, harder than was necessary. 'I knew I shouldn't have told you any of it. This entire business leads back to the cops, you see that by now, right? If you can't see it, Jaymie, you're blind.'

SIXTEEN

Monday evening, when I hobbled into the small concrete arena at the Earl Warren show grounds, cheers went up on all sides.

OK, it was just practice, and only twelve women were present: but La Macheesma got a round of whoops, whistles, and applause. I'd been wounded in battle, which meant I'd earned my stripes.

The Black Widow glided up to me and stuck out her hand. She gripped my good hand so hard I thought I heard a ligament pop. 'Way to go, bitch! You were awesome out there!'

I hadn't been awesome, I was sure of that. 'Sorry we lost, coach. I heard about the score from Clau – from La Diablita.'

'Yeah, so what?' The Black Widow snickered, showing her fangs. 'In three weeks we have a rematch. I got a few tricks up my sleeve. Those smart girls won't be able to add two and two after we use 'em to wipe up the track.'

'That's the spirit.' I looked around for Sylvia. 'Where's Hot Wheels? I want to thank her for taking me to emergency.'

'Called and said she couldn't make practice. Didn't feel good or something, the wuss.'

'Maybe she really is sick.' I took out my cell. 'Would you mind texting her contact info to me? I'll send her some flowers.'

'*Ohh*-kay,' drawled the Black Widow. 'Hey, you know she's got a boyfriend, right? And I don't think she's bi.'

The Black Widow might have thought I was interested in Hot Wheels, but Hot Wheels herself wasn't confused. 'I figured you'd try to talk to me. That's why I didn't go to practice tonight,' she snarled into the phone.

'Sylvia, was it something I said?'

'Don't play dumb with me. When I got back to the fairgrounds that night, Del was there. He told me all about you, OK? A nosy PI, that's what you are. You wanted to get info out of me, so you acted like you were my friend!'

'Hey, bullshit. Claudia asked me to sub for her, like I said. And If I remember right, you volunteered to take me to the hospital. I suppose you think the separated shoulder was a fake too!'

Hot Wheels laughed. Her laughter was real, throaty, and surprised. I actually kind of liked the woman, in a weird sort of way. But I did not like the company she slept with.

'Yeah, the shoulder was for real. But that shit about filling in for La Diablita? That was crap. You set it up.'

'You're being honest with me, Sylvia. So I'll be up front too. Yes, I wanted to talk with you. Sorry if I was sneaky. I didn't know anything about you, didn't know what kind of person you are.'

'And you think you do now?' Her had voice tensed. Del had tipped her off about me, and maybe she'd also talked to her brother. So why was the woman still on the phone?

'Not really, no. If you want to hang up, I'd understand.'

I was tired, I realized. Tired and impatient. I was trying to get by without any pain meds so I could think straight, but my shoulder ached liked effing hell.

'Look, Sylvia. I understand if you don't want to go against your boyfriend.'

'What, Del? What the fuck are you talking about?' Her voice changed again, taking on an anxious edge. 'It's my brother I'm worried about. If you don't know that, you don't know nothin'.'

I sat up straight. Sylvia had something to tell me, all right. 'Your brother. Steve Sanchez.'

'Yeah, that's the one.' Her tone had turned sarcastic, but something else, something real, lay underneath. 'Listen, Steve drives by my apartment two or three times every day. He says it's to keep me safe. But I'd feel a lot safer if he just left me alone.'

'If you have something to tell me, Sylvia, you don't need to worry.' I tried to keep the urgency out of my voice. 'I promise your name won't ever come up. You won't be dragged into anything.'

'Know what? I don't trust you. I shouldn't even be talking to you now. How do I know you aren't taping this call?'

'I'm not. But you have a point. Maybe Steve tracks your calls?'

'Wouldn't put it past him.' Sylvia made an exasperated sound. 'My big brother. He drives me crazy sometimes. Listen, can you think of some place to meet? Somewhere . . . where Steve won't see my car. Where he never goes.'

'I'll come up with something.'

'And in case you think I'm paranoid, get this. Del told me that when Steve's gone, he asks other cops to keep an eye on me.'

'I'll text you with a location. Tomorrow, what time?'

'I work ten to five.'

'Nine, then.'

'Nine's early. I'll think about it.'

She was backpedaling now, I could hear it. After nibbling the bait off the hook the fish was swimming away.

'Sylvia, I just had a brainwave. Do you know where the Botanic Garden is?'

'I've heard of it. Never been there.'

'I guarantee you Steve's never been there either. And the parking is hidden down off the road. It's above the old mission, in Mission Canyon. Nine a.m. tomorrow, I'll meet you there.'

I didn't give her time to think twice. I punched off the phone.

Sylvia needed to talk. I had no idea why, but she had a burning coal in her brain. She wanted to pass something on to me, to unburden herself. Something to do with her brother, Tejano Steve.

I tooled up Mission Canyon at quarter to nine the next morning. All the windows in the Camino were rolled down and cool air streamed into the cab.

The canyon smelled of damp loam and mushrooms, thanks to a few recent rains. It was generous, though, to call them rains. We'd had a few sprinklings, yes, but the drought continued to deepen. Summer loomed like a fire-breathing dragon lurking just over the mountains.

The Botanic Garden parking lot was set below the road, screened by oaks and other native trees and shrubs. You could count on the fact that anything growing in the Garden was native to our golden state. Any foreign plant, no matter how beautiful or rare, had long ago been yanked out by the roots and mulched.

I pulled Blue Boy into a slot next to a parking place reserved for electric cars. The lot was almost empty. The facility didn't open till nine, for one thing. For another, this was the month of February: the garden was drab at this time of year and received few winter visitors.

I climbed out of the Camino and went to stand near the entry gate. I wanted to get there before Sylvia. The garden employees and volunteers were good souls all, but I wasn't sure how Hot Wheels would feel about being instructed to keep her feet on the paths.

Promptly at nine, the entrance kiosk raised its green awning. The gate lady looked good: her smooth silver hair was cut in an artful bob, and her face work was up-to-date, which was more than I could say for mine. Her black and turquoise designer outfit, however, seemed less than ideal for dabbling in the dirt.

'Good morning. Are you a member?' Her expression implied she was sure I was not.

'Yep. Lifetime. I don't carry my card on me, but you'll find me in your computer. Jaymie Zarlin.'

The lady's brows knitted. Her earrings, tiny gold flowerpots set with diamond-studded daisies, quivered. 'Do you have identification?'

I pulled out my driver's license. What was it, I wondered, that made me look like I didn't belong? I could play in the dirt with the best of them.

'I'm bringing a guest. I think that's free for members, right?'

Her brow furrow deepened. 'If you are a lifetime member, then yes.' She peered at her iPad. 'Hmm. I do see you here.'

I could tell she was dying to know how someone of my ilk was a member. Oh, and a lifetime member no less. The morning was bright and I was in a generous mood, so I decided to indulge her.

'Jane Starkey gave me the membership as a gift. I don't use it much, but every once in a while it comes in handy.'

'Jane Starkey? Jane is one of our most valued benefactors.' She handed me two tickets. 'Perhaps you'd like to become more involved?'

'Ah. Well, the thing is—' As good luck would have it, Hot Wheels chose that moment to appear.

'Hey, Jaymie.'

In defense of the gatekeeper, whose jaw had dropped about a foot, I had to admit that Hot Wheels didn't look like a woman who was eager to meander down a gravel path. It's a challenge to look hot and sexy at nine a.m. in the month of February, but Sylvia had managed it, and with panache. Her mass of dark curls bounced, her fingernails glittered, and her boobs threatened to pop out of her tight V-neck top. The woman wasn't there to pull weeds.

'Hey, Hot Wheels, come on in. Let's go for a walk.' I waggled my fingers goodbye to my fellow garden member. I'd given her a gift, the way I looked at it: something to gossip about for months to come.

'Damn fucking dirt. What's the matter, can't they afford a little concrete?' Hot Wheels' four-inch stilettos were sinking into the damp decomposed granite path.

'Yeah, well. The paths used to be paved, the way I heard it. Then the Garden yanked all the pavers out. Not natural enough.'

'What the fuck?' Sylvia put a hand on my shoulder to balance herself, then checked her heels. 'If these shoes are wrecked by the time I leave, this place is going to hear about it. Fucking two-fifty.'

'Blahnik, huh?'

'A fucking good copy.'

Together we hobbled along to a garden bench. I noticed it was made of an exotic timber, teak. Definitely not a native timber. As a lifetime member, I would have to protest.

'Shit.' Sylvia grinned at me. 'The day's barely started, and already my feet are killing me.'

I eyed the shoes and her get-up. 'Where do you work?'

'Nirvana Spa. I do nails.' She held out her hands, to better display the lethal weapons springing from her fingertips. 'I can do yours if you want, but not for free.'

'I don't have any to do.'

'We'll glue on some fake ones, La Macheesma.' She studied my face. 'Fake eyelashes, too.'

I kept quiet. No need to inform Sylvia that, as far as I was concerned, my days as La Macheesma had come to a close.

'Shit.' Sylvia held back her curls to look up at the trees. 'Those birds are loud.'

'Mmm. Hey, thanks for agreeing to meet with me, Sylvia. I'd offer to pay for those shoes, but—'

'Jaymie, you couldn't afford it.' She started to smile, but then her face fell. 'I hate talking about this shit. What we're going to talk about, I mean.'

'I know.' I paused. 'Then why are you doing it?'

She looked out over the meadow. It was covered in thick black plastic, to snuff out any weed seedlings even thinking about having a life.

'Because I figured it out.' Sylvia shrugged. 'This is all about Chucha Robledo, right? I know her through work, actually. I'll bet you didn't know that. We've done a few weddings together. Quinceañeras too.'

Sylvia had caught me by surprise. 'No, I didn't know that.'

'Yeah. Chucha's nice. She referred me to some clients, good ones. I feel bad about what happened to her.'

Something occurred to me: maybe Sylvia Sanchez wasn't as tough as I thought.

'Listen, Sylvia. Wasson's your boyfriend. He's a cop. Aren't you taking a risk, talking to me?'

'Huh? I told you, Del I can handle.' She looked sideways at me and arched a heavy black eyebrow. 'I know how to keep him in line.'

'I bet you do. But your brother – he's a different matter, right? Are you afraid of him?'

'Yes and no.' She crossed her arms over her chest and scowled. 'Steve's my big brother. He's not going to like hurt me or nothing. But he wants to control me, and he can do other stuff.'

I knew I had to be cautious. I didn't want Sylvia clamming up on me. I was quiet for a moment, watching a Black Phoebe flutter through the branches of a manzanita bush.

'Other stuff? What exactly are you talking about?'

'Hey, don't worry about it. I'll deal with my brother. He likes Del and that helps. See, I was dating a guy Steve didn't like. The guy disappeared, and for three or four months after that Steve followed me everywhere. I mean *everywhere*. I couldn't get away from him.' She made a face. 'You know, I never found out what happened to that guy.'

'Steve's not going to spy on you this morning. He'd stick out like a sore thumb if he followed us in here.'

'No, this ain't his style.' Sylvia's laughter sounded like bells – brass bells – ringing out over the quiet garden. 'Anyways here's the deal. A couple of days ago I heard Steve and Del talking. We were all at my mom's place and I was helping her in the kitchen. They didn't know I could hear.'

Keep rolling, Hot Wheels, I thought. *Don't stop now.*

'They were talking about Chucha. Steve said she was fucking things up, getting in the way. That little girl, the one they're looking for? He said she's Chucha's daughter – can you believe that?'

'It's true, Sylvia. And I might as well tell you: it's my case, and I'm trying to find her for Chucha. Her name is Rosie Robledo.'

'Oh, so now I get it. That's why you wanted to talk to me.'

'Yeah.' I decided to lay my cards on the table. 'Look. I'm sure the police are involved in smuggling drugs. The thing is, I don't want anything to do with that business. All I want is to find Chucha's daughter. But it's possible the two things are connected. So maybe the cops kidnapped Rosie.'

'*What*? That's crap. I'm telling you, *no*.' Sylvia twisted around on the bench to face me. Now I saw the tough girl, the one who'd walked the dusty roads of south Texas, stepping up.

'Steve would not hurt a kid. Period. Got it? The same goes for Del. The drugs, yeah, I can see that. But kidnapping a little girl? No fucking way.'

'OK. I believe you.' The truth was, I suspected Steve Sanchez was capable of just about anything if pushed far enough. But maybe I could accept that he wasn't usually so inclined.

I decided to give my informant another prod, just to be sure. 'Sylvia? Maybe Steve or Del did take Rosie. Not to hurt her, but to protect her, you know?'

'No. Absolutely not.' She folded her arms across her chest and assumed an expression of defiance. But now Hot Wheels Sanchez didn't look all that sure.

I steered Blue Boy into the empty carport space behind 101 West Mission. The Santa Barbara Investigation Agency was at long last operating in the black, and Gabi had decided we could afford to add a parking spot to our lease. Most of the time her big old station wagon filled it, but this was a Sparkleberry morning and Gabi was out swirling up the dust.

As I lifted my Schwinn from the Camino's bed, my office neighbor pulled in beside me. 'Morning,' she trilled. Always pleasant on the surface, Repo Woman indulged in her dark side at work.

'How's Deadbeat? Haven't seen him out lately.'

'Too wet and cold for my lil chick. He's tucked up inside the office with a heating pad. Say, you've had some weird types around the place lately.'

I bounced my bike down on its tires. 'Are you talking about my clients, Val?'

'Maybe.' Repo Woman pouffed up her bouffant of split ends. 'Let's see, there was the woman that's a man, I've seen that one around a few times. Then there was the wetback hiding in the bushes. And last night there was the tough guy, lounging on your back patio.'

I swung my leg over the bike. 'Somebody was hanging around my office last night?'

'Yeah. I said I'd call the cops if he didn't clear off, and he told me he is a cop and to mind my own business. Don't know if I believed him.'

'Did he have an accent?' But I was pretty sure I already knew.

'Southern. Maybe Texas. Yeah, he was Mexican but he sounded like a tough-talking Texan. Anyway, I gotta go. First of the month coming up, and I'm freakin' busy this week.'

'Business is booming, huh Val? Lots of families to toss out in the street?'

'You mean scum, Zarlin. Deadbeats, leaches. At least I'm knocking them back instead of helping them stay out of jail.'

Surely this was one issue I didn't need to take on, not today. 'No doubt there's a need for your – ah – services.'

'That's right. Somebody's got to do it and whadaya know, I'm the one.' Repo Woman slammed her car door and strode off, into the breach.

So. Steve Sanchez was taking notice of me. That wasn't good, though it was interesting. My brain was whirling and I needed to talk, but Gabi wouldn't be back till late in the afternoon.

I set my bike on its old-fashioned stand, opened the Camino's passenger door and fished around in the glove box for the fresh sack of horehound candy I'd purchased. I tucked the bag inside my jacket, hopped on my bike and tooled on down the drive.

SEVENTEEN

I turned left on Mission and pedaled down State to the water. Then I turned right. I spotted Charlie's van from a distance: except for the Great American Novel, the Leadbetter lot was empty today.

I could hear Charlie's hacking cough from the far end of the beach lot. I wove my bike through the piles of seaweed and sand stranded by the latest storm and pulled up at the van.

'Charlie? It's Jaymie.'

The coughing ceased. Then it started up again as a scarred hand tugged at the ancient hopsack curtain and slid open the aluminum window. 'Jaymie?' *Hack, hack.* 'Jaymie, that you?'

'Yeah, it's me. Sounds like we need to get you back to the doc. You don't want to develop pneumonia again.'

'No docs, Jaymie. I told ya. All they do is put you in the hospital, then ya die. Hold on a minute, will ya?'

I heard a mighty nose-blow. 'Coffee?'

'What, with a dose of pneumonia germs? I'll pass.'

'Ya sissy. Germs is good for ya. That's what's wrong with kids today, it's the truth. Haven't you heard? Kids don't get dirty enough anymore.' Another round of hacking ensued. 'Why, I see these parents here at the beach. Always fussing, cleaning the kids. And the kids, they get a little dirty and bawl about it.'

I tugged the sack of horehounds from my inside jacket pocket and poked the offering through the curtain.

'Bless ya, Jaymie, bless ya.'

'So, you were saying. The new generation is puny and weak.'

'Aw, no. I'm exaggeratin'.' Several sucking sounds. 'Naw, I sound like an old fart. People don't change much.'

I stared out to the gray sea. A low fog obscured the islands. 'They don't, do they? Any improvements you think you see are nothing but varnish.'

'Jaymie? You don't sound so chipper today. It's the missing baby, right? But maybe ya don't want to talk. Last time you was here, I got the idea you don't trust me no more.'

I watched a fishing boat fight its way through the waves. A ragged scarf of gray birds trailed behind. 'Charlie, come on. I trust you if I trust anybody. But . . . maybe that's not saying much.'

'You got something on your mind, spit it out. Else why did you come down here? It's not exactly sun-bathin' weather.'

'Chucha Robledo. Did you hear?'

'Not a thing. Been pretty much keepin' the window shut lately.'

'She's up in Cottage, Charlie. She was beaten up bad. Brain damage. And I'm pretty sure it was the police.'

Charlie was quiet. In the silence I could hear a sea lion barking. It seemed to be voicing some kind of complaint.

'I'm sorry, Jaymie. Sorry to hear it. That's real bad.'

'And that's not all. It was Gabi's boyfriend, Angel, who ratted on Chucha to the cops.'

'What did he wanna go and do that for?'

'He wanted to get Chucha deported. If you can believe it, Charlie, he says he did it for her daughter's sake. He didn't think Chucha would be a good parent.'

'What the hell do you do with a idjit like that. Tell me somethin, Jaymie. What does the cowboy think about all this?'

'Mike's still not back.' I felt a pang of worry but pushed it aside. 'I'm on my own.'

'Got any ideas?'

'Yeah. But they don't add up.'

'But you are takin' a look at the ones who protect and serve.'

'First on my list. Everyone keeps telling me cops would never kidnap a kid. The thing is, though, they're involved in the marijuana smuggling. I'm sure of that. And who's to say what they'd do if they thought their enterprise was threatened? Not all of them, no. Not even most of them. But it would only take one.'

'Tell me somethin'. The little one that died on the way across. How do you think she figures in the story?'

'Oh God, I don't know. I honestly don't.' I slipped my hood over my head and drew the strings. 'It's cold down here, Charlie. Not where you should be hanging, not with that bark.'

Charlie waved my comment away. 'Anything else botherin' ya?'

'There is something,' I admitted.

'Figured as much. Shoot. If ya trust me, that is.'

I ignored his dig. 'It's about a woman named Laura Brautigan. She's a priest. A Catholic priest.'

'You're pullin' my leg.'

'No, I'm not. It's a long story.'

'Wait a minute—' Charlie took time out to cough. Then I heard the crinkling of cellophane as he unwrapped another horehound drop. 'Is that the one we call Sister Laura? Gives out sandwiches down here a couple days a week? Real pretty long silver hair, looks a little bit like an angel.'

'Yeah. She's the one.'

'You gonna try and tell me she kidnapped the little girl? Sister Laura's the last one I'd pick.'

'I know. But she's got a record, Charlie. A record for kidnapping.'

'What? All I can say is, it musta been for a good cause. Sorry, I'm not budging on this. I know a little somethin' about people, don't forget.'

'Yeah. I can't disagree with you.' I turned and looked back down Cabrillo Boulevard. The hotel parking lots were mostly empty. A Mission Linen truck had pulled up in front of one, the Seaside Motel. A man in a white uniform and cap scurried out of the motel office. He was bent double under a huge sack of dirty laundry.

'What about clues,' Charlie was saying. 'Good old-fashioned clues, ya know? Got any a those?'

'There's the dragon fruit, I guess.' I shrugged. 'Don't know how that fits in. And the silver cross. Other than that, not much.'

'Then here's what you gotta do. Peel your eyes for what looks outta place. Kinda funny or odd. Jaymie? You're maybe trying too hard to figure things out.'

'Just the facts, ma'am?'

'You got it. Now, as it happens I got something myself to run by ya. Something I been thinking about ever since you dropped by the other day.'

'Shoot.'

'It's gonna rock ya. Are you ready to hear it?'

'Come on, Charlie. You've got my attention.'

'See, I was thinking about Brodie. Then I thought about Sideview, what he saw out there at More Mesa. And I got to wondering.' Charlie stopped to cough. 'Wondering if your brother didn't see something like that too.'

My chest tightened. 'You mean the panga boat, don't you.'

'That's what I mean all right. Now Brodie, he was a quick one. If Brodie saw something like that, he'd figure it out. Off meds like he was, he coulda said something about it. Coulda? No, woulda. To somebody he shouldn't.'

I wasn't guarding myself. Tears sprang to my eyes.

'Jaymie, come on. You ain't crying, are ya?'

'No way. What good would that do?'

'Maybe I shouldn't a told ya. Anyway, it's just a wild idea.'

'No.' I swung a leg over my bike. 'No, Charlie. It's more than that.'

As I pedaled out of the lot, I glanced over at a dark gray older model BMW. It had pulled in while Charlie and I were talking, and parked with its nose facing away from the water. Why would someone turn his back on a 180-degree ocean view?

I tried to get a look at the person scrunched down in the driver's seat, but all I could make out was a man's head bent over a copy of the *Independent*. Was he, to use Charlie's words, 'outta place'? Maybe so: he'd caught my eye. Or maybe I was paranoid and he was just a guy who wanted a little peace and quiet.

The wind off the water had turned bitterly cold. I rode hard to warm up, over to the marina and out onto the breakwater. A row of flags snapped in the wind. Midway along, a green wave washed over the wall, dousing my right side in icy brine.

When I reached the end of the breakwater I halted, straddled my bike, and gazed out over the restless sea.

The fact was I couldn't afford to think about Brodie. I had to focus on Chucha's daughter. Later on, I promised myself. Later on I would tend to my brother.

My cell rang in my pocket. I'd barely heard the sound over the crash of the waves against the breakwater wall.

'Gabi, hey. Is something wrong?'

'Wrong? You tell me, 'cause I just got a message from you. The message said you wanted a call.'

'Huh?' I shifted the phone to my other ear. 'You'll need to speak up. The surf's running high.'

'I said you sent me a message Miss Jaymie,' she shouted. 'Not on the phone or a text or anything. The old way, from the brain.'

'From the – oh. You mean you got a message from my mind to yours.'

'That's right.' She continued to yell. 'It said to call you. And that's all I know.'

'I didn't send you a message, Gabi. But I'm glad you called.'

'See? You did send a message, even if you do not know it. Your brain sent the message, not you.'

Time to move on to another subject. 'I have stuff to tell you. When will you be back in the office?'

'Not till late. Maybe even not till the morning. I'm sorry, Miss Jaymie. But I have three houses today. And everybody is so dirty this week.'

'Gabi . . .' A gull dipped and screeled. 'I need you more than they do.' I sounded petulant, I realized, like a cranky three-year-old. 'Never mind.'

'Miss Jaymie, that sounded like a seagull. Are you down at the beach?'

'I'm on the breakwater, at the marina. I'm wet, and it's cold and miserable down here. Suits my mood.'

'But that is no good. You might get sick. Come and visit me, I'm only a few blocks away. I'm at Miss Francie's house on the Mesa. Miss Francie is the one who named her baby for a bear. The one with the husband who has a girlfriend, but Miss Francie don't want to know about it.'

'So how do you know he has a girlfriend?'

'I know 'cause I hear him talking to her on the phone all the time.'

Stupid man, assuming the maid couldn't hear. 'We need to talk in private, Gabi. It will have to wait.'

'Nobody's home. Ursula, the little bear, she is on a date. I'm not joking, Miss Jaymie. Miss Francie writes all the appointments down on the calendar. Ursula, she is one year old. But she is very popular. She has a date to play maybe four times every week.'

'OK. But first, I'm going home to get changed. Then I'll come by. What's the address?'

'1451 Las Ondas. Come to the kitchen door by the driveway, OK?'

I stopped off at Mrs McMenamin's on my way up El Balcon. When I opened the back gate I discovered Dexter and Blanca lying side-by-side on the grass, watching the clouds go by. The yard looked a little torn up.

'I hope you two have been behaving yourselves.' I saw Mrs McMenamin through her kitchen window and waved. Then I crossed the yard, opened the kitchen door and leaned in.

'I had to come back home for a minute,' I explained. 'Is Dexter driving you crazy?'

Mrs McMenamin placed a hand on her crossword. 'What? Oh my no, Jaymie. Blanca is so happy, and I love watching them play through the window. No trouble at all.'

Most likely she couldn't see what had happened to her land-scaping. 'Right. I'll come and get him at four.'

'We'll be here, dear. He and Blanca will be inside by then. It's so cold today, and I'm going to bring them in after my nap.'

'No, you can't live here,' I told Dex on my way back out through the yard. 'See you this afternoon, bud.' The wind was picking up, and I realized I was now chilled to the bone.

I pedaled hard on the hill to warm up, then dropped my bike in the breezeway. I let myself in through the front door.

It was quiet inside, cozy and welcoming. I went to my bedroom and peeled off my wet clothes. I was damp to the skin.

My injured shoulder ached and I was weary. I looked at my bed. I'd told Gabi I wouldn't be long, but what the hell. I slipped in between the sheets, doubled up my thin old pillow under my head, and curled into the hollow in my mattress.

I tried to let my worries about Rosie and Chucha go. I took in a deep breath, and with it came Mike's fragrance. I shut my eyes, and as I dozed off I thought of sunburnt grass, sweat, and hot sun.

Not long after, I woke with a start. For some reason, my muscles were tense. Then I heard it: the crunch of footsteps on the gravel drive. Farther away, down at Mrs McMenamin's, I could hear Dexter barking.

I lay still, listening. My bike was lying on its side in the breezeway, so whoever was out there would guess I was home. I was naked. Where had I left my damn clothes? They were in a pile, I realized, on the floor at the foot of the bed.

The thing was, I hadn't bothered to pull the drape across the bedroom window.

The footsteps approached around the corner of the house. If I jumped up and dove for my clothes, the prowler might see me through the bedroom window.

My head faced the window. So I saw him, when he stepped up to it. Steve Sanchez looked quite a bit like his sister, with one difference: his expression was cruel.

I watched him through partly-lifted eyelids. Sanchez stepped up to the window and cupped a hand to the glass. His eyes met mine. I just prayed he thought mine were closed.

After a minute he turned and retraced his steps. There was a heavy pounding on the front door.

I jumped out of bed and struggled into my wet jeans and T-shirt. Then I marched to the front door and threw it open. My eyes moved past the guy on my doorstep, to take in the dark gray BMW parked in my drive.

'What the fuck do you want, Sanchez?'

Surprised, I suppose, that I knew who he was, he stared at me without speaking. Then his eyes went to my chest. My shirt was damp and I'd had no time to put on a bra.

Sanchez returned his gaze to my face. When he spoke, I was the surprised one. Steve looked like a bruiser, but his voice was soft, almost feminine.

'I ask the questions, Zarlin. What the fuck are you doing, messing with my sister?'

I thought of Mike Tyson. Somehow Sanchez had figured out a way to make his girlie voice threatening, and it gave me a chill.

But Steve would have been better off appealing to my better nature. If somebody scares me, I get mad. That's just how I am.

'Mind your own fucking business. I'm on the Brawlers. If I want to talk to a teammate, that's what I'll do.'

'Don't make me laugh. You wanted info out of her, info about me. That, or you want to fuck her. Either way, Zarlin, you're way outta line.'

I realized Sanchez was inches away from shoving me into the house and roughing me up. I thought of Chucha, and wondered if this guy was her attacker. Now I *was* afraid – and pissed off.

'Why did you do it, you asshole? Chucha Robledo did nothing to you. Yeah, I know you were tipped off. And I know you beat her up.' I stepped over the threshold, hoping to make Sanchez step back. But he didn't, and I found myself nose-to-nose with a nasty-tempered pit bull.

'What, the tranny? That piece of she-it?' He tipped back his head and laughed. I was tempted to punch him in the voice box. Send that voice a few octaves higher. But the truth was, I didn't dare.

'Yeah, the tranny was getting in the way all right. Attracting too much attention. But somebody else took care of it, not me.' He grinned. 'Hey. Where's your boyfriend, Zarlin? Not around when you need him?'

'Back tonight,' I lied. 'He's been up in the forest, rounding up drug smugglers like you.'

Now all traces of amusement evaporated from Steve Sanchez's face. He leaned in close. 'The homeless freak, the one they call Sideview? I know you been talking to him. Get your nose outta my business, you hear? Or Sideview is gonna be chillin' up in Atascadero State Hospital.'

'Who the hell is Sideview?' Best to play dumb. Because of what Darren had witnessed, he was a serious threat to Steve Sanchez. I just hoped Sanchez thought I didn't know that.

'Who's Sideview? Don't play me. He's a freak, just like that other freak – Brodie. You know what happened to your brother, right?'

I felt sick. Charlie was right: Brodie had died because he'd known too much. Now for the first time I knew that for sure.

I opened my mouth, then closed it. I ordered myself to keep my eyes on the prize.

'You abducted a child, Sanchez. An innocent little girl. And another girl died on the boat, coming up from Mexico. That makes you—'

'You don't know what you're talking about, bitch. I don't hurt kids.' His soft voice twisted into a snarl. 'I'm done talking with you. Just remember what I said about Atascadero. I don't mess around.'

Before I could respond, Sanchez grabbed me by my injured shoulder. I grew faint from the pain.

'Atascadero. Or worse.' He leaned in close. So close I felt his breath on my cheek.

'That creep Sideview could end up just like your fucking brother, understand?'

EIGHTEEN

The Santa Barbara Mesa isn't a mesa, not as far as the geologists are concerned. In fact it's a marine terrace, built up over millennia from the shells and skeletons of a gazillion sea creatures.

After WWII, the GI Bill financed the construction of small two- and three-bedroom tract homes up and down the state. It wasn't

till fifty years later that Santa Barbarians noticed the tacky little
Mesa tract houses were perched over the Pacific, and thus provided
the city with its only seaside housing. There went the neighborhood
– and how.

Money dribbled into the Mesa from Los Angeles, then increased
to a gusher. One by one the bungalows began to be converted into
million-dollar-plus properties.

Number 1451 Las Ondas was one of those which had been 'done
up'. Now two-storied and roofed in blue-green copper, it loomed
over its modest neighbors. Either daddy indulged his Francie, or
hubby was a software designer.

I pedaled up the short drive, dismounted at the kitchen door and
set my Schwinn on its stand. While I waited for Gabi to answer my
knock, I looked into the backyard. A skinny lap pool, landscaped
with chocolate and lime-colored shrubs, ran the length of the back
fence. A granddaddy of a golden retriever was curled up on the
deck. He raised an eyebrow round as a penny, then shut his eyes.

'Miss Jaymie, come in. I got the coffee press on.' Gabi beamed
a welcome. Then her face fell. 'Miss Jaymie? You don't look so
good.'

'I had a visitor.'

'Not the nice kind I can see.' She took my good hand in hers
and drew me into the gleaming kitchen. Great steel appliances
loomed like cargo containers. Polished stone countertops gleamed.

'We are not gonna sit in here. See those chairs, they look nice.
But they will hurt your back.'

Gabi lifted a pair of vintage cups from a glass-fronted cupboard.
'Miss Francie, she is an artist, you know? All the cups, they are
different. Collectible. She says they have different personalities.'

I accepted my pink and red cup. 'So you've given me a cheerful
one, right?'

'Positively positive, yes.'

Gabi poured a slow steady stream of aromatic coffee into the
cups, then set them on a vintage aluminum tray. 'Miss Francie, she
don't cook. But she has lotsa parties and she pays me to help her.
I know where to find everything in this kitchen. She don't have a
clue.'

I followed my personal assistant – and Miss Francie's personal
assistant too, it seemed – down a tiled hall.

'Walker and Zanger.' Gabi pointed at the floor. 'All the houses I work at, they got Walker and Zanger, you know?'

'Gee, I need to get some of that.'

We entered the living room. I set my cup down on a smoked glass coffee table and lowered my butt into a black leather chair. As I did so, I banged my elbow on the steel armrest.

'Fuck!' I whined. 'That hurt.'

'You can't just fall into these chairs. Like Miss Francie says, you gotta think about how you're gonna sit down, you know?'

'Yeah, yeah. Very Zen. Maybe I'll just sit on the floor.' I looked at the Walker and Zanger. 'That doesn't look so comfortable either.'

'Miss Jaymie you have to relax. Here, have a French macaron. I don't buy them for the office cause they are too much money and they aren't very big.'

'My God.' I'd just taken a bite of rapture into my mouth. 'Who needs sex?'

'What?' Gabi stopped with her macaron halfway to her mouth. 'Miss Jaymie, sometimes . . . sometimes I think you don't make no sense.'

I licked my fingers. 'I mean, with French macarons in the world . . . oh, never mind.' We were quiet for a time as we sipped our coffee laced with real cream.

'I can tell something bad happened to you, Miss Jaymie. And I know you don't want to talk about it right now, 'cause that will make you feel bad all over again.' Gabi pressed a napkin to her lips. 'I also don't want to talk about some things.'

I set my happy cup on the table. 'You mean Angel, don't you?'

'Yes. I am so angry, Miss Jaymie. Angel asked can he come and talk to you, but I told him he better stay away. And I told him to stay away from me too.' She stared at a big artsy rock on the coffee table. The rock was sitting on its own carved wood stand.

'I don't want to hate Angel, you know? Hate is bad for the one you hate and also bad for you too.'

'Yeah, hate is bad. It's best to stop hating. But forgetting? I don't know how people do that.'

'Let's not talk about Angel, Miss Jaymie.' Gabi waved a hand in the air. 'Please tell me even if you don't want to say it. What is wrong?'

'Plenty. I don't know where to start.'

'At the beginning, not the end. That is always the best—'

The doorbell rang. At least I assumed it was the doorbell: it chimed like temple bells.

'Oh, I forgot!' Gabi jumped up and ran from the room. A moment later, she reappeared. She was dragging a large sack across the floor. A whiff of baby poo rose to my nostrils.

'It's the laundry man. I was supposed to put this on the front porch.' She disappeared into the hall, and I followed.

A guy dressed in a white cap, shirt, and pants stood in the doorway. Outside, a Mission Linen truck idled at the curb.

'Hi. Thanks, I see you've got it there.' He took the sack from Gabi and hoisted it to his shoulder.

I walked up to the open doorway and watched the laundry guy walk down the front path to the truck. Even after the truck had driven away, I stood there gazing into thin air. My mouth was open, I realized. I closed it.

Charlie was right: the clue was there all along. I hadn't recognized it. Just like Charlie said, the clue was the thing that was out of place.

Who used laundry services, besides commercial establishments?

People with babies, that's who. The dirty diaper brigade.

'Miss Jaymie? Is something wrong?'

'Gotta run!' Then I was off, racing around the corner of the house. With one hand I righted my bike, then kicked up the stand. I sailed down Las Ondas, in hot pursuit of the laundry truck.

I caught up with the guy at Shoreline Park and slammed to a stop beside his open door. The laundry man was pale, young, with a long aesthetic nose and a prematurely receding hairline. He was taking a break from his duties, leaning back in the driver's seat and reading a paperback.

'Hi! Say, I have a question for you. Does your route cover Hope Ranch?'

He could have been the type who'd have told me to mind my own business. But he wasn't that type. He was no doubt underemployed, bored stiff, and as it turned out, he was only too happy to gab.

'No, but my friend's route does. Why do you ask?'

Might as well do this the right way. I pulled a damp card from my jeans coin pocket and handed it over.

'Jaymie Zarlin, Santa Barbara Investigations. Wow, a PI.' He set his book facedown on the dash and grinned at me. 'I'll give you

Enrique's number. And ask me anything you want, investigator. Anything at all.'

I parked Blue Boy in the Arroyo Burro lot, trudged through the dry sand past the Boathouse Restaurant, and headed west. The tide was out and the beach was deserted. Evening approached, and a cold wind whipped in off the water. I zipped my sweatshirt to my chin and jammed my hands in my pockets.

It didn't take me long to arrive at the Hope Ranch beach, maybe ten minutes at most. Another ten minutes farther to the west was the beach below More Mesa, where the panga boat had landed. The puzzle was beginning to fit together.

Rosie's abductor, according to Darren, had grabbed her out of the boat and set off jogging east, down the beach. I was willing to bet my life on it: carrying Rosie, he'd left the beach at Hope Ranch, heading inland through the cut in the cliffs.

Following in what I now believed were the kidnapper's footsteps, I walked up the zigzag path to the road. A woman jogged past, giving me a suspicious stare. I accelerated my stride, to make it look like I was out walking for exercise.

It took me eight or ten minutes more to arrive at Agua Azul. I moved to the far side of the road. I was careful not to step off the asphalt, concerned I'd snap a stick and alert Greco. The hound had a bark that was as loud as a lion's roar.

The big gates were locked. But the fence on the right only extended four or five yards into the steep landscaped hillside. It was just there for show.

I made it past the infinity pool and the main house, unheard and unscented. I kept going. I was headed for the garden cottage, the miniature barn. That was where I'd spotted the maid, walking in with an armload of linen.

According to Enrique, the Mission Linen guy, the frequency of his pick-ups at Agua Azul had recently doubled.

A hundred yards on I halted. From this angle I could see that the garden cottage was occupied. Light glowed in the single window facing the road. I pulled my field glasses from my messenger bag and trained them on the window. All I could make out was a blank interior wall.

I continued on up the road to the parking area near Staffen Brill's office. A vehicle I didn't recognize, an old beige Honda Civic, was parked in one of the spaces.

The office windows weren't visible from the road. But I could see light emanating from this building, too: the skylight in Brill's office glowed in the dusk.

I needed a better vantage point. I moved along the path to the spot where I'd looked through the wall of bamboo and noticed the maid. Now I could see into the garden cottage window from a wider angle. Just as I raised my left hand to refocus the binoculars, I heard voices.

Someone was leaving Brill's office, saying goodbye. I retreated back along the path, up to the road, and stepped back into a big ceanothus bush.

A slim woman entered the parking area from the path. Her long silver braid glowed in the dusk. My breath caught in surprise.

Sister Laura climbed into the Honda and closed the door. She sat there for at least a minute, her head bowed. Then she turned the key in the ignition and backed out of the space.

The Honda swung around. The headlights caught me full in the face. The lacy ceanothus provided little cover, and the driver stepped on the brakes as her eyes met my own.

After a long minute the Honda continued in its arc and moved off down the road. But then it stopped, and backed up.

Laura lowered her window. She looked sad. 'Hello, Jaymie. Can I give you a ride?'

I walked around the Civic, climbed into the passenger seat and shut the door. A fresh sprig of orange blossoms was tucked into a small vase hot-glued to the dash. The car interior was filled with the sweet citrus scent.

We looked at one another. Finally, I spoke. 'We'd better move on. Brill – or whoever you were meeting with – might come out to see what's going on.'

Laura nodded. She slipped the car out of park and steered it back down the hill. 'Do you have your bike, Jaymie? Or a car?'

'I left my car at Arroyo Burro and walked in from the beach. Never mind about that. I have some questions for you.'

She nodded and stared straight ahead. 'I know you do. And you deserve answers.'

* * *

Laura pulled over at the top of Marina Drive. The ocean spread out far below us. The night was dark now. If there was a moon, it was hidden behind a cover of low cloud.

We sat close together in the small car. Too close: I rolled down my window. For a time we were silent, listening to the boom of the foghorn.

I wasn't sure how to start. After a while I just said what came to my mind. 'A close friend of mine is an attorney. He knows everything and everybody. He has a long memory, too.'

'Ah.' Laura let out a sigh. 'I suppose I knew you'd hear about it eventually. That day you came around to talk to Bernie and I, I realized you're too good an investigator not to figure it out.'

'Don't try to flatter me, Laura.'

'If you knew me better, you'd understand I wouldn't do that.'

'Maybe not. But that's what I don't get. You of all people, involved in this mess!'

She turned in her seat and looked at me. But I stared straight ahead into the dark. Laura, the priest. I felt angry, even betrayed.

'Jaymie. What are you saying?'

'Do me a favor, Laura. Don't play dumb. Brill, your old partner in kidnapping. She has Rosie there at Agua Azul. Don't try and tell me you don't know!'

'What!'

Now I did turn to face the woman. I snarled in her face. 'I can't prove it. But I'm pretty sure Brill's smuggling kids into the country for illegal adoptions. I don't know how you're involved, not yet. But I swear to God, Ms Brautigan, I'll figure it out.'

Laura's mouth opened, then shut. Her voice shook when she spoke.

'I have to take your word for it, that what you say about Staffen is true! But how could you think . . .' Her voice faltered. 'No. I do understand. How could you *not* think I had something to do with this? *How could you not!*'

'I just saw you, Laura. Coming out of Brill's office.' But a tiny worm of doubt squirmed in my brain.

'Jaymie, please let me explain. Staffen asked me to come out and meet with her. She wanted to talk about Darren. She said she had a way to help him at last.'

'Darren?' *The same Darren, of More Mesa?*

'Darren Hartek. He was . . . well . . . I might as well say it. He was the boy I tried to help. He was the reason I was arrested.'

So it was the same Darren. This I hadn't foreseen. 'I'm listening. What did Brill have in mind?'

'Not much, as it turned out. She claims she wants to get him into some program in Bakersfield. To be honest, I didn't like the sound of it. Oh, and she asked me if I knew where he was. I think that was the real reason Staffen wanted to talk to me. To help her find Darren, I mean.'

'And do you know where he is?'

'No. I hand out sandwiches every weekday to the homeless, in different locations. But I haven't seen Darren for months now. He's homeless himself, you see. I've tried again and again to help him over the years, but never succeeded. He has schizophrenia, poor man.'

'So your great rescue attempt didn't help him at all.'

'I'm afraid not. Sometimes I think it made matters worse for him. That's a burden I'll carry for the rest of my life.'

'They're after him, you know. They're after Darren. Because he saw something he shouldn't have.'

'Who is *they*? Jaymie, I don't have a clue what you're talking about.'

I opened the car door and stepped out into the night. My gut was telling me Laura Brautigan was innocent. I needed to calm down, so my mind could accept that fact.

She got out of the car and walked over to me. We stood there side-by-side, listening to the waves crash on the rocks far below.

I realized I had a choice: I could trust this woman or not. I decided on a middle path.

'OK, here it is. A ring of cops have been smuggling in marijuana from Mexico, most likely for some time. But that's not the only thing they're smuggling. They're trafficking in children.'

'Dear God! So Staffen Brill – you're saying she's part of this?'

'Yes. And I thought you were too.'

'I would never do such a thing, *never*. Jaymie, you have to believe me.'

'Yeah. I guess I do.'

'Good. That's a start. Now, how does Darren fit into all this? Staffen and I haven't discussed him for years. It can't be a coincidence that she wants to connect with him now, can it?'

'Darren witnessed something that incriminates the police. They have him in their sights.' I thought about Steve Sanchez's threat to send Darren on a one-way trip to Atascadero, and decided not to say anything more. The fewer people who knew where Darren was and how he was involved, the safer he'd be.

'That's bad news. Jaymie, tell me, how can I help? There must be something I can do.'

'I'm not sure yet. Just keep all this to yourself.'

'I will. And if you think of something, anything, give me a call. Even if I need to break the law.'

I looked over at her. 'You're something of a transgressor, aren't you, Rev?'

'I try to make sure it's not just my ego.' She smiled a little. 'You know, Jaymie, He works His will in surprising ways.'

NINETEEN

'Are you a close friend?'

A note of urgency in the nurse's voice alerted me. I rested my hand on Chucha's motionless wrist and looked up from the bed. 'Yes. I care a lot about her.'

'She has no known relatives. The hospital tried to locate someone in Mexico. But I'm not really sure . . .' She smoothed a gray strand of hair at her temple.

'How hard they've tried?'

The nurse pursed her mouth and nodded.

'Well, I can tell you where Chucha's from: Lake Chapala, outside of Guadalajara.'

'Thanks, I'll let them know that. It might . . . slow down the process.' She turned to go.

'Wait. Slow down what process?' I rose from the bedside chair.

The nurse clasped her hands and gave me a long look. 'It's not something I'm supposed to talk about. Except with relatives.'

But she wanted to tell me, that much was clear. 'Look, this sounds important. Can't you at least give me a clue?'

'Just – this.'

The nurse walked over to the wall, bent down over a wall socket, and yanked out an imaginary plug.

* * *

'Gabi, get over here to Cottage Hospital right away. Drop whatever you're doing – and make it quick.'

'What, is it Chucha? Is she getting bad?'

'She's stable. But they're planning to pull the plug.' I didn't want to talk about organ harvesting. Christ, I didn't even want to think about it.

'To – what? Oh no! They can't do that!'

'They claim they've looked for Chucha's relatives and haven't been able to locate them. But I'm not sure they've even tried.'

'Miss Jaymie, I am thinking fast. Now I gotta ask you a question. A hard one, OK?'

I sat down on a bench outside the hospital. Time was of the essence, and I felt the urge to move on. But I knew by the tone of Gabi's voice that I'd better comply.

'Here's what I want you to tell me. For Chucha, what do you think is the best thing to do?'

I knew what Gabi meant. And I knew her question was the right one to ask.

'I want her to hold Rosie in her arms. And—' I had to stop and swallow hard. 'And I want Rosie to see her mom. I want to take a picture, Gabi, of the two of them together. Something for Rosie to have when she's older. Do you see what I mean?'

The phone was quiet. I looked at the lunchtime stream of people ambling along the sidewalk: doctors in scrubs, moms and kids, an old man with a walking frame.

'Yes. I see what you mean. OK, I am ready. What can I do?'

'Come over here right away. Tell them you're Chucha's aunt. If you have to, Gabi, lie through your hat. In the end they might figure out the truth, but we're just trying to buy time.'

'I understand. But not the part about the hat.'

'Forget the hat, it's not important. Now, one more thing.'

'Shoot me.'

'Don't you mean "shoot"?'

'Miss Jaymie, just tell me. What is the one more thing?'

'Angel. I need to find him fast, before it gets dark.'

'Angel? But Miss Jaymie, you know what he did!'

'I can't explain now. Just tell me how to get hold of him.'

'Maybe I still got his work schedule in my phone,' she admitted. 'I'm gonna hang up now and send you a text.'

'Thanks. I'll meet up with you later today in the office. Then I'll explain.'

'OK. 'Cause I don't know what you are doing, talking to Angel. You got a real good reason, I hope.'

I spotted Angel's beat-up old pickup on Serena, a quiet street in the Samarkand neighborhood near the Lawn Bowling Club. I pulled up behind the truck and switched off the engine.

An ember of anger still smoldered inside me when I thought about what Angel had done. But I needed him, and I had to get over my emotion. I had to do it for Rosie's sake.

I got out of the Camino and slammed the door shut. Gabi hadn't known the exact address, just that on Wednesday afternoons Angel worked for a Mr Ishida on Serena. But it was obvious this was the house.

The front yard was an exquisite Japanese garden, sculpted and raked to perfection. I walked along a series of wide flat river stones, through an open bamboo gate to the back.

Angel stood beside a massive red-leaf Japanese maple. He held a pair of small clippers in his hand. He bent down to check the angle of an errant twig, then clipped it. I watched as it tumbled to the ground.

Angel straightened and looked across the yard at me. As I approached, he dropped his gaze.

'Angel. I want to talk.'

'Thank you for coming over, Miss Jaymie.' He slipped the clippers into a loop on his belt. 'Mr Ishida's daughter came to take him to a doctor's appointment. So we are alone.'

I nodded and waited. It wasn't my place to begin.

'I did something wrong. I made a terrible mistake.'

'Why, Angel? Why did you do it?'

'There is something I must explain. I will tell you, but it is not an excuse.' His arms fell to his sides.

'My mother, she was a very bad mother. She was a . . . puta, and she used heroìna. I'm not complaining, other people have the same problem. But I thought about that little girl, how she was going to be adopted, maybe into a rich family. And I thought maybe Chucha would not treat her that good.'

'It was none of your business. Besides, you were wrong.'

'I know now. And the police – why did I trust them? That was so stupid. I am a stupid man.'

'Angel? It can't be undone.'

'No.' He made several gasping sounds. Angel was struggling not to cry. 'I never thought they would hurt her! I feel sick when I think about what they did.'

'Chucha is going to die.'

He walked away to the back of the garden and stepped behind a hibiscus hedge. I heard him break into sobs.

I waited for some time. Then, when the sound of crying had stopped, I followed after him.

Angel stood at a low fence, looking out across the city to the terra cotta mountains. 'What can I do?'

'I'll tell you why I'm here, Angel. The fact is I could use your help. I want to ask you to help Chucha's daughter.'

He turned to look at me. There was a glimmer of hope in his eyes. 'Yes. Whatever it is, I will do it.'

I saw I was throwing him a lifeline, a way to redeem himself. And why not? I didn't like to think of the bad mistakes I'd made in my own life.

'All right. There's an estate in Hope Ranch called Agua Azul. Do you know where it is?'

'Yes. A guy who used to work with me, he's on the landscaping crew that has that job.'

'Here's the story.' But I paused. How much should I say? It was all very well to give Angel a second chance. But Rosie's life could depend on what happened next. Once again, I opted for a middle road.

'It's possible the owners are holding Chucha's daughter at Agua Azul. I could be wrong, but I don't think so. I can't get near the place – they know me. I need you to get onto the grounds, Angel, and take a good look around.'

'I'll talk to Jorge. I can pretend to be a new person on his crew.'

'Good. I'm hoping the owners won't notice you at all, but if they do, you'll have an excuse for being there. Now, in a minute we'll go back to my car, and I'll draw you a map of the estate. But there's something I have to warn you about.'

'I'm listening.'

'Angel, Gabi told me you're afraid of dogs.'

I had to hand it to the man: he squared his shoulders. 'Yes, that is true. But don't worry, it is my problem.'

'The dog's name is Greco, and he's a beast. Most of the time he's shut in the house, but not always.'

'Miss Jaymie? I will handle it. This is what I must do.'

'Here Miss Jaymie, drink this.' Gabi handed me a steaming mug of strong tea. 'I'm warming up a hot towel in the oven to put on your shoulder.'

'It hurts like a son-of-a-bitch.'

'Like a son of what? No, never mind.'

'It sounds like it went OK at the hospital.' I cupped both hands around the mug and took a sip.

'Yes, I think so. I do not know if the man believed me when I told him I am Chucha's tia. But he's gotta, you know, look into it. And I told him I am coming back to visit Chucha again tomorrow.'

'That's all we can do for now.'

Gabi pulled her chair around from behind the desk. Then she sat down and looked at me. 'About Chucha. I saw her and I got something to say.'

I set down the mug and looked out at the gray afternoon.

'Miss Jaymie, Chucha is already gone. She is not gonna come back.'

In the silence I could hear the *brr* of the old electric clock on top of the bookcase. 'But you know what I told you. I just want Rosie to . . .'

'Yes, I know.' Gabi reached forward and patted my hand. 'But even for Rosie, I do not think we should wait too long.'

I knew she was right. But this wasn't the time for me to dwell on the matter. 'Message received.'

Gabi folded her hands in her lap. 'OK. Now I'm gonna ask you about Angel. I don't wanna talk *about* him. But I wanna know what happened today.'

'We talked. I explained some of what's going on, but not all of it. I asked him if he'd go over to Agua Azul and look around, to see if he could find out if Rosie is there.'

She studied her hands. 'So what did he say?'

'He said yes. He was glad I asked. He's already there. We're going to touch base at around four p.m.'

'Did you tell Angel about the mean dog?'

'I did.'

'And he said yes even after he heard about it?'

'Yep. I'll say this for the guy. He wants to do the right thing.'

I was surprised to see Gabi's eyes well with tears. 'Angel is a good person in his heart. Sometimes, he don't think so good.'

'He needs you to help him with that.'

'Yes. That is why it is sad I'm not gonna see him no more.'

I was too smart to chime in on that topic. I drank down my cooling tea.

After a minute, my cell vibrated on the corner of the desk. I grabbed it and saw I'd received a text. It was from Angel, and I read it aloud:

> *Miss Jaymie – I just heard a little kid cry. It came from the shed you told me to watch, the one like a barn. I will keep watching till you tell me what to do next.*
>
> I texted back: *Good news. Keep watching as long as you can. Remember the dog.*
>
> A text flew back: *I am ready for the dog. I am going to stay here when it gets dark. Then I can see in the window when the lights go on.*

I looked up at Gabi. 'Sounds like Greco better keep an eye out.'

She frowned. 'Like I said. It is too bad I am never gonna see Angel again.'

I turned in early. I was anxious to hear from Angel, but I was exhausted and needed to grab a few hours of sleep. I set the phone on my bed stand and dialed the ring volume up to the max.

'No barking at critters tonight, understand?' I wagged a finger at Dex. 'I don't care if the raccoons boogie on the roof. Do not wake me up.'

I felt like I'd just dozed off when Dexter woke me with a deep nasty growl. I fought through the gauzy curtains of sleep and sat up in the bed. 'Dog, this better be good.'

By the time I'd thrown on a dressing gown Dexter had opened the throttle. His loud barks made my ears ring.

I opened the front door, and the three-legged heeler bolted off the threshold, clearing the steps in one bound. He messed up on the landing, but hopped back to his feet and raced over to the Camino. I'd left it parked outside the car shed, in case I needed to take off in the night.

I stepped back inside, grabbed a flashlight off the kitchen counter, and walked down the steps in my bare feet. I was glad to see that Dexter was silent now. The last thing I needed was for the heeler to bail up a skunk under my car.

The night was dark, the air oppressive. The temperature had risen, and it felt like rain. I shined the light over the steep bank behind my house. There were rustlings in the undergrowth, but they were small rustlings, sounds made by rodents or cats.

'Whatever it was, it's gone now. Let's go in.'

I raised my voice and repeated my command: 'Dexter, come!'

But the dog continued to circle the car.

Wary, awake now, I approached. I shined the light under the car, bending down to check: nothing. Then I stepped right up to the Camino and peered in. The vehicle was empty and the doors were locked.

I straightened up and glanced at the windshield. A flyer was slipped under a wiper. I circled the Camino and stared at the paper. It was folded in half.

It was just a sheet of paper. It wasn't going to bite.

I transferred the flashlight to my left hand and removed the page with two fingers. Then I flipped it open.

It was a mug shot from the Santa Barbara PD.

There was no name. There didn't have to be. I recognized Darren Hartek, and I recognized the sheer terror in his eyes.

'Fuck them. Fuck them to hell!' The paper was shaking as I bent close to read the date and time. *Feb. 23, 10:30 PM.*

Rage is one thing. It can compel you to action. But rage coupled with impotence is something else. It burns you from the inside out.

I stood in the dark for what seemed like an eternity. Five minutes passed, maybe more. Then I went back inside and shut the door.

My brain was jumping as I heated a cup of milk on the stove. Anything to calm myself down. Because the one thing I knew was that I must not go off half-cocked.

I heard my cell ring in the bedroom. I ran for it, nearly knocking over the nightstand as I lunged. Sure enough, it was Angel.

'Angel. What's going on?'

'Something's gonna happen.' His voice was little more than a whisper, and I had to strain to hear his words. 'All the lights are on in the shed. Two people are walking around in there. I don't see the little girl, but I hear her crying. What do you want me to do?'

'Go home now. Get out of there without being seen. What about the guard dog?'

'Miss Jaymie, I am sorry for the dog. But it died very fast. It did not suffer, I promise you.'

Yikes. 'Angel, was that really—'

'Miss Jaymie, I decided. The little girl, she is important. Not the dog.'

I was taken aback, but there was no time to dwell on it. I needed to get to Rosie, and fast.

TWENTY

In fact I had no clear plan. I only knew I could not allow Staffen Brill to move Rosie to another location. If she did so I might never find Chucha's daughter again.

But I had to do something about Darren. I couldn't get that mug shot out of my mind.

'Hello, Jaymie? Is that you?'

'Laura, I need you to do something. I know it's two in the morning. But they've arrested Darren Hartek. They've arrested him to get at me.'

Laura was quiet. But I was in a big rush and couldn't wait for her if she wasn't onboard. 'All right, if you can't help—'

'No Jaymie, I can. I'm thinking. What should I do?'

'Go down to the jail. Ask to see Darren. Try to find out what trumped-up charges they've arrested him on. Make as much noise as you can, Reverend Laura. They'll be more careful, I think, if they know you're concerned.'

'I'll go right away. I'll camp out in the lobby if I have to. Jaymie? Thank you for trusting me.'

'Yeah. I seem to be trusting everyone these days.'

'Is it paying off?'

'So far.'

'Good. In my case, you've made the right decision. Now, whatever it is you're about to do, take care and God bless you.'

I stuffed the cell in my pocket, called Dex inside and shut the door on him. The heeler protested with a series of sharp barks, but I ignored him and headed for the Camino.

Once I was rolling, I checked the time on my cell: two nineteen.

I told myself not to speed. No one was out at this hour but me and a few cops, and the last thing I needed was to get pulled over. I curved down El Balcon, and a minute later was traveling west on Cliff Drive.

I tried to work it all through in my mind. I was sure Angel was right: Brill was preparing to move Rosie. Did Brill feel pressured? Sanchez had sworn he had nothing to do with any abduction. Yet somehow Brill must have been alerted.

Babies and cops and drugs and attorneys. Darren Hartek . . . Steve Sanchez . . . and my brother. How did the lines connect?

I jumped out of my skin when the cell jangled. I'd forgotten to dial down the volume. I pulled over at the bottom of Cliff, near Las Positas, and slammed the Camino into park.

I saw the name on the cell. At that moment, everything else was wiped from my mind.

It was after two a.m., and Trudy Freitas was phoning me. It could only be about Mike.

'Trudy. What's wrong?'

'Mike is – Jaymie, he's going to be OK.'

I could tell by the sound of her voice that Mike was not OK, not at all.

'Trudy, tell me. What's happened?'

'They brought him out in a helicopter.' She began to cry. 'I'm at Sierra Vista Hospital, and I just talked to a doctor. Jaymie, Mike was shot.'

'What?' I'd heard what she'd said. But my brain had turned to Teflon: it repelled the news. Somehow I couldn't, or wouldn't, take it in.

'You've got to come up here, Jaymie. They're going to operate in a few hours.'

'Operate?' I heard my own voice as if it were coming from somewhere outside me.

'Jaymie, can't you hear what I'm saying? Mike got shot in the back!'

Mike was shot in the back. They were going to operate. At last reality burned its way in. 'Just tell me one thing. Is Mike going to be all right?'

'He's – he's not going to die. The doctor told me that for sure. He said that, Jaymie.'

'Good. Thank God. Trudy . . . what aren't you saying?'

'The bullet. It's lodged in his spine. They used the words "possible paralysis". So far that's all I know.'

I sat there in the dark cab, blocking out the fear. I knew I wasn't accepting what I'd just heard. It would be hours, or even days, before I let myself understand.

'Trudy, listen to me. I'll be there as quick as I can.'

'Trevor's home with the kids. It's just me here. Don't take too long.'

I switched off the phone. Adrenalin pumped through my body and my heart raced. Still, I didn't drive on.

I shut my eyes and spoke aloud. 'Mike. You matter more than anything to me, and you need me. Tell me what to do now.'

I waited, and after a minute his answer flowed into my brain: *I'm in good hands for the moment. Go and do what you have to.*

'But what if—' I left the words twisting in the dark.

I'll be here waiting for you. I promise. So go.

I shifted the car into drive and stepped on the gas.

I entered Hope Ranch and parked the Camino on a dead end road not far from Agua Azul. I got out and leaned against the door, closing it with no more than a click. Even so, the click sounded like a gunshot in the dark wooded lane.

I set off with a quick stride. A nearby dog heard me and erupted into a series of alarm barks. But no lights came on. Hopefully the owner would assume the canine was yapping at a coyote or a raccoon.

A few minutes later I came to the drive leading into Agua Azul. I continued on up the hill, thankful I'd dressed all in black, and grateful too for the lush landscaping all along the road. I could fade out of sight if necessary.

The method Angel had employed to silence Greco had shocked

me. But now I had to admit it was a good thing that the guard dog was out of the picture.

Before long I was in view of Staffen Brill's office. Light streamed through the screen of shrubs and live oaks.

A Lexus was parked in the turn-out. The trunk popped open, and I melted into the landscaping as someone – a man – approached along the path and walked up to the car.

A light inside the trunk had switched on, and I could make out the guy's face as he bent forward over the opening. It was Jack Morehead, Brill's husband. Morehead carried a small overnight case. A golf bag was slung over his shoulder.

He tossed the case in the trunk, then slid the golf bag off his arm to the ground. He leaned into the trunk, shifted something, then lifted the golf bag in beside the case.

Morehead stood there for a moment. He seemed to be waiting for something. After a minute, he stepped around and opened one of the doors to the backseat. The interior light came on. He walked back to the office path, leaving the car door wide open to the night.

Maybe all this was a false alarm. Maybe this was just Jack Morehead, getting an early start on an out-of-town golf engagement.

But before I could decide what to do next, I heard angry voices. A man and woman were haranguing one another. A floodlight on a pole switched on.

Now I could make out the Lexus's license plate number. Just in case, I entered it into my phone.

Eric appeared around the corner first. He carried something heavy in his arms. My breath choked in my throat: the bundle looked like a sack of flour, but I knew what it was.

Morehead followed Eric, and hard on Morehead's heels was Brill. She held a flashlight and didn't bother to switch it off when she stepped into the pool of white light.

'I mean it, Jack. I don't like this. I'm telling you, I don't agree.'

'Knock it off, Staffen. It's under control.' He was now carrying a duffle bag, and he set it down at his feet.

'But I have somewhere for her, Jack! It just took a while, that's all. It's arranged.'

'Fuck!' Morehead stopped in his tracks and spun around, forcing Brill to take two steps back. 'The kid's got somewhere to go, see?

Don't you get it? I had it set up all along. Don't worry, Staffen, you'll get your cut.'

'What are you talking about? Jack, where is she going? Tell me. I insist.'

Eric was standing beside the car, the bundle slung in his arms. I heard a weak whimper. It was all I could do to stay put.

Morehead turned to Eric. 'Put the kid in the back. You sit there too. I'll toss your bag in the trunk.'

Eric did as he was told, and Morehead slammed the door shut after him.

'I don't like this, Jack.' But now I could hear that Brill had given up.

'Come off it, Staffen. It's a little late in the game for all this concern.' He tossed the duffle in the trunk and slammed down the lid. Then he walked around the Lexus and got into the driver's side.

Staffen Brill stepped forward, but the Lexus growled to life and dovetailed out of the space, spraying gravel. It took off down the drive.

I was desperate to run back to the Camino and follow the Lexus. But Staffen Brill stood there, staring after the car, and I'd no wish to reveal myself. Finally she took the path back to her office, and I was free to go.

I took off jogging down the hill. But I realized it was useless. By the time I reached the Camino, Morehead could be anywhere.

I halted at the bottom of the drive. I wanted to scream with frustration. Rosie was gone, bundled into a blanket. She'd been so still – most likely drugged.

No choices, damn it! Where could I turn? The cops were out of the question – I knew they were somehow involved up to their necks.

I looked up at the main house. A light switched on, and then another. Staffen Brill was inside.

I could think of one slight crack in the wall. One way in. I'd have to make the most of it – I had no other options.

'Who is it? What do you want?'

I glanced up at the security camera perched over the massive front door. Brill knew perfectly well who was standing on her porch and ringing her bell.

'Staffen. We need to talk.'

There was a moment's silence. 'What about?'

'Rosie. The little girl.'

'Go away! I don't know what you're talking about. Go away or I'll call the police.'

'No, somehow I don't think you will.'

I could have said more, much more. I could have opened my mouth and let my anger pour out. But that wouldn't have helped me to get the woman to open her damn door.

Then, it did open. A sliver. I resisted a strong urge to shove it open in her face.

'Invite me in or come out. We have to talk.'

She opened the door farther. Staffen Brill stood there in her beautiful entry hall, lined with rich hardwood stripped from a faraway rainforest. She'd changed into a ratty old bathrobe, pale green. Her gray face looked haggard under her bright auburn hair. She reminded me of a caterpillar that had begun to entomb itself in a cocoon.

'Go away, will you? I have nothing to say.' But the door remained open.

'Talk to me, Staffen. Eric and your husband – I know they have Rosie.'

'I have no idea what you mean.' She wrapped her pale green arms around her chest and stepped back from the door. In other words, she gave me my chance.

I pushed in and pulled the door closed behind us. 'Listen up. I saw them take off with Rosie in the car. I heard you try to stop them.'

'I don't know any Rosie. Why can't you leave me alone?'

No way was this barracuda coughing up the hook. 'Did you know I have connections in the sheriff's department, Staffen? The police might not move on this, but I can promise you the sheriff's department will.'

I couldn't promise any such thing, but who gave a damn? 'You wouldn't look so good in prison orange. Not a good color with that red hair.'

I saw her falter. I saw it in her eyes: the instant when Staffen Brill began to be just a little afraid.

'I don't know anything about a kid, all right? I saw Jack and Eric moving something, yes. A package, that's what it was. I tried to get Jack to tell me what . . .' Staffen Brill stopped. She gave in.

'I don't know where they've taken her, and that's the truth. You'll never find out, not now. She'll disappear. Just go.'

'There's got to be a way to figure out where they're headed. We could follow the GPS. Staffen, listen. I know you didn't intend for it to go this far. Help me and things will go better for you.'

She stared at me, shaking her head. 'GPS? Do you think my husband's that stupid?'

But I could see she'd had an idea. 'You do know something, though, don't you? You thought of something, I can tell.'

'Maybe I have.' Brill started to walk away down the hall. I didn't need an invitation to follow.

Near the end of the hall was an elevator. Brill pushed a button. 'I'll be back. You can wait here.'

'I can, but I won't.' The elevator door slid open, and I stepped in on her heels.

The space was narrow, like a coffin standing on end. The door closed and the coffin crept upwards. At one point the elevator shook a little, and the woman bumped into me. I felt a wave of revulsion at her touch.

'I didn't invite you into the house, understand me, Zarlin? You forced your way in.' We were about the same height, and Brill looked me straight in the eye. 'You came to the house and I told you to get lost. Then you came back and broke in when I was asleep.'

She was afraid, all right. But not of the police. I figured Brill was afraid of her dearly beloved.

'I'm not planning on talking.'

'But if you do, Zarlin. If you do, I'll say that's how it was.'

The elevator door opened and I followed her into a carpeted hall. We appeared to be standing in a bedroom wing of the house. Brill turned to me.

'I want to help the child. That's why I'm doing this, understand?'

I understood, all right. She wanted to help herself. Staffen Brill was playing her cards with care, strategizing like mad for a range of possible outcomes. I doubted Rosie's welfare was one of her concerns.

We walked down the corridor to a closed door. She took a step back. 'Eric keeps his bedroom locked. Go ahead, break in.'

'Eric – he lives here in the house with you?'

'My husband likes to keep the help close.' Her voice had taken on a mocking tone. 'My bedroom is on the first floor.'

What did Brill mean – that Eric and Jack Morehead were lovers?

Somehow, I couldn't see it. Maybe my intuition wasn't quite up to snuff.

'You've got a key, Staffen. Right?'

She shrugged. 'Perhaps. I can't remember.'

Fine. The bitch wanted me to break in. I reached into my messenger bag for a pick. I thought of slipping on a pair of gloves but decided against it. I was in one hell of a hurry, and besides, what did it matter now?

The lock popped in a flash. I'd broken the locking mechanism, but who cared. I was torching all my bridges behind me.

The room was austere, painted tan, trimmed here and there in dark brown. I stepped in, and Brill followed.

The furnishings were sparse. If it hadn't been for their obvious cost, the room could have been the cell of a monk. A pair of tall cabinets stood against one wall, and twin nightstands flanked a small double bed. A clothes frame in one corner held a jogging suit on a hanger.

'My, Eric is tidy.' I walked over to one of the cabinets: three silver-framed pictures had caught my eye.

'Oh, yes. Eric is impeccable.'

I could hear the loathing in Brill's voice. I glanced at her in surprise. Eric was a guy she lived with, worked with, and spoke to nearly every day. And it sounded like she hated him.

I turned back to the photographs. The pictures were of three little girls. One looked to be around four years old, and the other two were perhaps five. 'Are these children relatives of his?'

Brill said nothing. The silence was heavy in the room.

I like to think I'm fast on the uptake. But when new information is something I'd rather not know, it can take ages for the penny to drop. I continued to study the photos.

The little girls didn't look at all alike. You could see they weren't sisters.

'You know all about this, don't you, Staffen? You've been in this room before.' I lost my cool. 'Goddamn it, answer me!'

'I have no idea what you're talking about. But if you go over to the chest of drawers on the right, you'll discover that the trim on the bottom is camouflaging a drawer. There's something in there. Something you are welcome to take away with you, as far as I'm concerned.' Her eyes slid away. 'None of this is my doing. None of it. Do you understand?'

'You let it happen, Brill. You must have known what Eric and your husband were up to.'

'I know what they *are*, if that's what you mean. It disgusts me. But believe it or not, I only found out tonight that they had plans for the child.'

'You know, I don't get it. Your husband isn't exactly hurting for cash. Why? Why the hell would he do something like this?'

Brill started to walk to the doorway. Then, just when I thought she'd spoken her last word to me, she turned back.

'Jack doesn't care about money, not really, except that it gives him power. He's a puppet master. He's only happy, even in that dirty little world of his, if he's pulling all the strings.'

'You're a bit of a puppet master yourself, Brill.'

'Maybe so.' She shrugged. 'But Jack is sadistic. You can't say that about me. He's only satisfied if he's causing somebody pain.'

She turned on her heel and disappeared into the hall.

I knelt down and ran a hand under the trim. It slid sideways to reveal a drawer that was no more than four inches high.

The drawer was locked. I wasn't in the mood to mess around. I grabbed it by the bottom edge with both hands, propped my feet against the dresser, and pulled. With a graunching sound, the drawer came away.

Inside was a laptop. I grabbed it and jumped up to go. Then I stopped. This wasn't just about Rosie, I knew that by now.

I set the laptop on the bed and lifted down the three frames from the dresser. One by one, I removed the photos. Then I opened the laptop, laid the photos flat on the screen, and closed it up again.

I ignored the elevator and hurled myself down the staircase. Staffen Brill was standing outside on the porch, calling for Greco. Peering into the black night.

It was the fastest turnaround I'd performed in my life. I didn't allow myself to debate, just raced the Cam home, grabbed Dexter, and drove downtown to the office.

I pulled up at the curb in front of the bungalow court, snatched up Eric's computer and jumped out. 'Wait here, bud. I'll be right back.'

The courtyard was dark, lit only by a porch light left on by the repo woman. I unlocked my office door, slipped in and locked it behind me. I checked that the blinds were all closed, then switched on a light.

I didn't bother with the safe. I couldn't recall the latest combination at the best of times, and I knew there was no way I'd remember it now.

Instead I raised a cushion on the craigslist couch, placed the laptop on the crumb-strewn base, and dropped the cushion back in place. On the spur of the moment, I hurried into the kitchenette, picked up a pile of papers stacked on my work table, and spread them over the couch. That would have to do.

I jogged back through the courtyard to the street, jumped into the Camino, and continued down Mission to the freeway. I hit 101 heading north.

TWENTY-ONE

The highway was quiet, almost dead empty. It was all I could do not to press my foot to the floor. Twenty minutes later, I picked up my cell and punched in a number.

'Gabi. It's me.'

'Miss Jaymie?' Her voice was blurred with sleep. 'Is something wrong?'

'Everything. Everything's wrong.' I stopped myself. Just speaking to Gabi made me let go, allowing the tears to form.

'Miss Jaymie. Come over to my place.' She sounded wide awake now. 'I hear you, I know you gotta talk.'

'I can't. I'm on the freeway heading north, to San Luis Obispo. Mike's in the hospital. He was . . . he was *shot*.'

'Shot? You mean with a gun?'

Under any other circumstances, I'd have smiled. 'Yes. With a gun.'

'Oh no! Tell me, please tell me – how bad?'

'He was shot in the back. In his spine. He's not in critical condition, they said he's stable, but they've got to operate. They're going to do it right away.'

As I said these words aloud, I realized they didn't make sense. The doctors were acting fast to remove the bullet – did they really see his condition as stable? They didn't know, and that was a fact.

'Miss Jaymie, you are driving right now?'

'Yeah. I just passed Buellton.'

'Slow down. I know you, Miss Jaymie, I'm saying slow down. One thing you can do for Mr Mike, is not get into a crash.'

I eased off on the accelerator. She was right. 'I've got a lot to tell you but it can wait. One thing that can't: I want you to phone Claudia. The two of you need to get over to the office quick as you can.'

'OK I will, but tell me why. Claudia's gonna wanna know why I call her in the middle of the night.'

'It's a long story, Gabi. But we need her tech skills. You know how good she is at breaking through passwords.'

'Yes I do.'

'I've hidden a laptop under a cushion on the couch. I need her to open it up, quick as she can.'

'OK. What is she s'posed to look for?'

'Anything. Everything. This has to do with Rosie. They've got her, Gabi. Eric and Morehead. They're moving her on from Agua Azul. And I've got to find out where they're taking her.'

'OK. A computer. Where did it come from?'

'It belongs to Eric, the guy who works for Staffen Brill.'

'Agua Azul – I gotta ask, did Angel help you?'

'He did. Maybe we should think about forgiving him.'

'Maybe. Forgiving, that's a good thing to do. But forgiving is only one thing, Miss Jaymie. Remember what you said? You can't make your head to forget.'

Dawn was just breaking as Dex and I pulled into the hospital parking lot in San Luis. An angry red line ran along the murky horizon.

As I switched off the engine my phone dinged, announcing a text. I peered at it: Claudia. *Call me as soon as you can.*

I let Dex out of the Cam. The heeler plunged into the flower beds, chasing down scents. I phoned Claudia, and she picked up on the first ring.

'Jaymie, what's this all about? I'm in the computer. All I see are some lists of names, and a few pictures of little kids.'

Pictures of kids. *Shit*! In all the confusion, I'd done something incredibly stupid. 'Are the photos head shots?' I held my breath.

'Yeah, head shots. They look like school photos, you know?'

Thank you, dear God. There could have been anything on that computer, including photos I'd never have asked Claudia to look at.

'Jaymie?' she prompted. 'So, what's this about?'

'I think we may be looking at lists of pedophiles.'

'*What?*' There was a long moment of silence. 'What they do, those guys, to little kids – I really don't . . . don't even want to think about it. But I want to help!'

'You are helping. I can't do this without you.' I watched an ambulance creep up the road. Its lights were flashing, but there were no sirens. The scene was painted in the lurid colors of the dawn.

'Claudia, here's what I'm after. Clues, any clues you can find, as to where they've taken Rosie. Names, addresses, phone numbers of anyone within a three-hundred-mile radius of Santa Barbara.'

'What about the three pictures? These little girls . . .'

'We'll pass everything on to the authorities once we've got hold of Rosie. Right now you need to concentrate on the lists. Got it?'

'Got it. When are you coming home?'

I watched as the ambulance pulled into a far entrance and stopped. 'Mike's in surgery. I'll be back as soon as I can.'

'Gabi told me all about it. I hope he's going to be OK! Jaymie?'

'Yes?'

'Just . . . well, you can count on me.'

'I know I can. And I'm sorry, Claudia. Sorry I have to put you through this.'

'No, I can do it. Just come back as soon as you can.'

'Is Gabi there?'

'Yeah. She's—' Claudia managed a giggle, and at that moment I knew she'd be all right. 'Gabi's making hot chocolate. Like that's going to solve everything.'

'Good for her. Put her on.'

'Miss Jaymie? Mr Mike, how is he?'

'Trudy called fifteen minutes ago and said he's still in surgery. I'm about to go inside the hospital. The operation seems to be taking a hell of a long time.'

'Don't worry, Miss Jaymie. That just means the doctors are doing a very good job.'

'Let's hope so. Listen, about Claudia. She might need your support.'

'Yes, I heard what she said to you. I will help her, Miss Jaymie. Do not worry about that. You take care of yourself and Mr Mike, OK?'

We signed off. I saw that the back doors of the ambulance were wide open now, and two EMTs were transferring someone to a gurney. The attendants were casual in their movements, almost careless, as if they had all the time in the world. I realized that the someone must be deceased.

I called for Dexter. Then my phone rang.

'Jaymie. I just talked to the nurse. All she would say was that Mike got through it. The surgeon's coming out to talk to me in about twenty minutes. Where are you?'

'I'm here, in the parking lot. I'll be right in.'

'Jaymie, the nurse . . . she wasn't smiling.'

My heart dropped. All I could do was echo myself. 'I'll be there, Trudy. I'll be right in.'

The surgeon's limp mask dangled around his neck. I tried to read his expression but saw nothing other than exhaustion in his eyes. He shut the waiting room door behind him. 'Mrs Freitas?' He looked at me.

Trudy stood. 'I'm Trudy Freitas, Mike's sister. This is Jaymie Zarlin, my brother's partner.'

He nodded. 'Mike's resting. His condition is stable. We were able to remove the bullet.'

'Thank God,' I said. 'Can we see him?'

'Right now we have him in the recovery unit. He's going to be heavily sedated, but he should recover consciousness in an hour.' The doc hesitated, and in that moment I knew there was more to come.

'I'm not sure how much they told you before surgery.'

'They told me about the bullet. They said there was the risk of infection . . .' Trudy's words trailed off.

The surgeon raised a hand, as if he were asking us for something. 'We don't know anything for certain at this stage. But there is nerve damage. They didn't tell you about that?'

'No, they didn't.'

Trudy was the one doing the talking. I was struck dumb. My brain was focused on making connections, filling in what the doc was leaving unsaid.

'Paralysis. Is that it?' I blurted out.

I wanted him to deny it, but he didn't. In fact, the surgeon seemed grateful that I'd supplied the word.

'There will be paralysis, yes. But it's too early to say how much. The bullet had lodged in a vertebra. He shouldn't be affected above the waist.'

This was crazy! Who the hell was he talking about? *Mike*?

I could see that the surgeon wanted to move on. Trudy was silent, but I refused to let the guy go.

'Do you mean he won't be able to walk?' I heard my own voice. I sounded incredulous, as if I were going to burst into laughter.

The surgeon rubbed his face. 'It's a possibility, yes.'

It was more than a possibility. It was a probability, maybe even a certainty. Otherwise he wouldn't be bringing it up. I covered my mouth with a hand.

Mike looked too large for the bed. And even though it was winter, he looked too dark and suntanned against the white sheets. He belonged outdoors, where he spent most of his time. Not in a hospital.

'Jaymie—'

I bent down and kissed him on the lips, then placed a hand on his cheek. 'I'm here. Trudy's here, too. Take it easy, sweetheart.'

'Jaymie . . . Sis—' He was asking us a question. Trudy took half a step back.

'Mike, everything's OK,' I said. 'If you want, you can go back to sleep.'

But I could see he didn't want to sleep, not yet. 'Mike, are you asking what happened?'

His chin tipped up. He was nodding a 'yes.'

'You were up in Los Padres. Going in after a meth operation.' I stroked his cheek with my thumb. 'One of the perps shot you in the back.'

He stared at me wide-eyed, like a kid. He wanted this explanation, but I couldn't be sure how much he was taking in.

'You're safe now, Mike. They airlifted you out. They took out the bullet.' I tried to fill my voice with confidence. 'Everything's going to be fine.'

Mike closed his eyes and drifted back into sleep. It had bothered me to lie. No matter what had happened between us, we'd always told one another the truth.

'I don't know how to do this,' I said to Trudy out in the hall. 'I don't know how to tell him.'

Trudy nodded. 'Mike's going to be asking, sooner than they think.'

'Maybe one of the hospital staff will tell him. But I'm not sure it should come from them.'

'Or maybe he'll figure it out for himself.' Trudy shook her head. 'Oh God, Jaymie, this is just the beginning. How am I going to cope?'

'I'm going to help you.' The words popped out of my mouth. I discovered I didn't regret them. 'We'll do it, you and me.'

'This could be a long haul, Jaymie. Sure you two can stay together for more than a week?'

'I'll be there for Mike. Even if he tells me to get lost.'

'You two.' She gave me the trace of a smile.

But ten minutes later, back in the room, I was telling Trudy I had to return to Santa Barbara that night.

'We're trying to locate a child who's been abducted. I know Mike would want me to get back on the case.'

She looked crestfallen. 'When will you be back?'

'As soon as I've found her. In a few days, I hope. Then Dex and I will be spending some time up here.'

'Our house is a zoo, but you're welcome to stay with us.'

I bent down and kissed Mike on the cheek, then the mouth. His eyes opened. 'Jaymie—'

'Shh. It's all right.' I didn't know if I could smile. As it turned out I could, but only through a film of tears. 'I told you, Mike, you're going to be fine.'

I was amazed at how easily the lie slipped out this time. Maybe it was easy because I knew he needed to hear it.

'Jaymie, stay—'

It hurt to hear him ask me for that. 'Sorry. I'm always leaving you, aren't I?'

He was drugged to the eyeballs. I had no idea how much he understood. 'Mike? Trudy will be here with you till I get back. I have to go, just for a little while.'

He stared at me. How the hell could I explain? 'Dexter's waiting for me out in the Camino. We have to go and find Rosie, OK?'

Mike's lips curled up in a smile. 'Yeah, Dex . . .' He closed his eyes and slipped back into sleep.

I looked over at Trudy. 'See? I always knew Mike liked Dexter better than me.'

She shook her head. 'I'd say you and your dog are a package deal.'

I felt guilty as hell as I made my way through the halls to the parking lot. Guilty because I was leaving Trudy with all the responsibility, yes, but that wasn't the main thing. I felt guilty because I was abandoning Mike.

One hour later, I hit the coast. The early morning light over the ocean was slick and mean as cold metal. As I approached Santa Barbara, I could just see the tops of the islands piercing a long line of gray barrier-shaped clouds.

Twenty more minutes and I was charging up Mission, then pulling up in front of the bungalow court. I jumped out, raced through the garden to the office, and banged my way in through the door. Dexter was hot on my tail.

Gabi was sound asleep on the couch, and Claudia sat slumped at the desk with her head in her arms. Both of the women jumped when the front door banged against the wall.

'I got something, Jaymie,' Claudia mumbled.

'Good job.' I threw my messenger bag down on the hot seat. 'I need to get some coffee down me, pronto.'

Gabi sat up and combed her hair with her fingers. 'Miss Jaymie, are you sure? Maybe you better take a nap.'

'No time.' I circled the desk. 'Claudia, show me what you've got.'

She tapped the mouse and the screen lit up. 'OK. There are only two folders on the computer. And there's only one file in one – that's the school photos of the kids – and two files in the other.'

'Got it.'

'So, the first of the two files contains a contacts list. It's huge. It's an email list, I'm pretty sure, but the thing is, it's all in code. Here, I'll open it and show you.'

I stared at the odd combinations of letters and numbers. 'A list of the people this guy communicates with. That's dynamite.'

'Right. The thing is, I fiddled around with the code, but right now my brain's too tired to crack it.'

'But Claudia is smart enough to do it,' Gabi reminded me.

'Oh, I know that. The thing is, we don't have time to figure it out, not if we're going to find Rosie. The sheriff's department can do that later on.' I walked into the kitchen, picked up the ladder-back chair, and carried it to the desk.

'So. How about the other list?'

'Yeah. That one's gold.' Claudia closed the first file and opened the second. 'Here, take a look.'

'Hm. Fourteen or fifteen names. I wonder why? I mean, why isn't it in code like the longer list?'

'I don't have a clue. But this file is a lot newer than the other one. It was created just a few months ago – last year, in November. Maybe the creep didn't think he needed to be careful anymore.'

'Could be. Maybe Eric got complacent. He figured no one was ever going to find this laptop. Staffen Brill found it, though.'

Gabi paused on her way through to the kitchenette. 'Miss Jaymie, that woman, is she one of the bad people too?'

'You bet she is. Brill's been smuggling children in from Mexico for illegal adoption. I'm certain of it. But I don't think she's part of the sex trafficking ring – that's something different. Her husband, on the other hand, is guilty as sin.'

'Turning little kids into sex slaves,' Claudia muttered. 'I'm going home to get my knife.'

'No, no!' Gabi said. 'You leave that knife with your ma.'

'What we need to use is our brains. Gabi, how about that coffee?'

'Right away.'

'Claudia, you said you've located addresses for these guys?'

'Yeah, and it took me over two hours. I trolled through the internet. This desktop is freakin' ancient.' She reached for the yellow legal pad on her right. 'Nobody can hide their address these days. I had to dig deep for two of them, but in the end I got all fifteen. Here.'

I scanned the locations. Six of the fifteen were located in California. Of those, two lived in the LA basin, one was in Stockton, and another was in Palm Desert. The last two were close by, one in Santa Maria and the other in Camarillo.

'Right. Let's focus on the California addresses first. The guys in Santa Maria and Camarillo, we can cross them off for now.'

Claudia frowned. 'How do you figure that?'

'Eric had a duffle bag and Morehead had a small suitcase. Overnight bags. Santa Maria and Camarillo are too close – they wouldn't need to stay overnight.'

'Makes sense.'

'And Los Angeles, it's not all that far away either. I suppose it's possible they planned to spend the night down in LA, but it's unlikely.'

Claudia turned to me. 'That leaves Stockton and Palm Desert, right?'

'Yeah. Two cities in opposite directions. I'm running out of time – I've got to choose one.'

'Maybe I could go to one address and you could go to the other?'

Gabi set down a coaster and a cup of coffee in front of me on the desktop. 'You mean me and you could go to one together, mija,' she said to Claudia. 'I'm not letting you go alone. Look at you – drinking that Coca-Cola. Not even old enough to drink coffee.'

'I don't like it, that's all. And anything Jaymie can do, I can—'

'OK, OK.' I took a sip of the coffee. I could almost sense the elixir bridging the synapses in my tired brain. 'I'm not sending either of you anywhere. We don't have time to mess around. We have to be sure.'

I got to my feet, opened the front door and stepped out onto the porch. The dawn had seemed threatening, but the clouds dissipated and now the sky was fresh, sparkling with birdsong. Somewhere a little girl was being transported to captivity, and Mother Nature seemed to be ridiculing her fate.

I gripped the porch rail with one hand and shut my eyes. I had to think hard.

Last night, at Agua Azul. Was there anything I'd missed? There must have been something to indicate Morehead's destination, some sort of clue.

Step by step I replayed the scene, but in reverse:

Morehead, barreling down the drive, with Rosie and Eric in the back seat.

Staffen, protesting.

Rosie stuffed into the BMW, along with Eric and his duffle bag.

Morehead placing his own case in the trunk. His case, and – *fuck*! My eyes flew open.

Morehead hadn't just dropped a small suitcase into the trunk. He'd added a golf bag. I could even recall the sound it had made – a dull clank-clunk – as the clubs thumped against one another.

Every town in the state had a golf course. But I could think of only one town which no golfer would travel to without bringing along a set of clubs.

'Claudia. The guy who lives in Palm Desert – he's the one. Here's my phone. Enter that address into the GPS.' I swallowed the remaining hot coffee in three gulps.

'Gabi, can you keep an eye on Dex? I've got to run.'

TWENTY-TWO

I motored into a seedy section of Palm Desert late in the afternoon. The light was mellow, the temperature a lazy eighty-one degrees. The cacti, snug in their beds of quartz gravel, bloomed in splashes of cerise and tangerine.

All the homes on Silver Spur Drive were early sixties tract houses, built in angular modern designs. Back in Santa Barbara houses like these would have been snapped up and renovated. But here in the desert they were left to the elements. Peeling paint, cracked stucco, and trash in the gutters prevailed. In oil-stained driveways, a few disabled vehicles awaited future repairs.

I cruised up Silver Spur in the Camino. A man in his seventies stood in his front yard, watering from a hose in his hand. In his other hand he held a cigarillo. A thin spiral of smoke rose upward in the stagnant air.

I slowed to a crawl as I approached 153 Silver Spur. An old blue Accord hunched in the drive.

A thin woman wearing navy canvas pants and a pink and blue top stood at the curb, peering into the mailbox. She pulled out a handful of mail and leafed through.

I didn't want Mrs Ronald Goretz to see me. But I did want to get a good look at her. As I passed by, I took in her straight shoulder-length brown hair and navy blue headband. Her blouse featured a peter-pan collar, a design element I hadn't seen for years.

I adjusted the rearview mirror. Mrs Goretz looked up from the mail, glanced at the receding Camino, then looked away. She hadn't seen my face, I was sure.

But I had seen hers. Her expression was defensive, gullible, and perhaps just a little afraid.

I located the nearest car rental agency on my cell, then headed straight for it. Mrs Goretz had noticed my bright red Camino. Of course she had – it shouted out for attention.

I left Blue Boy in the agency lot and drove off in an unremarkable mouse-gray sedan.

Next stop was an office supply store. I grabbed a clipboard, pen, and a packet of official-looking forms. It didn't matter what the forms were intended for: they would become part of a magic trick, a sleight of hand.

Back in the sedan I grabbed a comb from my toiletry kit and ran it through my snarled hair, then re-did my ponytail. I figured my standard black jeans and dark-colored T-shirt would do.

I pulled down the visor mirror and met my own eyes: they looked kind of wild. I sucked in a slow breath to calm down. I was about to put on a performance, maybe the performance of my life.

I slowed to a stop in front of 153. The blue Accord still hunkered down in the drive. The house faced west, and though summer hadn't yet arrived the blinds were shut against the blaring sun.

I attached several of the forms to the clipboard and stepped out of the car. Assuming what I hoped was a semi-official air, I walked up the mottled-red concrete path and knocked. As I studied the paint blisters on the door's surface, I rehearsed what I was about to say.

'Yes?' The lady of the house peered at me around the edge of the door. Her forehead was puckered.

'Mrs Goretz?' I glanced at my clipboard. 'Mrs Ronald Goretz?'

'Yes?' she repeated. Her mouth smiled but her brow tightened.

'Is Mr Goretz at home?'

'No. No, he doesn't get home till at least six.'

I made a face of disappointment. 'Six? I'm afraid we don't make inspections past four thirty.'

'What – who are you with?' She opened the door a little wider. Behind her I could see half the living room: a couch, armchair, and the corner of a droning TV.

'I'm Christine Knight. I contract with the city, the water department. Your husband should have received a notice. They were sent out over two weeks ago.'

'Notice? What for?'

I glanced again at my clipboard. 'Water consumption. Your usage is over the third tier. Whenever that happens, we like to come out and inspect the property. To work with you, not against you. To give you some tips.'

I was confident Mrs Ronald Goretz did not pay the bills. If she did, I was sunk: the property looked as if it hadn't been watered in months.

'I think Ronald is pretty careful.' She ran a finger under her headband. 'We hardly use any water. Are you sure?'

'Yes. And if you are as careful as you say you are – and I believe you – then I'm afraid it means there's a leak.' I was growing impatient and told myself to slow down. 'The leak could be underground. If you don't mind, I'd like to do a walk-through of the premises.'

'Oh.' Her face closed like a drawstring sack. 'No, my husband doesn't like people coming around.'

'I don't need to go inside your *house*, Mrs Goretz.' I'd have loved to look in the house, but would take whatever I could get. 'I'll just walk the property. Nobody ever objects to that. Or – is there some reason it's not OK?'

'I . . . I guess you can.'

'Thank you.' I gave her my most radiant smile. 'Mind if I start in the back?'

'OK.' She still looked unsure. 'I'll unlock the gate for you.'

'Great. Do you mind if we hurry? I have two more houses on my list and I want to finish before dark.' I needed to move quickly, in case wifey decided to give hubby a call.

I followed the woman across the front of the house to the gate at the side. The fence was constructed of ordinary sun-bleached cedar boards, but the gate was another matter. Custom-built of powder-coated steel, it was mounted on a stout post. I watched over the woman's shoulder as she entered in a combination on a keypad, but I couldn't make out the numbers. The gate swung back.

'Thanks. I appreciate your cooperation, Mrs Goretz. I'm paid by the house, not the hour.'

'I'm Patty.' For the first time, the woman smiled. 'I used to work in sales. I know how it is.'

I stepped into the back yard. And halted. Because *fuck*, my stab in the dark had been right: Ronald Goretz was the one.

The yard looked abandoned: unwatered, untended, fast reverting to desert. But there was nothing abandoned about the rock-solid new shed. The structure, gleaming with white paint, stood in the southeast corner of the block-walled lot.

The shed wasn't prefab. It was large, about twelve by twelve, constructed of lumber, and taller than any shed needed to be. The roof was shingled in sheets of gray asphalt. A tubular skylight, no more than a foot wide, projected several inches above the roof. There was a door, but no windows at all that I could see.

I turned to the woman. 'Patty, do you have a dog?'

'No, my husband doesn't like pets. I like dogs. If it was up to me . . .' She trailed off.

'Then you don't need to stay out here with me, do you? I'm sure you have something better to do. I'll just go through my checklist. Shouldn't take long.' I nodded at the yards of black tubing arcing up out of the sand. 'I'll start with those old drip lines. Bet you've got a nasty leak somewhere in there. Could be costing you plenty.'

'Oh. All right then. Will you close the gate when you leave?' Poor Patty. She looked disappointed and sad. A lonely woman, she seemed to think she'd found someone she could talk to.

'Sure will. Thanks.' I turned away.

There was no point in messing around. As soon as Patty had closed the back door to the house, I walked straight over to the structure and circled behind it.

Between the shed and the block wall, out of sight, stood a brand new air-conditioning unit. It was silent, switched off for now.

I continued around the back of the shed to the south side. There, a new wooden trellis was fixed to the siding. A shrub, some sort of thorny desert specimen, was planted in front of it.

I circled back around and stopped to study the shed door. Dried paint bridged the gap between the door and the frame. It hadn't been opened since the structure was painted.

When I looked over at the main house, I saw a crooked finger holding back a drape. I moseyed over to a nearby faucet, dropped to one knee and made a show of switching it on, then off. I got to my feet.

Enough. It was time to go.

I was out of the yard and into my rental car before Patty could exit her house to approach me. In a matter of seconds I'd turned the key in the ignition and pulled away from the curb.

I wasn't so sure I felt sorry for Mrs Goretz. Maybe the woman knew nothing, but on the other hand, maybe she wanted to know nothing. Either way, her world teetered on the brink of change.

I drove a few blocks away from Silver Spur Drive and parked at a strip mall. I'd planned on grabbing something to go while I waited for six p.m., and Ronald Goretz to return home. But the thought of food somehow repulsed me.

I leaned back in the sedan and stared at the shop in front of me: a swimming pool supply store. The sign in the plate-glass door read *Closed*.

Pedophilia. I knew I should feel some compassion for the perps. Because so often they were passing on the poison that had been dosed out to them as kids. And I *could* be compassionate, if I kept that in mind – and if the pedophile asked for forgiveness, and was determined to cease and desist.

The thing was, Mr Ronald Goretz was not on that path.

I didn't hate the man. It was worse, in a way: he was nothing to me. One day, perhaps, I'd be able to see Goretz as a human being. Right now though, he was less than a rat in the road.

It was Rosie I needed to think about, Rosie and Chucha. I reached for my cell.

'Gabi. Thought I'd check in.'

'Miss Jaymie, I am so glad this is you. I couldn't decide, should I call you or not? First tell me, what is going on?'

'We've got the right guy. I'm waiting for him to get home from work.'

'Good, that is so good. And Rosie? Did you see her?'

'No. She hasn't been handed over to him yet, I'm pretty sure. And so far there's no sign of Morehead and Eric.'

'Miss Jaymie . . .'

'What is it?'

'Like I said, I thought, should I call you? Then I decided no, you had to focus, you know?'

'Gabi, right now I'm kind of on edge. Just spit it out.'

'Chucha. It's Chucha, Miss Jaymie.'

I'd been so focused on my own situation that I'd missed the anxiety in Gabi's voice. 'Chucha – is she—'

'No, no. But I went back to the hospital today. And the

administration guy, he figured out she isn't my sister's daughter like I said. But one of the nurses, she *is* my sister's daughter's . . .' Gabi stopped. 'Miss Jaymie, she told me in maybe three days, they are gonna do it. They decided for sure. Pull the plug.'

The sun slid down behind the strip mall. Right away I could feel the desert chill creeping in through the open window. 'Three days. I have to make this work *now.*'

'Yes, you gotta find Rosie and bring her to Cottage right away. Even if Chucha cannot hear or see, I think she will know.'

I wasn't sure about that. But for Rosie's sake, I wanted a photo of her with her mother. I knew she would cherish it one day.

'I'll do my best. Keep your phone switched on just in case. The sun's setting. I need to get ready to roll.'

'Vaya con Dios, Miss Jaymie.'

I drove a few blocks away to Home Depot and picked up a crowbar, a file, and a small set of screwdrivers. Power tools would have been useful, but the noise made them out of the question. Even using hand tools might be a risk.

Back in the car, I checked my phone: five thirty-seven. Soon it would be time for hubby to return home.

But something nagged at me. I'd gone to see Mike, and I'd checked in with the home team. Even so, I had the feeling I'd left something undone.

And if I were honest with myself, I knew what it was.

I got out of the car and paced through the dusky parking lot, stopped still and dialed.

'Hi Doreen. It's me. How are you?'

'Jaymie? Jaymie, is that you?'

I heard the loneliness and the panic in my mother's voice. But sure enough, in her next sentence she covered it over.

'How am I? I've been sitting by the phone for days, waiting for you to call. Days, do you know what that's like? Didn't your father tell you I'm not well?'

'Yes, I'm sorry, I—' But then, maybe for the first time in my life, I stopped myself. If this was going to work at all, I'd have to change.

'Let's not worry about that now. How are you feeling?'

'How am I feeling?' Now she tried outrage. 'I have – I'm ill! Of course, what do you care? What do any of you care? Most people, when they hear their mother has – has—' She stopped, unable to say the word.

'Mom, I have to go. But I wanted to let you know I'll be coming up to visit you, soon.'

I heard her start to cry. Was it because she had cancer, or because I'd said I would come to see her? Or was it because, for the first time in my life, I'd called her 'Mom'?

I drove back through the streets of Palm Desert to Silver Spur Drive. The red-orange spires of a flowering ocotillo fence glowed like candles in the fading violet light. No one was out in the neighborhood. Nobody noticed or cared when I parked five houses up from 153.

My window was open, and I heard a clackety-clack approach from behind me. I glanced into the side mirror: a girl was dawdling along on a skateboard, staring at the rented sedan.

I grabbed my phone and started fake-talking into it, keeping my eyes on the kid. By the time she clattered past, the girl had lost interest. Once she'd turned the corner I relaxed down in my seat, keeping an eye on my rearview mirror.

Five minutes later a van pulled into the driveway of 153. An overhead sensor switched on, flooding the driveway with light.

So Ronald Goretz drove a van: what a cliché. The van wasn't white, though, and it wasn't a panel van. Two-tone, maybe beige and brown – it was hard to make out the colors in the half-light. The windows appeared to be tinted, reflective. I turned in my seat and studied the vehicle. Could Rosie be inside?

As I reached for my field glasses, Goretz got out. He slammed the van door shut with more force than was necessary. Goretz was pissed off about something. He reached out a hand, and I heard the faint beep-beep of a door lock.

Goretz stood there for a moment more in the glare. The guy was of average height and build, the kind of person you'd pass in the street without giving a second glance. His light brown hair was thin on top and he wore it clipped short. Even his clothes were nondescript: brown slacks and a long-sleeve light blue shirt. I wondered what he did for a living: hotel manager, maybe? High school teacher?

Goretz was ordinary, except in one detail: he'd buttoned his shirt all the way up over his Adam's apple, and it made him look as if he were choking.

I was still peering at him through the binoculars when he turned and stared up the street. I froze in position, the glasses raised to my eyes. It seemed as if we'd locked gazes, Goretz and I.

But then he turned again and looked in the opposite direction. I knew he hadn't seen me, thanks to the shadowy darkness of the street and the bright light pouring down all around him. I was pretty sure, though, that he'd noticed my car.

After a moment the guy walked up to the gate, punched in the code, and stepped through. The gate closed. I sat there, waiting for the sensor light to switch off so I could get out of the car and walk over.

The damn floodlight lit up the entire front of the house and part of the right-hand neighbor's house, too. How long was it set to stay on? Five minutes, ten? My hand drummed the console, and I ordered myself to stay calm.

Yes, it was possible Rosie was locked in the back of the van. But my guess was that Morehead hadn't handed Rosie over – not yet.

Then, a minute later, something odd happened. The lights came on in the Goretz's living room, and Ronald himself proceeded to lift up all the blinds.

Soon the interior of 153 Silver Spur was illuminated like a stage set. Goretz switched on the TV, then set up two tray tables. As I watched through my binoculars, it occurred to me that the scene looked like something out of the 1950s. June Cleaver, a.k.a. Patty Goretz, minced in with hubby's dinner and set it on one of the tray tables, then returned to the kitchen and reappeared with her own plate.

They both settled into their easy chairs and stared at the big screen TV as they forked food into their mouths.

Was this something the Goretzes did every evening: put on a show for the neighbors and passersby? If so, why?

I lowered the glasses and stared at the brightly lit fishbowl. And after a moment, I thought I understood. Ronald Goretz was showing everyone that he had nothing to hide.

The Goretzes were every bit as normal and boring as their neighbors. More so, in fact. As anyone could see, they never argued, drank, smoked, or touched.

By this time the sensor light had switched off. But my instincts told me to stay put.

It wasn't long before Ronald finished his supper. Was dessert to follow? It seemed not. He picked up his cell and looked at it, then wiped his mouth with a napkin and walked out of the room.

After a few minutes, Patty got up and cleared the dishes. Then she took possession of the remote and settled back in her chair.

TWENTY-THREE

Ten minutes later the floodlight poured down once more and the side gate opened. Goretz carried a tennis racquet bag now and seemed to be in a hurry.

He glanced up and down the street, his eyes pausing again on my rental sedan. Then he stepped over to the back of the van, opened one of the doors and shoved in the bag.

Goretz climbed into the driver's seat, backed the van out of the driveway, and motored down the street at a good clip. I started my engine but waited before I switched on the headlights. As I cruised past 153 I saw Patty at the window, closing the blinds.

I followed the van through the residential streets of Palm Desert, taking care to keep my distance. Not many cars were on the road and the last thing I wanted was for Goretz to notice he had a tail. No, I wanted his plan to flow without a hitch right up to the end.

He turned into the main drag and headed in the direction of Cathedral City. Now there were more cars on the road and I could hide in the pack.

I figured Goretz was heading for a meet up with Morehead and expected him to turn off the highway and into a hotel parking lot. But instead, after a mile or less he entered the glitzy Los Zorros Restaurant lot and pulled up in an empty far corner. I chose a spot that provided me with an unobstructed view of the van.

An overhead light illuminated Goretz as he spoke into his cell. Then he climbed out of the van and headed for the restaurant. His movements looked jerky, as if he were angry, upset.

When Goretz didn't return after several minutes, I got out of the sedan, crossed the lot and pushed in through the tall sand-blasted glass doors.

'May I help you?' The host, who looked more like a bouncer, knew how to make his words sound like mini slaps in the face. He ran an eye up my body, from my black tennies to my pony-tailed hairdo.

'I'm meeting up with a friend in the bar.' Goretz had already dined, at home. I figured the bar was the best bet.

Bouncer Boy allowed me to pass. When I stepped into the bar, I could see why I'd been scrutinized. Everyone in the room was dressed in their best duds, as if they were out on the town in Manhattan instead of the dusty Sonoran Desert. But nobody bothered to give me a second glance, which was just how I wanted it.

It took me a moment to locate Ronald. He was seated at a high top table with another guy whose back was to me. Goretz looked agitated. He leaned forward over the table, making a point.

I sidled along the curve of the long mahogany bar and took a seat at the far end, in shadow. Then I swiveled around on my stool to face Goretz's table. And that's when I found myself looking straight at Jack Morehead.

Morehead was leaning back, away from Goretz. He'd assumed an easy attitude, with his cashmered arm draped over the chair back. But he was listening, all right.

The barman approached me and I ordered a beer. I kept an eye on Morehead and Goretz while pretending to study my phone. Goretz didn't know me from Adam, but I'd met Morehead at Agua Azul and he was too sharp not to recognize me. Luckily at the moment his attention was elsewhere.

When the IPA arrived, foaming over the lip of the glass, I ignored it. That had to be a first.

It was difficult to follow Morehead and Goretz's every move while pretending to look elsewhere. After a while I gave up the show and focused on the two men. They were negotiating, I could see that. Was it Rosie they were haggling over? If so, Morehead and Goretz were no different from slave traders, bartering over a child on the block.

Morehead raised both hands, palms outward. The bartering had come to an end.

But Goretz was pissed off. He shoved his chair away from the high top and got to his feet. He looked like he wanted to leave, but he hovered near the table. Morehead was cool and bided his time.

Then Goretz lifted a hand in a sharp upward motion, and at the same time dropped his head. He wasn't happy – but it looked like they had a deal.

I dropped a bill on the bar and followed Goretz out of Los Zorros. I couldn't lose him, not now. I had to take the risk of being seen.

I entered the lot in time to see Ronald Goretz open the passenger door of Morehead's black BMW. He removed a white envelope from an inner pocket of his jacket. He leaned into the vehicle, and when he straightened, the envelope was no longer in his hand.

I'd just made it to my sedan when Jack Morehead strode into the lot and over to his vehicle. Before Goretz started up his van, Morehead had turned left out of the lot, heading south for Palm Desert and La Quinta.

I jumped in my rental, pressed the ignition button and backed out of the space. Then I waited for Goretz's van as it passed through the lot to the highway. Just as I began to move forward, Goretz made a right turn. Unlike Morehead, he was headed north toward Palm Springs.

God damn it, which way to go? Morehead had Rosie in his possession – didn't he? But Goretz had apparently just paid to procure her. On the spur of the moment, I decided it was better to keep Morehead in view. I turned left and accelerated.

A few seconds later I realized I'd made a mistake. I'd forgotten about Eric.

Jack Morehead was smart enough to protect himself. Smart enough to collect the money and let Eric do the mop-up. In fact, Morehead hadn't even collected the money: he'd merely found it in his car. Topnotch attorney that he was, the asshole had covered all the bases.

I glanced once in the rear view mirror, made a sharp U-turn across the highway, and stepped on it. Three minutes later, I came up on the boxy shape of the van.

The van didn't turn into Palm Springs as I'd expected. Instead it headed away from the valley floor, in the direction of Indian Canyons. A sign announced I had entered the land of the Agua Caliente.

I rolled down all the windows. The desert was mysterious in the dark, the night air delicate and perfumed. I was driving up a bajada, but instead of rising straight up the slope the road was taking a zigzag path. Goretz's tail lights winked in front of me. I dropped back and switched off my own headlights, so I wouldn't be observed.

Goretz showed no sign he was thinking of anything but the road ahead. He kept on at the same steady pace without surging or braking. A car approached, and the driver blinked his headlights to tell me to switch mine on. I ignored the suggestion. So far, I was doing fine.

We were three miles into the reservation when Goretz jammed on his brakes. The rear of the van flared scarlet. I slowed, then stopped. Goretz had turned off the road.

I watched as the van juddered over the rocky desert floor, then dropped down into a wash and disappeared. I realized the sedan had been a poor choice: I needed a vehicle with higher clearance to follow Goretz.

But one way or another I had to make it happen. The guy was meeting someone, and I'd bet my right arm it was Eric. If my hunch was correct, Ronald Goretz was about to take possession of Rosie.

I moved on past Goretz's turn-off point, rounded a bend, and slowed. Then I made a U-turn so that the sedan was pointing back the way I'd come, and pulled off onto the shoulder.

I got out of the sedan and eased the door shut, leaving it unlocked. Then I jogged back down to the turn-off. Here I discovered an unpaved road, covered in a thin layer of flinty rock. The sharp gravel crunched under my feet as I ran. My footsteps sounded like small explosions.

I jogged up a steady incline for perhaps a hundred yards. As I crested the hill I slowed to a walk, then came to a standstill. Below me lay an oasis.

A pair of vehicles were parked near a cluster of fan palms. One was the van, the other a large SUV.

Two men stood near the SUV, arguing. One held a powerful flashlight. The beam was pointed up and away, illuminating the dried skirts of the palms. I inched forward in the dark until I was close enough to make out their words.

'You made a deal, that's what I'm saying.' Goretz thrust his head forward like a snake. 'What you did – that's called bait and switch.'

'Shit happens, Ronnie. You know that.' It was Eric. Eric the delivery boy. His tone was familiar: he seemed to know Goretz. I thought about the computer list: maybe Eric and Ronald were members of the same nasty club. The little bastard was in it all right, up to his neck.

'You sent me her picture! Fuck it, Eric, you promised her to me.

What, now you guys are saying she's not available? You sold the kid to a higher bidder, is that it?'

'Take my advice, Ronnie. Let it go.' Eric swung the flashlight so it pointed straight in Goretz's face, and the guy stumbled back. 'For one thing, you already paid Jack. No refunds, bud. So what the fuck are we arguing for?'

'Get that out of my face. I don't like the look of the replacement, all right? Jack showed me her picture. She looks like a fox or something. Not my fucking type, that's for sure.'

'Can't hurt to take a look, can it? Take a look, you might change your mind.'

'Tell you what, I might take my money back. You're not pushing me around.' Goretz's voice turned stubborn. 'I might make a stink.'

'A stink?' Eric's high laughter snapped like the breaking of dead sticks. 'There'll be a stink all right if you try and screw the deal. You have no idea, Ronnie, what Jack can be like. I'd let it go if I were you.'

'I just want to know why.' Goretz sounded peevish, like a kid determined to get his way. 'The other guys in the club, they'd want to know about this!'

'You'll keep your fucking mouth shut if you know what's good for you.' There was a drawn-out moment of silence.

'Eric, come on—'

'All right. I'll tell you what happened. To shut you up once and for all. Just don't let on to Jack that you know.'

'I'm listening.'

'She died. The kid you're talking about didn't make it. So you're lucky, man. Lucky to get a sub.'

'Died? How?' Goretz's tone was chilling. It sounded like he was asking about the death of a gerbil or something.

'Fuck, I don't know. They gave the girls some sedative on the trip, some fruit they use in Mexico to calm kids down and keep them quiet. The one kid, she got too much of it, or maybe she was allergic, who the hell knows? One made it and one didn't, that's all there is to it.'

The dragon fruit. In a flash, the last piece of the puzzle slipped into place in my mind.

But in my shocked surprise I forgot to keep still. I must have lurched forward. I tripped on a rock, tried to catch myself and failed.

The pain from a dozen barbed needles shot though the fabric of my jeans and into my knee.

'What – what was that?' Eric swiveled the beam of the light in my direction. I hunkered down, unable to lift my knee from the cactus patch. I tried to ignore the pain and control my breathing, but it came in short gasps.

'Some animal,' Goretz said. 'They're out in the desert at night.'

'It sounded more like a man.' Eric swung the powerful beam back and forth over the hillside. Thank God I'd dressed all in black. The light passed over me, continuing on in a low arc.

'A man?' Goretz snorted. 'People don't wander around in the dark, not on the res. You scared?'

'I don't know. Do you have mountain lions around here?'

'Sometimes. Around these oases, yeah. OK, let's get it over with. Let's see the little bitch. Maybe I need to make sure she's alive, after what you just told me.'

'Oh, she's alive all right.'

The deal was about to be concluded. Eric sounded relieved.

The light beam retracted. At last I was able to get to my feet. I brushed a hand over my knee: half a dozen spines protruded. I yanked them out one-by-one, bracing myself against the stinging pain.

Goretz followed Eric over to the SUV. Goretz was right in one thing, I thought: there were predatory animals out here tonight. I was looking at two of them.

Eric opened the SUV tailgate, reached into the back, and dragged a bundle forward. The bundle gave a cry: the cry of a terrified child.

Stay put, I ordered myself.

Little kids have many different cries. Some cries are annoying. Others can be ignored. But the cry that came from the back of the SUV: that was the kind of cry that lassoes the mind and the heart and yanks you off your feet. The sort of cry that makes it impossible to stand your ground.

But I had to bide my time. I bit my lip so hard I tasted blood.

I watched as the two men unwrapped the bundle. They muttered together, but I could no longer make out their words. No doubt it was just as well. Rosie wailed in the cold air.

After several minutes Goretz wrapped up the little girl again. He slung her over his shoulder like a sack of flour. Meanwhile Eric slammed down the tailgate, climbed into the SUV, and switched on the big engine.

Then, in the glare of the SUV headlights, I saw Ronald Goretz climb into the back of his van with Rosie. I knew what I had to do.

Careful this time to avoid the cactus patch, I dropped to the ground again as the SUV roared up out of the wash. Then I took off jogging along the gravel road, heading back to my car. I listened hard for the sound of the van behind me, ready to fall to the ground once more. I tried not to think about what was taking Goretz so long.

I'd almost reached the paved road when I halted. I was so focused on my plan, so hell-bent on achieving it, that it was hard to make myself stop and reconsider. The problem was, Goretz wasn't doing what I'd expected.

My strategy was to follow Goretz straight back to Silver Spur Drive and watch him lock Rosie in the shed. I would rescue Rosie, then call the Riverside County Sheriff's Department. Goretz would be caught. And with the evidence on Eric's computer, the whole sorry lot of them would be rounded up and arrested.

But now Goretz was taking his time returning to Palm Desert. And he wasn't reading to Rosie from a storybook, that was for sure.

I pressed a hand to the small of my back, reassuring myself that I was packing my gun. Then I began to jog back to the oasis. Forget the plan. Right now, Rosie mattered more than anything.

I was a hundred yards short of the oasis when I heard the van rumbling up the wash. For the third time, I hit the dirt. My frustration was mounting: I was two steps behind.

The van rumbled past. Once it had disappeared from view I jumped to my feet and ran after it. My adrenaline pumped like a gusher, and it wasn't long before I reached the paved road.

The van was long gone by the time I climbed into the sedan and took off. But now I was certain Goretz was headed home, to his cozy place on Silver Spur.

I wound back down through the dark desert bajada, then turned onto the highway heading south. I thought about what I'd overheard.

At last the pieces fit into place. Milagros had been intended for Ronald Goretz. The lead pangero had given the little girls what he no doubt assumed was a mild narcotic – the dragon fruit. He hadn't intended to kill Millie, but that was exactly what he'd done.

And Rosie. Rosie Robledo was just along for the ride. The pangero had agreed to transport her too, for some extra cash from Chucha.

When Millie died at sea, the pangero saw an opportunity to salvage the situation. Millie, no doubt, had a sizable price on her head, and the creep wasn't about to let his cut slip away. The pangero knew who Chucha was, and he guessed she wouldn't be in a position to do a goddamn thing about it.

And so he'd delivered Chucha's daughter to Agua Azul, in Millie's place.

TWENTY-FOUR

The one hundred block of Silver Spur Drive was quiet. A cat darted into the street, then changed its mind and shot back to the curb. Here and there a porch light emitted a fuzzy glow. I rolled past 153. Sure enough, the two-tone van was backed into the drive, nose pointed out to the street. A gleam of light shone from inside the house, leaking around the edges of the blinds. Funny, I thought, how dead-stillness can seem like peace.

I continued on down the street and around the corner, into Riata Way. Then I pulled up just past the house that stood behind Goretz's place. I'd driven down the street earlier in the day and taken a close look. I knew that an older man lived in the concrete block home at 176 Riata, and that he didn't have a dog.

Palm Desert isn't big on streetlights, and there were none on Riata. I stepped out of the sedan and looked up. The black sky glistened with a silvery wash of stars. I paused for a moment, praying without words.

Then the time for prayer was done.

I hopped the low block wall enclosing the yard of 176. Hugging the fence, I crossed a graveled area and headed for the back property line.

Goretz had erected a massive block wall behind his home – I judged it to be seven or eight feet high. But the man hadn't been able to control everything in his world. The perpendicular side wall running down the neighbors' property was no more than five feet high.

I hoisted myself up onto the side wall, then edged along to the point where the two walls met, behind big shed. A faint light glowed at the ridge line: light was seeping out through the tubular skylight on the west-facing flank of the roof.

I cautioned myself to hold back. Goretz might be inside the shed. I couldn't hear a sound – the structure was too well insulated for that. I couldn't be sure.

My phone vibrated in my pocket. I pulled it out and glanced at the screen: *Gabi*. I switched it off. I was sure it was important, but my partner and friend would have to wait.

I shifted my weight a little and tried not to think about what might be happening in the room below me. My knee stung like hell, but now it was a welcome distraction.

As I waited, I challenged myself. Maybe I should call local law enforcement immediately. They could trap Goretz – if not in the shed, then on the property. That's what Mike would have counseled. But I knew it wasn't a good move – not for Rosie, not in the long run.

She needed to be with Chucha, if only for a short time. And after, she needed to be with someone who would care for her with love.

Rosie was what they called 'an unaccompanied minor.' ICE would snag her – and then what? Would the little girl be shipped back to the mother who'd mistreated her? Or would she disappear into a gulag of temporary foster care, with no one to give a damn?

I knew all about neglect. I knew neglect could make it difficult, or even impossible, to trust another human being – maybe for the rest of one's life.

No. I didn't need anyone to tell me what was right.

I pulled myself up onto the seven-foot wall. Then I dropped to the ground with a soft thud.

Now I stood in the narrow gap between the wall and the back of the shed. I edged around to the south side of the structure and glanced over at the main house, where a faint interior light glowed. Nothing had changed.

Rosie was inside the shed, I'd stake my life on it. But was she alone?

I moved around to the front of the shed, switched on my cell light and shined it along the edge of the door. The old paint still bridged the seam where the door met the frame. What the fuck? No one had entered through the door since it was painted. *Or maybe,* I realized, *that was exactly what Goretz wanted the casual observer to conclude.*

I stepped back out of sight to the side of the shed. I had to think. Did Goretz access the shed through some kind of tunnel leading out from the house? But that would mean Patty was in on it, which I doubted. Besides, this ground wasn't loam or clay. A tunnel would collapse in the desert sand.

I shifted a foot and felt something under my sneaker. I switched on my light again, cupping it in my hands, and looked down. What I'd stepped on was the desert shrub planted in front of the new redwood trellis.

As I stared at the spiky bush, it occurred to me that the choice of plant was odd. It wasn't trained on the trellis. In fact, it was a good foot shorter than the bottom edge of the trellis. For that matter, it wasn't even the kind of plant that could grow on a trellis. So what was the point of having it there?

A bell dinged in my brain.

The man was fucking clever, all right. Clever, meticulous, and paranoid. I shined my penlight up and down the redwood strips.

Goretz had jig-sawed a door into the wall and hidden the cuts under the lath. The door was shaped like a giant puzzle. It was a masterpiece of trompe l'oeil.

Now I knew how Goretz accessed the shed. I was desperate to enter it myself, to grab Rosie and run. But it would take me some time to get through the door, and I'd no intention of being surprised halfway through the process.

I thought about the skylight. It was far too small for me to fit through. But a light was on inside the shed, and the skylight should give me a view. I'd find out if Rosie was inside, and if she was alone.

If I could just hoist myself back up onto the seven-foot block wall, I could climb to the roof from there.

I stepped out into the star-lit yard. Right away I saw what I needed. A stack of concrete blocks, left over from the construction of the shed, tilted against a side fence. Just four blocks should give me what I required: a step-up to the wall. I carried them across the yard, one by one.

In a flash, I was up and onto the wall, then the shed roof.

Making as little noise as possible, I stretched out flat and put my face to the skylight. At first I couldn't figure out what I was looking at in the dimly lit room below. When I figured it out, my breath grew shallow and fast.

A tiny child lay directly below me in some kind of homemade crib. She wore a nightgown and was curled into a fetal position. Her eyes were closed, but her hand moved a little.

As I studied her, trying to see if she was OK, the light went out. Then, with a graunching sound, the trellis door opened. Goretz had been inside, all right. After a moment, the door clacked back into place.

I lifted my head and watched over the roof ridge as the man crossed the yard to the house.

He shut the back door behind him and the lights came on. I could see his shadow behind the blinds, moving around in the kitchen. This was my chance to break into the shed.

But Goretz could be making something for Rosie to eat. He might return. I was debating whether or not I should make a move when the kitchen light switched off. After a few minutes the softer interior light was turned off, too. Goretz must have gone to bed. All was quiet and dark at 153.

Now I couldn't move fast enough.

I backed down off the roof, dropped from the fence to the ground, and hurried around to the trellis. The inset lock was one I hadn't come across before. I gripped my phone in my teeth, shining the light on the lock as I worked with both hands.

In the end, I had to break the mechanism. Then I grabbed the trellis and pulled. I didn't have the knack of it, and there was a graunching sound as the siding caught at several points. Then the door gaped wide open.

I stepped inside the single room, pulled the door closed behind me, and raised my light.

A chair and a chest of drawers stood against one wall. A shower curtain was pulled back, revealing a toilet and washbasin. That was all there was in the room, except for the crib. The wooden bars rose to within three or four feet of the ceiling.

Rosie's curled-up body lay on the mattress. She lay very still, with her back to me. Thank God I'd seen her move. I knew she was alive.

I didn't point the flashlight at her. There'd been enough of that. 'Rosie,' I whispered. 'Rosie, everything's going to be OK.'

She understood Spanish, not English: but did the words matter? I hoped she'd understand the gentle tone of my voice. But Rosie didn't turn to me. Instead, I heard the tiniest of whimpers.

The crib was secured with a goddamned combination padlock. I took one look at it and went for the bars instead.

I suppose I'd have hesitated, if this had been just any old day. Stopped to be sure I could climb out carrying the child. But something told me I could do it, and I wasn't about to argue with myself.

A stabilizing rail was nailed about a foot down from the tops of the bars, at just the right height. I grabbed it and managed to lever my body up and over on the first go. I eased myself down to the mattress, and took a breath to calm myself.

'Hey, Sweetie, somebody's waiting to see you. Rosie—' I put out a hand.

Again, she cried a little. She didn't seem to have the will to either reach out or to pull away.

The best thing, I knew, would be to gain her trust step-by-step, to wait for hours or even days before grabbing her. But that was time neither of us had.

I knelt down, reached out and took her into my arms. Dear God, the child weighed nothing. I pressed my lips to her ear.

'You are going to need to be a brave little girl, Rosie. But only for a very short time.'

When I laid her down on the mattress again, she whimpered. I took that as a good sign: she wanted to stay close.

I pulled off my sweatshirt and yanked the cord out of the hood. Then I zipped Rosie in, and used the cord to tie the bottom hem shut. So far so good.

'Just for a few minutes, I promise.' I swung the cocooned child to my back and tied the sleeves around my neck.

Rosie had grown still. Was she too terrified now to make a sound, or did she feel safe? I didn't know.

I jumped for the cross rail and missed. Shit. The little girl weighed nothing, but the problem was the mattress, which had too much give. I tried again, throwing everything I could muster into the leap. I caught the bar, and my grip held.

Using my feet as well as my arms, I managed to swing a leg over. Rosie hung down to one side of my back. Somehow I managed to get my left arm around to support her. Then the two of us slipped over the bars and down to the floor.

Just as my feet hit, the door opened and the light switched on. Goretz loomed in the doorway.

'What the hell – who the fuck are you?!'

'Get out of my way, Goretz.' I reached behind me and straightened Rosie on my back. 'Get out of my fucking way.'

'You – you're in my shed, you – *stupid bitch*.' He sounded flummoxed, even unsure of himself. Except for the stupid bitch part: that sounded like he meant what he said.

'*Your* shed? I wouldn't admit it's yours if I were you, you dumb fuck. This is no shed – it's a fucking prison.'

I was beginning to see more clearly now. And I could tell, by the expression on his face, that Goretz was beginning to understand the situation he was in.

'I don't know who the hell you are. But if you think you're going to come in here and take my kid—'

'*Your* kid?' I took a step forward. 'What, she's yours because you bought her? Keep talking, you asshole.'

That's when the man surprised the hell out of me. He reached into his cargo pants pocket, and when his hand reappeared, it held a small gun.

'Yeah, that's right. I bought her. Now get the kid off your back. Put her down on the floor and move over to the sink.'

'You need to think about this, Ronald. Use that gun, and you'll be in deep shit.'

'Shut up.'

'You don't think I'm doing this on my own, do you? I'm a detective with the Santa Barbara Police Department. Santa Barbara: that's where this little girl came from. We know who you are, what you've done.'

'I haven't done anything.' The gun wavered. 'All I did was take her in. I'm hiding her, you know? From – from immigration. Yeah. Call that a crime if you want, I don't see it that way.'

'Yeah? OK, we can work with that.' At all costs, I had to get Rosie out of there. 'It isn't you we're after anyway – it's Morehead. If you cooperate you might be able to skip the jail time. And in your case, that would be a damn good idea.'

I saw that Goretz was believing me. But I saw something else that had me worried: he hated me, too. As I watched his expression grew guarded: he'd had an idea.

'Like I said, lady, take the kid off your back.'

'Sure, no problem. That's something both of us don't want, right? For Rosie to get hurt.'

I reached behind my back – and drew out my own gun from my waistband. I didn't hesitate for a second: I shot the creep in the foot.

Goretz screamed and crumpled. I heard him moaning through the open door as I hopped up onto the stack of concrete blocks and climbed the wall. Then Rosie and I dropped down into the backyard of the house on Riata.

We'd done it. For the moment, we were free.

I lifted the papoose over my neck and hugged the child close. 'My brave girl.'

Holding her against my chest, I jogged through the yard and hopped the low wall, climbed into the sedan, and drove five or six blocks away. Then I pulled over and checked to make sure the GPS tracking was still turned off on my cell.

Next I phoned 911. 'Go to One-fifty-three Silver Spur Drive. You'll find a perp named Ronald Goretz in a shed in the back. He's been shot in the foot. Even with the bad foot, Goretz is a major flight risk. Phone Detective Deirdre Krause of the Santa Barbara PD for more information. That's it for now.'

I switched off the cell and tossed it in the back seat. Then I sat Rosie in the passenger seat beside me, angled it back, and belted her in. Her sweet little lower lip trembled.

I brushed her straight black hair off her forehead. 'We're hitting the road, Rosie. I'm Thelma and you're Louise, and we need to hightail it out of town.'

Whatever sedative Morehead had given the child was wearing off now. Rosie was uncomfortable, tired, and scared, and she needed a bottle and a diaper change. But that would have to wait. I rested my right hand on her chest to calm her and took off, steering with my left.

I headed for the freeway. Of course, the cops would catch up with me sooner or later. Later, if we were in luck.

I hoped nobody would take notice of the Camino languishing in the rental car lot. The last thing I needed was to fork over a thou or two, to bail Blue Boy out of impound.

But none of that mattered now. I kept on driving, grateful for the chance to put some miles between us and the desert. All that mattered was that I deliver Rosie home to Santa Barbara, to Chucha – and then to somehow spirit her away.

TWENTY-FIVE

L uckily for me, Rosie's exhaustion was greater than her discomfort. I was compiling a baby things shopping list in my mind when she fell fast asleep. Her little hand remained locked on my thumb.

I didn't know much about babies. Of course, I'd babysat when I was young, but I felt as if I'd forgotten anything I'd ever learned. Still, I had a feeling Rosie was going to make her needs crystal clear when she woke up.

Once I got to Santa Barbara, I would ask for guidance from Gabi. My office manager had no kids of her own, but she seemed to have raised dozens of brothers, sisters, nieces, and nephews.

Rosie's grip relaxed. The freeway was empty at this hour and I felt myself relax, too. I glanced down at the sleeping child. She looked a lot like Chucha, all right. They belonged to one another.

But I was in la-la land, I admitted. In the end Chucha wasn't going to make it. Then what? What would happen to Rosie?

I knew two things for sure. First, Rosie was not going back to her abusive birthmother. And second, she wasn't going to tumble down into the gaping maw of ICE.

The little girl slept on and on. Dawn was breaking when we hit the coast. When we reached Camarillo, I pulled into a CVS parking lot.

I didn't want to attract attention, but on the other hand I didn't like the idea of locking Rosie in the car on her own. Trying not to wake her, I wrapped her in my sweatshirt and hugged her close to my chest.

I grabbed a cart and entered the store, located the baby aisle and began to load the cart with diapers, wipes, formula, and baby bottle paraphernalia. I knew Rosie needed more than a bottle, but this would have to do for now.

As I walked down the aisle, a cute little outfit caught my eye. It looked about Rosie's size, so I snagged it. Then I noticed a collection of bright plastic toy keys, and I dropped that in the cart, too.

Shit, I was acting like an indulgent auntie already.

By the time we got back to the car, Rosie was wide awake and bawling.

'Hey, girl! Let's get something into you.' I switched on the radio, and found a station playing light classical music. Then I rinsed out the bottle, filled it with formula and water, unstrapped Rosie and took her into my arms.

She seemed a little confused about the bottle – or maybe it was my ineptitude that made things confusing. But man was she motivated. I tried to take the bottle out of her mouth at one point, thinking she might need to burp or something – but she made it clear she'd have none of that.

After she'd polished off the formula I cleaned her up, then dressed her in a fresh diaper and the new outfit. She put up with my awkwardness with grace. The clothes were too big on her, though: little Rosie was all skin and bones.

'Wow. You are one pretty little girl. Once we get some fat on you, you'll be a stunner.' I strapped her back in the seat, ignoring her protests. 'Time to go meet Mama, baby girl.'

I handed her the plastic key ring, and after a few minutes she settled down. We were on the road again.

The new day was just beginning as Thelma and Louise pulled into the Cottage Hospital visitors' lot.

Rosie needed another change. I needed a change, too. I felt dirty and exhausted among all the freshly showered citizens arriving for work at the hospital.

But there was no time to waste. Cradling Rosie in my arms, I walked in though the main doors and up to the desk. 'We're here to see Chucha Robledo. Jesus Maria Robledo,' I corrected myself. 'This is her daughter.'

This receptionist wasn't a candy striper but an employee. She shot me a scathing glance, then studied Rosie. 'Robledo?' She tipped back her head to look at a computer screen through the lower portion of her smudged bifocals.

'There's no Robledo.' She continued to peer at the screen, then pushed another button or two. 'No, I'm sorry. No one of that name.'

'She's here.' I shifted Rosie to my other hip. 'Maybe you're not spelling it right. Would you check again?'

'I can, but it won't change anything.' The woman looked again at Rosie, and frowned. 'Are you looking after this child?'

Rosie didn't appear to be very well looked after, I had to admit. 'It's a long story. But Chucha Robledo, she's very ill. She wouldn't have been discharged, I can tell you that for sure.'

Something was bothering me, tugging at the edge of my mind. 'Know what? I need to talk to someone in charge.'

I was surprised when the woman didn't argue. She kept one eye on me as she made a call.

'Somebody will be out to talk to you.' She replaced the desk phone in its cradle. 'Please have a seat.' She pointed across the foyer to a dark blue couch.

I hadn't reached the couch before I heard the door open behind me. I turned.

The tall and thin middle-aged guy didn't need to say anything. His expression said it all: *the one you are looking for is gone. You will find her nowhere: you must stop looking now.*

He motioned me to follow him into a side room, a kind of half-chapel, half-waiting room. At least it was quiet in there. Not too clangy, efficient, or bright.

The man dabbed at his nose with a balled-up tissue. He seemed to have a very bad cold. So the guy had a cold – why was I even bothering to notice such a thing?

But I knew why. My mind was reaching for anything to think about except the truth. Yet only the truth mattered, not just to me but to the child snuggled in the crook of my arm.

The hospital administrator motioned for me to sit down beside him. He asked a couple of questions. Who was I? Who was Rosie? Then he said a few things about Chucha – but not too much.

The man wasn't under any obligation to talk to me. I knew that. But I also guessed the last thing he wanted was trouble. He would say just as much as he thought he needed to say, in order to move on with a minimum of fuss.

Chucha's organs were on their way to helping others now, the hospital guy was explaining. He even smiled a little. It was a discreet smile, practiced, conveying just the right amount of sadness.

He dabbed again at his nose. Then he sniffed and said that Chucha now had a new kind of life.

That was nice, I replied. Nice for those others. But for Chucha Robledo, it was the end of all hope.

Sure, there were some harsh questions I had for the guy. But what was the point of asking them now? The answers wouldn't help Chucha or Rosie, not anymore.

Then the guy looked at Rosie. I could see he was trying to work out my connection to the little girl.

The best thing, I decided, was to not stick around. I felt empty inside, reluctant to leave or let go. But there was nothing here for us now.

When I stepped outside with Rosie, we were greeted by a baptism of light rain. I tipped back my head and let the moisture fall on my upturned face.

The sprinkle of raindrops felt good. But we were out of time and had to get going. Soon the cops would be searching for Rosie and me.

I opened my sweatshirt jacket and tucked her inside, then hurried for the car. I slammed the door shut, then switched on the engine and the heater. The windows misted over.

Rosie and I hunkered down inside our cave. For the moment I felt safe, safe enough to take time to make a call.

'Miss Jaymie, I waited all night with the phone by my bed. What happened, are you OK?'

'Yes, I'm OK. Rosie too. She's here with me – we're in Santa Barbara now.'

'That is good, good news! But why do you sound so sad?'

I didn't want to dump the news on Gabi like a ton of bricks. I tried to be gentle. 'We've just been to Cottage. We went to see Chucha, but . . . she isn't there.'

'Not there? Then . . . where?'

'She's gone, Gabi.'

'Gone?'

'I'm sorry to have to tell you. Chucha died.'

'No. No. They said it would be next week. Next week! They told me that one day ago.'

Rosie began to fret. I nudged my finger into her hand. 'Who knows what happened. Maybe some rich person somewhere needed an organ in a big hurry.'

'I don't think – that is so ugly! Miss Jaymie, is that how it works?'

'I have no idea,' I admitted. 'I just know I can't afford to think about it right now.'

'Miss Jaymie, I understand. Tell me what you want me to do.'

Gabi's question galvanized my mind. 'You need to take Rosie and hide her. Can you meet us in ten minutes, over at Five Points?'

'In the shopping center, you mean?'

'Yes, the parking lot. Park out by the hedge dividing the lot from the back of Peet's Coffee. Do you know where I mean?'

'Yes. I'm gonna go right away.'

'Gabi, wait. I need to explain right now, so we don't have to talk there for long. I want you to take Rosie to Angel's place. The police will never look for her there. Stay with her at La Rosaleda till I contact you. Got it?'

'Yes, OK.' She hesitated. 'Miss Jaymie? Are the police gonna take Rosie away?'

'Not the fuck if I can help it. See you in ten.'

I spotted Gabi's big old station wagon as soon as I pulled into Five Points, and was able to park right beside it. I looked around: no cops in sight.

Motioning for Gabi to stay in her car, I took Rosie into my arms and stepped out of the rental. Then I handed the child in through Gabi's open window.

'She's hungry. I gave her a bottle two hours ago, but she needs real food.'

'Don't worry, Miss Jaymie. I will send Angel out with a shopping list. I know everything a baby needs.' She peered into the little face. 'Oh! She gives me bumps all over. She looks just like Chucha.'

I stood there for a moment more, gazing down at the little girl. I knew what Gabi meant. It was tempting to think Chucha's spirit dwelt in Rosie now. But the child wasn't a stand-in for anyone: she deserved to just be herself.

'Gabi, I'm going to send Trudy's cell number to you when I get back in the car. Call her for me when you get a chance, OK? Tell her to tell Mike . . .' I stopped. Tell Mike what? What was it I needed him to know?

'Miss Jaymie, why do you want me to call Mr Mike's sister, not you? Are you going somewhere?'

'On an errand. Just something I need to take care of.' If I told

Gabi the truth, I knew she'd try to stop me. 'I want to make sure Mike knows I love him. That's all.'

'Oh Miss Jaymie, Mr Mike knows that! If he didn't, he would already leave you a long time ago.'

I marched into the lobby of the Santa Barbara Police Department and up to the 'pay parking tickets' window.

The young woman had a nice smile. 'Can I help you?' Her voice was muffled behind the thick glass.

'I want to see Chief Wheeler.' Asking to see the boss should get me attention. I figured the right person or persons would step into the light.

'Chief Wheeler doesn't deal with parking tickets. What can I do for you?'

I dug into my damp jeans pocket and pulled out a business card. 'Hand him this, will you?' I pointed at a wooden bench. 'I'll wait over there.'

Who wanted to pay a parking fine? No doubt the young woman dealt with plenty of cranks in her job. 'I will pass this on to one of the officers.'

Maybe she thought I'd see that as a threat, but it was exactly what I wanted to hear.

A few minutes later the clerk returned to her station. I saw her sneak a glance over at me. I wondered how long it would take for my calling card to wind its way to the target.

As it turned out it took no time at all.

Two young cops burst into the lobby through a side door. One grabbed me by the wrists and zip-cuffed me. 'You're under arrest,' the other barked in my face.

I didn't bother to argue. I figured I was headed where I wanted to go.

The two guys bundled me through the side door and down a hall. They were rough, trying to scare me. I was scared, all right. But not of them.

I wondered where they were taking me. An interview room or an office? No way. They frog-marched me through more doors and down a ramp, to a basement lined with walled cells. All the cells we passed were empty: apparently the entire floor was reserved just for me.

Then we stopped, in front of a cell that looked no different from any of the others.

'Hey,' one of the thickheads announced. He sounded like he was reading lines from a script. 'Remember that mental, Brodie Zarlin? This was his cell, right?'

'Yeah, you got it. This was the one.'

These two hadn't thought up this charade. I knew they'd been coached. Answering them back would mean nothing, so I limited my response to two words: 'fuck off.'

They walked away laughing. I stood in the center of the cell and resolved to be strong.

But after several minutes had passed, my resolve crumbled. My eyes filled with tears as I looked around the small ugly space my brother had died in. Concrete block wall. Cement floor. Hole in the ground for a toilet. I knelt down and cried.

Then one of those wordless prayers filled my mind. And again, somehow it worked.

My tears came to an end. I got to my feet and dabbed at my eyes with my sleeve. I had a job to do.

Of course I knew I was being watched on a camera. And that was just fine by me. I resisted the urge to give the watchers the finger. Better if those in charge thought I was broken and bowed.

I'm not sure how long my composure would have lasted. It would have been smart for my captors to leave me there in the cell to stew. But they had no time for that.

The authorities in Palm Desert would have already contacted the Santa Barbara PD. Now they had to find out what I knew.

They. Who exactly were 'they?' Sanchez and Wasson for certain. Beyond that, I could only guess.

Some ten minutes passed before I heard jackboots stomping back down the corridor. The same two gentlemen appeared. The big one, the one with the heavy jaw and too much testosterone for my taste, had the bulging eyes of a Boston terrier.

The smaller guy, he was a snake. You could see it in his blank gray stare. 'Hey, bitch. How did you like spending time with your crazy dead brother?'

I let the snake's words roll off me like beads of venom. He was the one who was dead – dead in his heart.

This time around they each grabbed one of my arms. I felt a stiletto of pain in my injured shoulder.

'Take it easy. My shoulder's injured.'

'Good to know,' the big one said.

But in fact, they eased off. I was escorted – almost politely – down the hall to a service elevator at the far end. Something was up.

Even though they'd backed off, standing inside the tight elevator with my handlers was a little scary. They stared me down like mad dogs about to latch onto my throat.

I knew it was all an act. But when I looked down at my feet, I saw what looked like real blood stains on the elevator floor.

I watched the floor indicator as we rose. One, two, three levels up from the basement. Well, I'd be damned: we were headed straight for the top.

TWENTY-SIX

The third floor seemed peaceful. Most of the doors off the hall were open, and we walked by pleasant offices with potted plants and windows with views of the mountains and city. Detectives I recognized looked up as our entourage passed.

I spotted Deirdre Krause behind a tidy glass-topped desk. When our eyes met, her mouth formed an 'O' of surprise. I said nothing. Why drag her down with me, after all?

We reached the end of the corridor. The door to the corner office. We halted and snake man knocked.

The door was opened by guess who – Steve Sanchez. His acne-scarred face was a hard and closed version of his sister's. I now knew for sure that he shared none of Sylvia's generosity – not a shred.

'I'll take her.' My escorts released my arms and walked away.

Sanchez looked hard at me for a moment. Then he stepped aside and motioned me in.

A massive oak desk stretched across the back of the room. Seated behind the desk was a man I recognized from his official photo, which appeared frequently in the local paper: Chief Wheeler.

Of course it was Wheeler, the chief of police. Why should that be a surprise to me? With the stakes as high as they were, how could Wheeler not be involved?

'Shut the door, Sanchez. Lock it.' The chief's voice was kind of warbly, like a bird's. But there was nothing funny about it. It only made him sound on edge.

The guy studied me. He seemed to be trying to figure me out. I didn't blink, just looked him straight in the eye.

Wallace Wheeler was ugly. He hadn't started out that way: there was nothing all that wrong with his looks. His upper lip was a little too long, and his ears had large lobes, like LBJ's. Otherwise his face was regular enough. Yet the ugliness was there, maybe in the slack wet way he held his mouth. You knew he'd done cruel things in his time.

To not be afraid of him, I tried to imagine Wheeler with his grandkids. But that was a little upsetting too.

'You dumb cunt,' he began. 'You walk right in here and what, you think we're gonna give you a fucking hug or something?'

'Think I'd want a hug from you?'

I was surprised to hear Sanchez, behind me, give out a short laugh. So Steve wasn't afraid of his boss.

Wheeler didn't react. I realized he didn't give a fuck what I said one way or the other.

'You want something, Zarlin? That it?'

'I want something, all right. First, get these cuffs off me. They're cutting into my wrists.'

Wheeler stared at me for a minute longer, then lifted his chin at Sanchez. 'You heard the little lady.'

Sanchez snatched something from his belt and stepped up behind me. Before he sliced the cuff, he grasped my forearm and gave it a light squeeze. He seemed to be trying to tell me something. But what?

'All right, cut the crap.' Wheeler leaned back in his chair. 'You want something all right. Why the hell should I listen to you?'

'Palm Desert, that's why. I know plenty, Chief Wheeler. And it's not just in my head. I've got witness statements, photos, and a laptop crammed full of data. If anything happens to me, half a dozen letters will go out in the mail. They're already stamped and addressed. Here's a short list: the *Independent*, the *News-Press*, and the *LA Times*.'

'I don't give a fuck about shit like that.' But his gaze slid away. I had him by the short hairs: publicity would ruin the man and he knew it.

There was no way Wheeler could know I was lying. The letters were a grand idea, but they were just that, an idea. I hadn't had enough time lately to even lick a stamp.

'You smuggle drugs, Wheeler. You've been doing it for years. And you smuggle kids, too.'

Wheeler heaved up like a tsunami from behind his desk. He was big all right, both in height and girth. The chief must have weighed at least 300 pounds.

He shoved back his chair and strode around the desk. 'We don't hurt kids. Get it? I will fucking hurt *you* for that!'

'What, for saying the truth?'

The slap was hard. So hard I felt my neck bend farther than it should. Tears of pain stung my eyes.

'It's a fucking lie, Zarlin.' Wheeler leaned in close to me. His face was inches from mine. I smelled the man, and the smell was rank, repulsive.

'Drugs, so what? Junkies are worthless, trash. They deserve what they get. But kids, kids we help.'

'You smuggle children into the country. One died. You can't change that fact.'

I steeled myself for another slap. But Wheeler took half a step back.

'Sanchez, go take a walk. The PI and me, we are going to have a private talk.'

My head still pounded. I looked over at Sanchez as he turned for the door. His face was impassive, but just for a moment his gaze held my own.

'Sit down.' Wheeler pointed at a chair. He stuffed his hands in his pockets and paced the length of the room. 'Know what? I could make you have an accident.'

'Sure.' My tongue felt thick from the slap. 'But there are those letters. All written and addressed.'

'Fuck the letters.' He waved the topic away. 'I'm talking to you for one reason, Zarlin. What you're saying about the kids is a lie – but the thing is, you think you're telling the truth.'

'There's evidence. A little girl died.'

'I don't know nothing about that, OK?' His voice exploded and his words sprayed through the air like shrapnel. 'Drugs. Like I said, so what? And Morehead, yeah, I let him bring in a few kids. But it's for their own good. So why the hell not?'

A few kids. My God, what did that mean?

'I don't know why I'm wasting my time talking to you, but lemme tell you something, Zarlin. Morehead, he takes kids outta some Mexican slum, he gives them to people who adopt them. He gives those kids a better life.'

'No. You've got it all wrong.' The room was quiet. The sounds of traffic filtered up from the street below. 'Morehead and his assistant, Eric? They traffic kids and sell them for sex.' I couldn't help it: the more I talked, the louder my voice got.

'I don't know about Brill. But Morehead and Eric, they're pedophiles, part of that sick world. Don't take my word for it. Morehead's probably already gone, holed up in Cancun or somewhere.'

'That's fucking crap.' Wheeler growled something more under his breath. Then he walked over to a window. His back was to me when he spoke. 'But let's say you're on to something. For the sake of argument, what is it you want?'

'Four things.'

'Just four?' He coughed up a laugh. 'Speak up fast before I send you back to the basement.'

'Stop the trafficking in kids once and for all. The Riverside County Sheriff's Department will see to the immediate problem. But you need to make sure Morehead never starts it up again.'

'I'll handle Morehead, that fuck. What else.'

Wheeler believed me now. I could hear in his voice that he did. 'Darren Hartek. Let him go.'

Wheeler turned to look at me. 'Who?'

'The guy your people picked up on More Mesa to put pressure on me. Darren's never hurt a fly.'

'The loony? What the fuck, sure.' Wheeler waved a hand and turned back to the glass. 'Besides you, who the fuck cares?'

'Number three. I want to know what happened to my brother while he was in custody. I want to know all of it – how Brodie died.' I walked up to Wheeler. 'I want to know all the names. And maybe yours is one of them, Wheeler.'

His laugh was forced. 'Number four, you want me to give you a kiss on your ass?'

'Number four. Chucha Robledo's daughter – the little girl. Promise me you'll leave her alone. I'm going to give Rosie a home.' I stopped then and listened to my own words. They spun in the air like honey bees, humming notes of pure gold.

I realized I did want that. Somehow, without consciously thinking about it, I'd made up my mind.

'You're weird, Zarlin,' Wheeler was saying. 'You should see a shrink. Oh by the way' – he lit a cigarette, tossed the lighter on the desk, and turned to face me – 'Hear the latest about your boyfriend, that poor prick? Too bad Deputy Dawson won't walk again. Gonna be in a wheelchair for the rest of his life.' He blew a stream of smoke in my direction. 'Too bad for you too. Maybe his dick won't work either.'

Wheeler didn't take his eyes from my face, and what he read there seemed to please him. 'Yeah. I thought you'd want to hear that news right away.'

I stood there like a tin soldier, clamping down hard on my feelings.

'What, for once you got nothing to say?'

'I've laid it all out, Wheeler. Take it or leave it.'

'Sure. You shred those letters. I don't give a fuck about the crazy guy or the girl, and Morehead, that sonofabitch, I'll deal with him. But the one about your brother?' He took a slow drag on his cigarette. 'Forget it. That was a few years back, and you don't need to know.'

The asshole was tormenting me. And I was on the verge of losing control.

I thought about Darren, Rosie, and all the other children, the ones I'd never know. For their sakes, I had to give in.

But it was hard, dear God it was hard: I'd have to let my own brother go.

'Yeah, Wheeler. We've got a deal.'

'Don't cross my path again, Zarlin. You'll regret it, I promise you.' He stubbed out his cigarette in an ashtray, reached across the desk and picked up his phone.

'Sanchez. Come and get the bitch. We're letting her go.'

Wheeler walked around the desk and dropped down into his oversized chair. He picked up a letter opener and dug at a fingernail. Neither of us spoke. There was nothing more to say.

The office door opened and Sanchez stepped into the room. 'Come on, Zarlin. Let's go.'

At that moment, I realized there was something else I wanted to say to Wheeler. Call it pig-headedness – I wasn't going to let it end there.

'What you just said, Wheeler, about me not crossing your path? The same goes for you.'

'Get her the fuck outta here!'

Sanchez grabbed me by the wrist, and a few seconds later I found myself out in the hall.

'Don't be so goddamn stupid,' he said under his breath. 'You got what you wanted.' Still gripping my wrist, he moved me down the corridor at a trot.

The elevator doors closed on us, and he put his mouth to my ear.

'The elevator's bugged, understand? I'm driving you home. I got one or two things to say to you.'

I pulled my arm from his grasp. 'I drove here. I don't need a lift.'

'Like I said, don't be stupid.'

The elevator door opened. Together we walked down the hall to the lobby. Just before Steve Sanchez opened the door to my freedom, he leaned close again.

'Trust me and everything will turn out OK. You're gonna get in my car, in the backseat.'

I followed him through the lobby, down the front steps, and around to the police lot in the back. Sanchez clicked open the doors to a dark green Camaro. I halted in my tracks. Was it smart to get in? My experience shouted *no*.

'There are cameras everywhere, Zarlin, even out here. Don't make a scene. You and me, we'll take a drive. After I tell you one or two things I'll circle back and drop you off at your car.'

Still, I balked.

'Hey, La Macheesma. Too scared to take a dare?'

'I heard it all. I heard you ask about your brother.' Steve Sanchez studied me in his rearview mirror.

I didn't try to mask my surprise. 'You have Wheeler's office bugged?'

'Something like that.'

'Do you know what happened to Brodie?'

'Yeah. Yeah, I do.'

We were driving along East Beach. Sanchez turned left and pulled in near the bird refuge, the old estuary. He switched off the engine.

I stared at the back of his head. 'Tell me. 'Cause the truth is, when it comes to my brother I'll never give up.'

'I know.' He rolled down his window and lit a cigarette with a Zippo before he began.

'Wheeler had three cops beat up your brother. The idea wasn't to kill him. Just to hurt him, to scare him near to death, so he'd keep his big mouth shut.'

'Because Brodie knew too much.'

'He knew about the smuggling. He'd seen us out at More Mesa, just like that guy you asked Wheeler about.'

'Darren.'

'Yeah. Thing was, your brother was nothing like Hartek. He was more like you – wouldn't shut up. Kept telling people what he'd seen. Let's just say, he wasn't a fan of the police.'

I felt like a statue – no emotions at all. Just concrete or stone. 'So they beat him. And something went wrong.'

'They left him there. And your brother, he vomited and choked. Choked to death. So Wheeler, he had them string him up. To make it look like suicide.'

Everything had gone numb: my mouth, vocal cords, even my brain. 'Why are you telling me this?'

'Sylvia.' Sanchez turned around in the seat to look at me. 'I love my little sister, you know? I'd kill anybody who hurt her. So I figure I know how it feels.'

'I don't know how it feels. Right now I can't feel a thing.'

Steve turned forward again. 'No. But you will.'

I looked out the side window. At that exact moment, a great blue heron lifted up from the far bank of the refuge. 'Look,' I said without thinking. 'Look at that bird.'

Higher and higher, its great wings stroked the air as it climbed.

Sanchez started the engine. We remained silent as he drove. When we arrived back at my rental car, he pulled up alongside it.

'The other things you asked Wheeler for? They'll all happen, I can promise you that.' He looked at me in the rearview mirror.

'Just for the record, I didn't know nothing about the kids. No way would I ever allow that, not on my watch.'

'So, why? Why do you do it?'

'What, the drug smuggling?' He curled his lip. 'That one's easy. Been to south Texas? Ever lived in a shack with dirt floors?'

'Were you—' I stopped. I was afraid to ask.

'What?'

I broke eye contact. 'Were you one of the three who beat up my brother?'

'No, I wasn't. But . . . I could have been. Yeah. Could have been me.'

I put a hand on the door. 'I'm not going to thank you, Sanchez. I don't owe you a thing.'

'Fine. But you owe my sister. She likes you, Zarlin. She's the one who told me I needed to help you. And I like to try and give lil sis what she wants.'

'Then you can thank Sylvia for me.' I opened the car door. 'Tell her if she ever needs a favor, I'm good for it.'

'I think she's already got something in mind. A rematch, maybe. Yeah, Hot Wheels told me to say she'll be in touch.'

POSTSCRIPT

S tanford University crashed in flames, and we celebrated the incineration to the hilt following our victory.

I passed Gabi's apartment on my way home from the team party. A light was on, but though I was tempted I decided not to stop in. Rosie was spending the night with her Tia Gabi, and it was better if I didn't interfere.

I drove up El Balcon and pulled into the car shed. There was no moon, and the shed interior was as dark as the bottom of the sea. I edged out of the shed and stepped into the yard.

The house was unlit. Mike must have gone to bed.

I crossed the yard and stood at the bottom of the steps, fumbling for my key. When I opened the door, Dexter was right there waiting for me. He pressed his wet nose against my bare calf.

I felt along the wall for the switch, then flooded the living room with strong light. I closed the door behind me and stood there for a moment, listening.

All was still. Just as it should be, I reassured myself. And Dex was wagging his stumpy tail: there was no bad news for him to report.

No bad news that the heeler was aware of, at least.

Stop that, I ordered myself.

For over two weeks, I'd felt a slight touch of dread each time I entered the house. Two weeks and three days. That's how long Mike had been staying with me.

He'd been desperate to get away from Trudy and her family: said he couldn't stand seeing his nephew and nieces feeling sorry for him. But Mike's own second-floor apartment in Santa Barbara wasn't an option, not anymore. Not for a guy confined to a chair.

I busied myself by picking up the bright plastic toys scattered over the living room and tossing them into the basket. I didn't want to go into the bedroom. I was afraid of Mike's depression, afraid it would one day drag him away.

I opened the door into the dark hall. The bedroom door was shut, just as Mike had told me to leave it. I switched on the hall light, took a deep breath, and turned the glass knob.

'Mike? Are you awake?'

To my relief, he shifted in the bed, then rolled over onto his back. 'Hi, Jaymie. Did you have a good time?'

'I had a blast.' The moment I said that, I felt guilty. 'Are you OK?'

'I hate that question. I told you, remember?'

'Sorry.' Then, to change the subject, to make him smile, I began to jabber away in a fake-happy voice.

'We won hands down – those college girls got a lesson! You would have enjoyed it. I wish you'd come along.'

'Turn on the light, will you? I've got to sit up.'

As it happened, I was looking at Mike as I turned on the overhead light. I saw his dull expression change, in an instant, to one of horror.

'Jesus,' he croaked. 'What the hell happened to you?'

'Huh? It's nothing. I thought I cleaned myself up.'

He was struggling, dragging himself to a sitting position. 'It's nothing? You need to go look in the mirror.'

I fled out of the room to the bathroom. Shit, no wonder I'd given Mike a scare. My bottom lip was swollen to twice its normal size, and my left eye socket was turning an inky blue. Dried blood encrusted my nostrils and spread in a cracked smear across my cheek.

As I stared at my ghoulish image, I heard a choking sound coming from the bedroom. It grew more frantic. I spun on my heel and ran back to the doorway.

Mike was bent forward at the waist and he was choking, all right. Choking with laughter, the jerk.

He looked over at me, and his choking grew louder.

It was the most beautiful sound in the world.

Then, just as I joined in, his laughter turned to tears. I climbed into the bed and put my arms around him. Mike began to sob.

At last he cried, for all he'd lost. I started to cry along with him, and that's when he started laughing again.

Dexter jumped up onto the bed and licked our faces. Those poor crazy humans of his!

At last Mike's laughter slowed. He wiped his eyes with the sheet and shook his head. 'Yeah, Jaymie. I can see you had a blast.'

He looked like he was going to start laughing or crying again. I stopped him with a hard kiss on the mouth.

When we came up for air, I kept my eye – my one good eye – inches from his. 'I want you back.' When he started to answer I interrupted him.

'No, you listen to me. I am so sick of this! I want you back *now*.'

'You want me back, huh?' He placed a hand on my cheek. 'You might as well know the truth. There's another girl in my life.'

My heart tumbled down a steep hill and hit bottom. I knew Mike pretty well, and he didn't look like he was kidding around.

'What, some fucking nurse? That's a man for you! I guess the saying is true – when guys get old, it's the nurse or the purse.'

'You're neither one, that's for damn sure.' He had the nerve to laugh. 'Nope, I'm talking about a bruiser of a girl who tried to twist the nose off my face this morning. She plays a mean game of peek-a-boo.'

He'd fooled me for a minute, goddamn it! 'Sorry. The bruiser won't be back till the morning. Tonight you only have me.'

'Looks like you'll have to do.'

'Yeah. Looks like I will.' I couldn't tell him how happy I was. I'd show him, instead.

'Do me a favor, go wash the blood off your face.' He gave me a gentle shove. 'Tell you what – you can leave on those fishnets, though.'